Renee 2:

The Protégé

Renee 2:

The Protégé

Brandie Davis

www.urbanbooks.net

Urban Books, LLC
300 Farmingdale Road, NY-Route 109
Farmingdale, NY 11735

Renee 2: The Protégé Copyright © 2019 Brandie Davis

ISBN 13: 978-1-64556-168-2
ISBN 10: 1-64556-168-2

First Mass Market Printing June 2021
First Trade Paperback Printing December 2019
Printed in the United States of America

10 9 8 7 6 5 4 3 2 1

This is a work of fiction. Any references or similarities to actual events, real people, living or dead, or to real locales are intended to give the novel a sense of reality. Any similarity in other names, characters, places, and incidents is entirely coincidental.

Distributed by Kensington Publishing Corp.
Submit Orders to:
Customer Service
400 Hahn Road
Westminster, MD 21157-4627
Phone: 1-800-733-3000
Fax: 1-800-659-2436

Renee 2:

The Protégé

by

Brandie Davis

*I dedicate this book to the strongest woman
I know, my mother.*

Chapter 1

"You're a fool if you get out now." Dane threw a piece of steak into her mouth without bothering to look at Renee.

Renee didn't respond right away. Instead, she looked out at the ocean, marveling at its beauty. Jamaica was stunning. A week after meeting with her newly introduced stepsister, Carmen, whom she had appointed as her protégé, Renee jumped on a plane with Dane and Metro and headed to her mentor's secluded beach house dropped on the edge of a luxurious green forest. She needed some time away, and if she truly wanted it, she had to get out of the U.S.

"No one stays on top forever, Dane. I have to get out while I can." Renee never took her eyes off the ocean, even as her hand searched the patio table for her drink. Finding her glass, she took a sip of her wine, then slowly inhaled a deep breath.

After almost being raped by a childhood friend, stalked by a loyal worker, and nearly murdered by her younger sister, Page, months prior, Renee now appreciated life and strove to live in peace. Temporarily staying with Dane and Metro was a necessity. She trusted them and could completely drop her guard without fear of betrayal. Those two had taken her under their wings and given her wealth along with knowledge. They were the married couple who'd introduced and guided Renee through the drug world when Metro saw it best to retire and crown her his protégé. Every day at sunset, Renee and Dane sat out on Dane's bedroom balcony and had dinner, just as they were doing now. The breeze and smell of leaves took Renee away to a place from which she didn't want to return.

"You're a fool to leave now, and you're a bigger fool if you actually believe your reign over New York will ever end. You're built for this. Why do you think Metro and I handed everything over to you?" Dane's plate was left without a crumb, and her piercing, dark brown eyes burned right into Renee.

Renee shifted in her seat. She was tired of having the same conversation with Dane repeatedly. However, once more she'd give Dane the satisfaction of repeating herself. Focused on the waves crashing into one another, Renee spoke clear and without error.

"I appreciate all that you and Metro have done for me. You entrusted me to run New York's drug trade when Metro laid down his crown and went legit. You two gave me all of your connections and protected me like I was your blood even when I was capable of protecting myself." Renee paused and nodded her head. "It's not common for an assassin and kingpin to befriend someone and give them the world. All I had going for me was school and Julian, so for you to expand my circle was uncanny yet needed."

Watching as the sun sank deeper into the ocean, Renee took another sip of her wine before continuing. "But as much as I would like to continue to show my allegiance to you both by staying in the business you trusted me with, I can't do it anymore. I can't continue to live the life you've given me when my spirit and heart are no longer in it."

Dane leaned over in her seat, her upper body near Renee's. "When did you grow a conscience? When did the cold bitch who ruled with an iron fist turn into"— Dane quickly looked her over—"this?"

"When I grew sense," Renee spat. Finally she placed her attention on Dane. "I'm done hiding and sinking further into darkness. This shit is depressing and lonely. It makes you numb, and I'm tired of feeling nothing!" Renee banged her fist into her chest. "There's more to life. There's peace and happiness, and I want it, dammit. I deserve it!"

Spit flew from her mouth. Her lips trembled, and redness covered her cheeks.

"What you think you want is not meant for you," Dane ensured, shaking her head from left to right. "That life is not meant for people like us. Besides, you're far from lonely. You have Metro, me, and Julian."

Renee blinked away tears. "As much as I love Julian, he'll never fully have me if I continue with this lifestyle. I've had to sacrifice any sign of weakness, including our unborn child, in order to remain cold and survive whatever was thrown our way. I should have been his wife by now. We should have had a family." Renee cleared her throat and squeezed the bridge of her nose with her thumb and forefinger. "I'm retiring."

"Over my dead body." Dane's face twisted and her lips curled. She was established in the love department, comfortable with killing, and had no desire to bear children. Therefore, Renee getting her to understand where she was coming from was futile.

Renee pointed at Dane. "So you're telling me that Metro's the only one who's allowed to retire?"

Dane's eyes lowered until they appeared to be nothing but slits. "We're not talking about Metro. We're talking about you. You're making a big mistake if you give it all up, and by all, I'm talking about the money, the respect, and most importantly, the power."

Drink still in hand, Renee set it down on the table. "I'm not giving up anything, except for the stress and bullshit of the game. I'm doing just fine in the money department, and as for the power and respect, that's nothing you can ever lose as long as you know when it's time to get out."

"So that's how it's going to be? You're out and handing it all over to a stranger?" Dane got straight to the point. "I don't trust her, Renee. There's something grimy about that girl."

Renee snatched up her glass and guzzled the remaining liquid. She then grabbed the bottle of wine from the middle of the table, refilled her drink, and devoured that as well. Dane was tap dancing on her last nerve. Renee had flown to Jamaica for peace of mind and to begin transitioning from a life of chaos to a world of happiness and joy. She was preparing to be normal. However, Dane was doing everything she could to talk her out of it.

"How can you want to give everything to someone you don't know, someone who acts so thirsty? This is a family business!"

Renee slammed down her glass. The bottom chipped and fell to the floor. Dane had officially ruined her moment of peace. "She saved my life! Did you forget if it hadn't been for Carmen showing up when she did that night on the terrace, Page would have killed me? And enough with the stranger bit. She's family! She's my sister!"

Dane's eyes widened and appeared to bulge from her face. "She's not my family! And why the hell must you claim your father's illegitimate child, whom you met not even six months ago?" Dane hollered. "She's a stranger! Open your fucking eyes! She's someone you recently discovered was your father's love child because Lyfe decided to come clean! Oh, yes! Lyfe! How could we forget about Lyfe? Your top goon who recently told you that he's your uncle!" Dane banged her hand down on the table, causing Renee's glass to crash to the ground. "This is some dysfunctional, soap-opera shit, and you're not giving Charmaine, or whatever her name is, what Metro started and you maintained just because you feel you owe her and need a scapegoat to get out of the game sooner!"

Dane slammed her back against her bamboo chair and tried to catch her breath.

"My aunt and uncle . . ." Dane stopped talking because her voice had temporarily gone out. She cleared her throat. "My aunt and uncle have parts in this business, big parts. If anything goes wrong, their asses are in hot water, and I will not have that," she reminded Renee.

Renee's leg shook.

Dane aggressively dug her hand through her hair, turned away from Renee, and mumbled incoherent words. Dane didn't know Carmen. All she knew was she didn't like her. Carmen's energy was off, and she came across as desperate and clingy when trying to get to know Renee. All were signs that she wanted something.

Dane replayed the "illegitimate" and "love child" comments in her mind and instantly regretted them. There weren't many people she cared for in the world, but the

few she did included Renee. Twelve years Renee's senior, Dane viewed the 25-year-old as her younger sister.
She had taught her so much and watched her grow. The
last thing Dane wanted was for yet again another family
member to break Renee after she had opened up to them.
For years, Lyfe was a loyal goon of Renee's, and even
he had deceived her by not revealing he was her father's
brother. That alone led Dane to wonder whether there
was something Carmen wasn't telling.

"Listen, Renee, I took it too far by saying—"

Renee cut her off midsentence. "She's taking over,
and that's that." Renee refocused her attention on the
vast body of water in front of her. Far away in the bluest
part of the ocean, she thought she'd seen a dolphin's fin.
However, the more she thought about it, the more she
questioned whether it belonged to a shark instead.

"Over my dead body," Dane repeated, her voice hitting
its deepest tone.

Renee's head fell into her right shoulder, her cheek
resting on her richly tanned skin. The ocean had just
become partially lit by the golden moon.

Calm and empty of any emotion, Renee responded,
"After I show Carmen the ropes, I'm thinking of moving
here if Julian agrees to come with me."

Dane's maid came out on the balcony. Seeing the
shattered glass on the floor, she immediately proceeded
to remove the empty dishes occupying the table before
rushing off to retrieve a broom and dustpan.

"You're not moving anywhere," Dane snarled after the
maid scurried off. "You're going to stay in New York and
do what you do best. You'll have no choice after I expose
Carmen for who she really is." Dane kicked a piece of
glass off the balcony. "I'm going back to New York with
you, and I won't leave until she's out of the picture."

Renee placed two fingers on her temple and closed her eyes. "Let it go, Dane. Besides, shouldn't you be thinking about retirement yourself? You've been a hit woman long before I knew you and before you married Metro. Based on what you make and the chunk of change he retired with from selling, you don't need to continue killing."

"It's not about the money. Unlike you, I know my place in this world, and it's to continue doing what I'm doing—killing. And if you know what's good for you, you'll continue to be queen and reign superior."

Chapter 2

When the hell does this end? Renee continued to walk down the slippery, overly waxed wooden stairs where one misstep could cause her to tumble down flights of stairs and break her neck. When the stairwell's light bulbs weren't flickering, they supplied a weak amount of light. Through the dim lighting, Renee struggled to see beyond the three stairs in front of her. Without a railing to guarantee her balance, she used the ashy brick wall for assistance. After descending four flights of stairs, Renee looked up at Dane, who stood at the very top of the staircase with her body jammed in the doorframe.

"When do these stairs end?"

Dane laughed as she used her foot to hold the door open, leaning her upper body farther out into the stairwell. "You're almost there. Keep going."

Renee squinted her eyes in search of the bottom. Still unable to see more than a few steps in front of her, she continued to use the wall as a crutch while grasping the electronic earmuffs and polycarbonate glasses in her left hand tighter. Renee looked down and took in a large crack in the following step. Carefully she avoided it and rolled her eyes.

He better be down here, Renee thought.

"Renee! I'm going back in the house. Don't be too long. Dinner's soon!" Dane's voice echoed down the hall followed by the slam of a door.

Oh, hell no! His ass better be back home. I'm not having dinner alone with his wife for two days in a row so she can constantly tell me how wrong I am for wanting to retire.

Renee's ponytail swung from side to side from the opening at the back of her baseball cap. She concentrated on the sound of the wood creaking beneath her sneakers. The eerie, uncomfortable sounds associated with haunted houses distracted Renee and took her focus off the journey that would lead her to her destination. Ultimately, Renee reached the bottom of the stairwell, where a large steel door met her. After she placed her glasses and earmuffs on, she pushed the door open.

Gunshots erupted, welcoming her to the home shooting range buried deep underground. Inside the room, glass cases displayed firearms organized according to their size. The multiple keypads and steel structure of the room's walls and floors were reminiscent of a panic room, minus the bottles of water and canned foods that most would have in preparation for the end of the world.

Two shooting stalls stood tall and secure in the middle of the room. Laid out in one of the stalls was a tray full of ammo situated in front of Metro, who wore the same protective gear as Renee while shooting at a blue full-sized silhouette. Holes saturated the middle of the silhouette's chest and forehead. Metro lowered his weapon to his side and observed his work. Renee stood on the sidelines, admiring his aim.

Metro raised his weapon and trained it back on the target. His finger was on the trigger ready to be pulled, but instead of injecting the blue man with more bullets, Metro turned around to see Renee planted on the side of the room. He nodded toward her and then, without hesitation, returned his concentration to the paper and fired. After emptying his magazine into the head of the silhouette, he placed his firearm on the tray and removed his earmuffs.

"You're dressed to shoot," Metro commented.

Renee pulled the right earmuff off her ear a little and sat down on the metal bench. Its coldness seeped through her pants. "Huh?"

"You're dressed to shoot, so grab a gun."

"Nah, that's not why I'm here."

Metro pointed his finger at her, moving it up and down. "Then what's with the getup?"

Agitated with holding one earmuff up so she could hear, Renee removed them from her head completely. "I'm taking precautions. Had I remembered my bullet-proof vest, I'd be wearing that, too. We all know your aim sucks."

Metro laughed. "Take a closer look! This shit is perfect!" He stretched out his arms and pointed toward the body target. His posture was identical to a game show host revealing the winning prize.

"I've seen better," Renee teased. "Dane hit the head and chest dead on. You're an inch or two off." She shrugged and fought to hold back her amusement.

"What do you expect? She's an assassin!"

The two shared a laugh. Once Metro finished snickering, Renee tried to regain her composure. However, her amusement could not be contained. The more she laughed, the more tears formed at the corner of her eyes and clouded her vision. She removed her glasses just as Metro took a seat beside her. He, too, took off his glasses, followed by his earmuffs.

Renee's laughter decreased. Once she caught her breath, she leaned back against the wall and looked over the shooting range. "It's not every day you see a range built in someone's home. Dope." She zeroed in on the silhouette printed on the large paper. "I thought targets came in black. What's with the blue?"

"I'm not using one of my own as target practice. Too many black figures are targets in real life."

Renee looked down to the floor, her mind reverting to the daily news reports that revolved around African Americans being gunned down by law enforcement.

"What brings you down here?" Metro asked, breaking her thoughts.

"I came to get your opinion."

"On?"

"On me retiring."

The sound of air releasing from his mouth resembled air seeping from out a balloon. "I have questions about that," Metro expressed. "I'm going to start by asking, why now? What's changed?"

Renee's shoulders rose and fell as she took a deep breath. "Why not? I'm at the end of my rope. This isn't what I want anymore. My rage, it's . . . it's dying down."

Metro smiled. "Your rage? Now that's why I mentored you. Rage is what brought you alive when the rest of you died." The day Metro met Renee ten years ago fell from his mouth.

"I never thought I'd live to see the day."

Dane briefly looked up from chopping onions to glance at her husband. Her facial expression demonstrated a questioning glare. "What are you talking about?"

"I never thought I'd live to see you have a friend."

Dane tossed a piece of onion at him. Metro dodged the vegetable and broke into a fit of laughter.

Dane chopped the onions faster. The chopping board vibrated yet held strong. Her eyes began to burn, and she could feel moisture developing at the bottom of her lids.

"I can see why you felt that way. Your ass is old. You can croak at any minute." She erased a fallen tear with the back of her hand.

"You got that. I'll let you have that one. Your comebacks are improving." Metro slapped his wife's behind. She stopped cutting to wipe away more tears.

"I fuckin' hate onions." Dane grabbed a napkin from the napkin holder and dabbed beneath her eyes.

Metro shifted the cutting board over to him and proceeded to sever the onion Dane had yet to complete. "This alone shows the girl is your friend. You cut onions for no one."

Dane rubbed her eyes, balled up the used napkin, and took the stance of a basketball player before aiming and shooting it into the garbage.

"There's another reason why I want you to meet her." Dane leaned back against the frosty glass door cabinets and folded her arms.

Metro looked up at her, his eyes red.

"I think she's the one."

"For?" Metro asked.

"To take over the business," Dane replied, her right leg crossed over the left. Her fingers relentlessly tapped against her arms.

Metro's cutting slowed. The onion was now small, and had he not been careful, he would've cut the tip of his finger. "My heart . . ." Metro began.

Dane rolled her eyes. Nicknames were a clear indication that whatever Metro had to say, she wouldn't like.

"I don't know her. Today would be my first time meeting her, and for me to even consider her, I'd have to—"

"Put her through the vetting process," husband and wife said in unison.

Dane rolled her eyes. "I know."

"If you know this, you wouldn't be bringing up this topic so soon." Metro dropped the knife on the counter, his onion slices cleaner and smaller than Dane's. Metro grabbed a dish towel from a rack and cleaned his hands.

"I've done that already. I wouldn't allow her to meet you had I not done so." Dane waited for Metro to speak. When he didn't, she kept on pleading her case. "She has no record, is incredibly intelligent, and has no family and friends but lots of rage and pain waiting to be released."

"What happened to her family?" Metro took a seat at the table filled with a lobster platter and bowls of mashed potatoes, greens, and shrimp. He snatched a shrimp and tossed it in his mouth.

"Father's dead, and she doesn't get along with her mother and stepfather, which is why she left home without a word after receiving her scholarship to NYU."

Metro's eyebrows dropped, and his faced scrunched up. "Her mother doesn't know where she is?"

"Doesn't know, doesn't care, in Renee's words. No police reports were filed, no attempt to find her. It's like she never existed."

"Shit."

"I know." Dane opened one of the double ovens and examined the baked chicken. She then sprinkled the additional onions inside the juices and on top of the chicken.

"No siblings?"

Dane closed the oven door and wiped her hands, covered in the stench of onion, on her jeans. "A younger sister. She wishes they were closer, but they're not."

"What if the sister were to look for her?"

The doorbell rang. Dane looked at the time on the microwave. "Shit! She's early."

She began scrambling around the kitchen, working as hard as possible to clean up behind herself and transport the finished dishes from the kitchen table to the dining room, where they'd feast.

"Should have had our chef cook," Metro said as he stole another shrimp just as Dane grabbed the dish.

She gave him a dirty look. "Get the door, please."

Metro strolled to the front door. His loafers barely rose off the floor while he buttoned the top buttons of his striped shirt. Out of all the homes that he and Dane had lived in, his New York condo was one of his favorites. It felt homey and calm. It reminded him of the environment he grew up in when good times transpired.

He opened the door and was finally met with the face he had heard so much about. Bullshit! This can't be her.

Renee didn't smile, nor did she hold a covered dish or bottle of wine in her hand as a gesture of thanks for allowing her into their home. Neither spoke. They both stood there staring at one another, waiting for the other to speak first. Renee penetrated Metro with her hazel eyes. Her caramel cheeks were a shade of red. Metro could not figure out if the color was from makeup or nerves. Big, bouncy curls contained her black hair, a hairstyle Metro's mother called Shirley Temple curls back in the day. Renee's eyes were big and almond shaped, her mouth and chin small.

This girl next door cannot possibly be Renee. She looks like a baby doll, for crying out loud. *Tired of having a staring match, Metro broke the silence. "Can I help you?"*

"My name is Renee. I'm here to see Dane and Metro."

Metro held out his hand. "Call me Mr. Row. Only my friends call me Metro." There was neither politeness nor hospitality in his voice.

"Metro!" Dane yelled from the back of her home. "Is Renee inside?"

Renee looked down at Metro's hand, then back up at his face. She had no idea where Dane's voice had come from. However, that didn't stop her from squeezing herself past Metro and into his home.

"I'm here, Dane! I'm just introducing myself to Metro!" Her neck snapped in Metro's direction.

He slammed the door shut and stomped his way toward her. "You hard of hearing? Didn't I tell you—"

Dane barged through the swinging kitchen doors and inside the dining room, her hands covered with oven mitts and carrying the baked chicken surrounded by potatoes. Dane smiled, set the food down on the table, and removed the mitts. "Renee, you're early."

"Sorry about that. Just didn't want to be late." Renee stood with her one leg behind the other and arms crossed.

Metro walked past Renee, his shoulder brushing against hers on his way to the dinner table.

"Have a seat, Renee. We'll start eating as soon as I return with the wine," Dane said before dipping back inside the kitchen.

Metro pulled out a chair at the head of the table. On the verge of sitting down, his body suddenly jerked for-

ward, and his stomach jammed into the table. He looked at Renee, who was already comfortable in her seat.

"I'm sorry, Metro. Did I bump into you?"

Metro was confused. He thought this dinner had been arranged for Renee to woo him and lead him to agree to give her his business. Not so he could sit there listening to his wife and her new friend chuckle and yap for a total of twenty minutes about things he couldn't care less about. But as dinner went on, that's exactly what happened.

"Do you think there will be a season two?" Dane poured herself another glass of wine, then refilled Renee's.

"Better be. That's damn good TV, and finally an actual television show. Not that reality TV garbage."

"As much as I love my ratchet TV, I am getting tired of it. It's frying my brain cells," Dane admitted.

Both women laughed. Dane covered her mouth, which was full of food, while Renee allowed her jaw to drop, giving Metro a clear view of her half-chewed shrimp coated with mashed potatoes. Metro pushed back his seat and got up.

"Dane, the meal was delicious." He kissed his wife on the top of her creased forehead.

"Where are you going? We're still in the middle of dinner, and you barely spoke to Renee."

"I don't need to speak with Renee." Metro planted his palms flat on the table and leaned down close to Renee. "She's an uncouth, raggedy little girl who will never lead my business, and after today, she is a friend you will no longer have."

"Fuck you say to me?" Renee rose to her feet.

"Metro!" Dane shouted. "How dare you talk to her that way!"

Metro's head snapped in Dane's direction. "How dare you bring this disrespectful cunt into my house!" he roared. "She's rude and needs to learn her place or else I'll teach it to her!"

No other sound was heard inside the condo. Not the low playing music in the background, not the air conditioner roughly pumping out cool air, and not the television Dane left on upstairs in her bedroom. All of those noises were canceled out by Metro's wretched howl. His chest tightened, and his breathing became ragged. The sight of the blade protruding from his bloody hand pushed his psyche to the limit. Spit slithered out the corners of his mouth. Using his other hand, Metro pulled at the knife. It took several attempts before he was able to rip the blade from his hand. Blood gushed out of the wound, and the red liquid stained Dane's new tablecloth. The entire time Renee stood there smiling.

Renee's mouth was slightly agape. Her eyes blinked nonstop before she shook her head. "I completely forgot I stabbed you." She became flushed, and the saliva in her mouth dried.

Metro laughed a hard, hearty laugh.

"I remember being so angry, so enraged when you said you'd put me in my place," Renee continued. "I took that as a threat, and at the moment, all I saw was that sick fuck Curtis. When you've been abused, you vow never to let anyone hurt you again." Renee sniffled and folded her arms.

"And that's exactly why I made you my protégé. Your pain is what fueled you and made you a monster. It takes a coldhearted, withdrawn person to survive this life, and you've endured more misery than half the people I know who've lived shitty lives." Metro paused. His eyes caught a glimpse of the scar on his hand. "Never has anyone been able to assault me and continue living, let alone have Dane defend the attacker. She didn't speak to me for a week because she swears I was the aggressor."

"I'm not the same person. Maybe I achieved closure after killing Sheila and Curtis, because now I want more of a normal life. I want peace, a family. Fuck, I want to be able to live without stalkers and my house being turned into a morgue. I've run my course and want out." Renee stretched out her legs. "I just wish that basket case wife of yours could understand that."

"I'll tell you why. You're the daughter we never had, and we refuse to let go of you. Outside of myself, Dane has never loved or trusted anyone who wasn't blood. In Dane's head, you walking away from the business that helped strengthen your bond is equivalent to her losing another family member."

Renee banged her head against the wall and threw her hands in the air. "I'm not doing that at all! I'm trying to be someone saner, happier!"

"And that scares the shit out of Dane. She doesn't know this Renee who you're striving to become, and she doesn't do well with change. If you walk away from the business, her question is, what else will you walk away from? Dane has lived inside the darkness for a long time. Seeing the light alarms her."

"I'm leaving the stress and pain of my life, not our friendship. And because I value the friendship, I'm trying to bring in family to take over and not some random person."

Metro placed one leg on top of the other, his left ankle resting on his right knee. "That alone is a bad decision."

"How? What's the difference between Dane bringing in me and me bringing in Carmen?"

"Dane knew you. She took the time to scout you, learn you, and our decision was made outside of emotion. We did what was best for the business, not ourselves. You're working off emotion."

"Carmen's no stranger to this life. Grooming and training will do her nothing but good. The night she saved my life, she handled it better than some of these motherfuckers you've done business with."

"If you want my opinion, I think you're making a big mistake. A mistake by leaving and a bigger mistake by handing it over to a stranger."

"What the fuck do you two want from me?" Renee shouted, jumping to her feet. "Why do you both act like I'm the only woman for the job? I'm handing it over to blood!" Renee gave Metro her back and took a deep breath. After collecting herself, she turned to face her mentor once more, and in a calm, stable voice, she told him, "I'm beginning to think no matter who I choose, they'll never be good enough for either of you."

"Because they won't." Both of Metro's feet hit the floor. "You've taken what I started and given it a new look. You've made it yours, and now a bulk of my foundation has your fingerprint on it. You doubled profits, sustained and added valuable connections all while taming some of the most untamable beasts. Not everyone can do that. You're in too deep to leave. You're close to reaching your peak. We only trust you."

"Close to reaching my peak?" Renee's hands found their way on her hips. "Bullshit! I've surpassed what we thought I'd accomplish."

Metro stood and walked over until he was standing in front of Renee with his hand outstretched, his pointer finger and thumb close but not touching. A smile laced his face. "You did, and now you're this close to reaching billionaire status. You can surpass me. You can't stop now."

Renee's face hardened. "How could I have not seen it sooner?" Renee paused and chuckled. She covered her eyes with her shooting glasses and positioned herself in front of the gun display in search of a weapon. "The longer I stay, the more money you and Dane gain. I get it. No other dealer would agree to give you a percentage to show their appreciation."

Renee slid open the door of the display case and reached inside to grab the Heckler & Koch VP9. Suddenly, the door slammed on her hand. Shooting pain shot through her hand and up her arm. She tried to pull her hand free. However, Metro held the glass door in place.

"You insisted and begged to show your appreciation for a fuckin' year of us rejecting your pennies."

Metro pushed the door harder against Renee's hand. She flinched and internalized her pain.

"Keep your money. I don't want or need it." He let go of the door, and with a balled-up fist, he created distance between him and Renee.

Renee rubbed her hand. "My decision is made," she huffed. "I only asked your opinion out of respect."

Back in front of the stall, Metro reloaded his weapon and put back on his shooting glasses and earmuffs. "You want to show me respect?" he roared. "Meet with a few friends of mine, some who stayed and some who left this world. It would be in your best interest to understand what you're about to get yourself into from those who have done it first. Let this decision be based on logic and not emotion."

Renee snatched extra ammo and a handgun from Metro's shooting tray, her interest in retrieving one from the display case long gone. She moved behind the station to Metro's left.

When Renee trained to take over the business, one of Metro's requirements was that she must visit the shooting range five times a week. So she did. She got so good at shooting that she made a game out of it and would shoot with her eyes closed. Shooting at the range was one of Renee's best life moments.

She covered her ears with her trusty earmuffs, followed by covering her eyes with her glasses. She loaded the firearm, aimed, and shot. The power she felt the first time she released a bullet into the paper returned. Sadly, no spark for life pumped into her soul. Now all she felt was exhausted and downright tired. Renee shot another bullet into the target's neck. It was perfect, a hole directly in the center. She released the remaining rounds into the small X located in the middle of the blue man's chest. She kept squeezing the trigger even though she ran out of firepower. Slamming the gun down, she snatched off the glasses.

"I bet your friends will have great things to say concerning staying, so no, thank you. I don't have time."

Metro emptied his clip inside the target's head, his aim better than Renee's. "As long as I'm alive, you're going to be fully aware of all your options so you'll do things right, whether I agree with your decision or not. I'm still your mentor, but more importantly, I'm your father figure. You have to go about things correctly."

Renee swallowed and blinked back emotions. She craved moments like these from her biological parents, and now that she had friends giving them to her, she damn near broke down. Nodding, she agreed to appease Metro and take him up on his offer.

"In two days, we'll fly with my friends to Bora-Bora in a private jet."

Light sparkled in Renee's eyes at the mention of the island Bora-Bora. Immediately, Metro crushed her vacation dream of traveling to one of the few places she hadn't visited.

"We won't be vacationing with them. That's not why we're going there. The commute will be your opportunity to pick their brains. Focus, Renee. It's all about the information."

Renee did not look at or respond to her father figure/mentor. Instead, she picked up the gun and reloaded it.

Chapter 3

There were things such as flying that Renee hadn't noticed she missed until she was back in the air. There was something freeing about watching the clouds float by and being thousands of feet above ground, away from the daily city riffraff.

"Would you like a drink, miss? Perhaps some champagne?" The stewardess, wearing white gloves, held the distinct dark bottle of champagne out in front of her so Renee could view it comfortably. Smiling, she displayed the bottle proudly, her smooth, dark, powdery skin glowing.

Renee nodded, her bottom lip slightly projected. "Good brand. Fill me up."

The flight attendant stretched a little while pouring the bubbly. Her orchid-colored, long-sleeved, plunging V-neck button-down top and swinging skirt, equipped with a large belt, failed to move with her from the thighs up. She fought to maneuver in the spandex material all while standing tall in six-inch heels. A cap atop her head completed the look.

Renee's champagne-filled flute weighed heavy in her hand.

"If you need me, do not hesitate to ring." Orchid gave Renee a friendly smile, followed by batting eyes and swaying hips meant for Metro. Orchid's departure sent her to the men who sat cross-legged on the couch across from them.

"I'm glad Dane's not here. I don't know how well we would hide a body on this jet," Renee commented, then sipped her champagne. Liking what she tasted, she drank a little faster.

"Trust me, she's not my type," Metro assured her.

Renee tilted the flute and studied it. "This shit goes for forty thousand a bottle?"

Orchid and another curvaceous woman clad in the scandalous modern-day version of the 1940s flight attendant uniform were leaned over, their breasts in the faces of the elderly men who were unbuttoning their tops.

"And this"—Renee surveyed her surroundings, from the leather sectionals to the flat-screen televisions and decorative gold-plated tree branches that stretched from the floor to the skylights—"had to have run him millions."

"Jaxs is a billionaire," Metro stated. "Something you'll be if you stay."

"Motherfucker!" Murry shouted. "This bitch has a bedroom with a king-sized bed and a bathroom with twin showers and tiled floors!" He looked from Renee to Metro.

Metro smiled. "I know. Jaxs didn't want carpet, so he had the floors custom made. She's a beauty, isn't she?"

"Bombshell is more like it," Murry whispered. "I go away for a month, and Jaxs gets a new toy. Aye! Aye! Jaxs, I'll pay you five million for this plane."

Muffled by the double-D breasts his face was planted in, it was almost impossible for Jaxs's words to come out intelligibly. "This jet is worth over thirty million!"

Murry folded his arms over his chest, lowered his eyes, and ignored another near-naked sex object in the sky pulling on his arm. The six foot two Dominican woman, who had icicle white hair pulled back into a long ponytail and bangs covering her broad forehead, pulled harder on Murry the longer he ignored her.

"Ten million, a bag of chips, and a box of chocolate bars. I know you like your chocolate," Murry offered Jaxs.

Prostitute number one looked over her shoulder at Murry. The tips of her wavy hair hit the edge of her behind when she threw her head back in laughter.

"There's plenty I'll do for ten million," the Dominican giant publicized. She licked Murry's right cheek and purred into his ear, her animalism winning over his attention.

"Lead the way," Murry instructed, allowing the woman wearing a cropped top and booty shorts to walk in front of him. He watched every inch of her before they vanished behind the bathroom door.

Renee and Metro were left behind to listen to the snickers and kissing sounds coming from both steward-esses as they smothered Jaxs on the couch.

Renee's eyes were locked on the public acts of affection. "So he's Jaxs?" she asked.

"Sticks out, doesn't he?" Metro replied.

"Very much. He's albino," Renee said, before sipping more champagne and swooshing it around in her mouth as her taste buds sucked it all in.

Renee had seen a lot but never had she met an albino. Jaxs was bleach white. His beard and eyebrows were snow white, yet his short, thick, wavy hair was as vibrant as wheat. He was slim and considered a giraffe among average-height folks.

"Jaxs is worth more than us all. He has his hand in every lucrative pot there is, from pharmaceuticals to diamonds and the black market. He's the smartest man I know and the reason why you push a majority of your work from drug stores." Metro paused. "We met in junior high. One day he was being teased, and I defended him."

"You despise bullies," Renee said more to herself than to Metro.

"Always have. I pick his brain now and then. Each time, his financial advice made me millions."

Through the spaces between arms and legs created from their human pretzel, Renee saw bits and pieces of Jaxs. *That colorful Hawaiian shirt doesn't scream savvy billionaire.*

"And him?" Renee gestured toward the heavyset Indian man who rubbed the two women's legs and occasionally palmed their asses.

"That's Neel. He came to the U.S. thirty years ago, and from the moment he stepped foot on American soil, he used all of his family's connections to grow and distribute his own genetically engineered weed, legal and illegally."

"How much is he worth?"

"$10.5 billion."

Renee's mouth fell open. "All from weed?"

"That and he struck oil, literary." Metro chuckled.

Murry and his Dominican woman reappeared from the back of the jet. Following close behind the disheveled two was a stench of body odor and lust. Light years away from taking on the role of a real flight attendant, DR picked up a bottle of gin.

"Gin for the man?" Pouring the liquid into a short, fat glass, she picked up where Orchid left off, flashing her pearly whites and deep dimples.

Metro didn't answer, let alone look at who offered the drink. However, when the prostitute placed the glass in his hand, Metro immediately indulged in the harsh yet surprisingly soothing poison. Lounging on his tongue, the gin burned into his taste buds. Trying to escape the raw, scorching flavor, he swallowed and felt it transform from a cruel and intense experience into a gentle and sweet flow.

Renee drank her bubbly while watching above the rim of her glass as Murry zipped up his jeans then flopped down on the edge of the sectional and sucked in a glob of air. DR plopped down on his lap and wrapped her arms around his short neck. Their lips intertwined and formed a glob of spit on the corners of their mouths.

Renee pulled the flute from her mouth long enough to ask, "What's his story?" Then she lifted it back up to her lips. When no champagne spilled out, she rolled her eyes and ditched the glass on the small, high table next to her.

Metro swayed his head slowly from side to side. "Murry's the oldest of us all."

Renee experienced a fit of laughter that resulted in her covering her mouth and shutting her eyes. "You have got to be kidding me."

"It's true. He acts like he's the youngest, but he's very much the oldest. What makes it more ironic is that he entered our type of lifestyle last. His mother, Liza, started out washing money for crooked cops and wound up marrying one, Jodi Dial. Jodi and his partner stole money confiscated from the largest drug bust back in the eighties, and they all ran off. When Jodi died, he left Murry eighty thousand dollars. Liza went to live in Hawaii, and Murry got into business with his best friend, Jaxs."

Renee looked at the albino Jaxs's empty pills from a prescription bottle.

"He's Jaxs's right hand, which makes him—"

"The second richest person on this jet," Renee filled in.

"Exactly." Metro polished off the rest of his gin. "After retiring, Murry spends his time traveling. He just came back from Abu Dhabi."

"You have to be shittin' me. Someone like him seems money hungry and starving for attention and the thrill of life."

"I can see where you see that. However, Murry is the cheapest son of a bitch you will ever meet. The only thing you have right is his hunger for attention."

"Met, you done giving Ms. Renee the lowdown on all of us?" Murry yelled from underneath DR.

"You two have been whispering for some time. Say anything about me?" DR's long tongue flicked from the slight opening between her lips and forced itself back inside Murry's mouth.

After gnawing away at the thick piece of pink flesh, Murry took a break, laid his forehead against hers, and placed his hands on both sides of her face. "You're not that special, honey. So do me a favor: keep your mouth shut and do your job."

Murry's thin fingers applied pressure to her face, her tan cheeks turning red. She tried sliding her face from his grasp. However, his grip tightened, keeping her in place.

"Say yes." His toothpaste-commercial smile never wavered. It only grew in length.

Strained and against her will, DR put on a smile all while pushing out an alluring and racy, "Yes."

Murry crashed his lips against hers, slapped her ass, and with a wave of his hand, sent her off.

"Ms. Renee, have you heard enough to feel a part of the family? We've never had a sister. Well, other than Dane." Murry stretched his arms and settled them on the top of the sectional behind him.

"I will," Renee answered. "Once I'm told about him. What's his name?"

Next to Neel sat a mute, slim man who wore large black glasses. He had one leg crossed over the other, and his hands were relaxed in a folded position. His thin beard and sideburns connected, and the cleanliness of his eyebrows led Renee to believe he got them waxed.

"Does he speak?"

"I'm blind, not mute," the well put-together man answered for Metro and Murry.

"Hell, I would have thought the same thing if I didn't know you. Your ass looks and acts like a mortician. Give the all black a break, my brother."

"Ha-ha, Murry, and to answer your question, Renee, my name is Spencer. I build and sell legal and illegal firearms. These fools, along with hundreds of other fools, get their weapons and other electronics of mine, from burner phones to night-vision goggles to home security. I offer hacker services, as well. My team handles my clients' overseas accounts and makes them invisible to the government. We're in a high-tech world, so we must change with the times all while protecting ourselves. I supply that protection."

Spencer reached inside his suit jacket's inner pocket, pulled out a pint of vodka, and took a mouthful. His cheeks bloated and quickly deflated after he swallowed the clear substance.

A prostitute waltzed over to Spencer. She sat on his lap and rubbed his facial hair. "I like a man who's into electronics. What else do you do?"

Spencer reached down between her legs.

"Ah! A man who knows what he wants!" she shouted and giggled.

Spencer proceeded to feel around down there, and then without hesitation, shoved her off. "Get off of me! I don't do dicks."

Like a prune, Renee's face shriveled up.

"I bet Metro didn't tell you that he and I are the only heterosexual men on this jet. The others are bisexual."

"Damn straight!" Murry yelled while the other two continued giving the other transvestites their undivided attention.

"Normally, I don't come along on their erotic vacations, but we're headed to Bora-Bora, and I wanted to meet the woman Metro speaks so highly of. I hope I can be of assistance with your decision."

It was impossible for Spencer to see, but Renee felt he was staring straight into her soul.

Chapter 4

Meanwhile in New York

Lincoln looked into the mirror and was happy with who stared back at him. In the last month, he had done a total 180 and changed his style. His clothes were no longer oversized or colorful. They now fit properly and matched. Lincoln hadn't seen or spoken to Shelia in months. She was an older woman he was involved with who turned out to be Renee's mother. She was nothing but trouble. After calling the relationship off, he never saw her again. He should have been okay with that, since he was the one who ended things, but for some reason, he wasn't. He missed her and wanted to hear her voice one more time, but as time passed, he realized it would never happen. The relationship was over, and wherever Shelia was, it was apparent she didn't want to be found.

With Sheila absent from his life, Lincoln took a serious look at himself. He was incapable of keeping a woman, and he was tired of it. Throughout high school, no girl wanted to date the nerdy kid. Then Electra, his first girlfriend and the love of his life, cheated on him and left him for her lover. Hurt and confused, he hooked up with Sheila. The goal was to forget his pain. What Lincoln had with Sheila was not supposed to be serious.

It was only something convenient for the both of them. However, Lincoln developed feelings. Now that another relationship had died, he thought he would change himself, starting with the way he looked. He didn't want to be alone. He wanted to catch a woman and keep her, and he was willing to do whatever it took to do so.

Lincoln smiled at his reflection. He was pleased with the crisp white T-shirt, dark blue jeans, and white low-top Nikes he sported. He grabbed his blue fitted Yankees hat off his dresser and slapped it on his head. His past relationships were exactly that: the past. He was ready to move on and start from scratch.

Lincoln drove into a McDonald's parking lot and took his place in line at the drive-thru. After ten minutes of waiting, he became impatient and continuously sighed while shaking his head.

"What the fuck is he ordering?" he asked himself.

He looked out his window at the Nissan Altima two cars in front of him. The driver seemed to be ordering the whole menu. The more Lincoln stared at the car sitting at the intercom, the angrier he became. He took his eyes off the Altima, and they landed on the rearview mirror of the vehicle directly in front of him. The driver looked back at him the entire time. Her hazel eyes were hypnotic and stared deep into his soul. Lincoln felt as though the wind had been knocked out of him. This stranger was the most gorgeous woman he had ever laid eyes on. Her skin was the color of caramel and appeared to be as smooth as silk. Her makeup was immaculate, and Lincoln pictured himself kissing her pouty lips.

While Lincoln daydreamed about the beautiful woman, the Altima finally moved, and the mystery woman followed suit. If it weren't for the three cars behind him honking their horns, Lincoln would have never snapped out of his daydream and moved up.

He watched the woman order her food, and when she was done, she looked back at him. Once again, their eyes met, and she smiled. Her red lipstick sparkled in the sunlight, enhancing her beauty. Lincoln smiled back, his heart pounding against his chest. This beauty took over his very existence, and within seconds, all confidence and self-assurance vanished. This woman, whose name he didn't know, had stolen his heart and locked it inside a vault all while dismantling whatever pride he had.

Five minutes later, Lincoln had ordered, paid for his food, and exited the lot. He watched as the lady's silver luxury car drove down the street and stopped at a light. Without giving it a second thought, he followed her and didn't stop until she pulled over in front of a corner store. For ten seconds, no one got out of his or her car. They both sat there, waiting for the other to make a move. Lincoln's mouth grew dry, and his nerves kicked him from the inside out. He wanted this stranger and, without understanding why, needed her. Never had a woman taken hold of his soul without saying a word. That alone scared him. The unknown, undeniable connection and appeal came so strongly it baffled him. This appeared to be love at first sight. The feelings he'd prayed for and set out to achieve had come sooner than he expected, and it paralyzed him.

Minutes passed. It was obvious Lincoln would not or could not budge, so Ms. Red Lipstick got out of her car, and with her arms crossed, she leaned against her vehicle. Lincoln took a deep breath. He knew she made the first move, and although his feet were cemented to the floor, he had to get out. He had no idea what he'd say to her, but

he'd think of something. He could not have her wait forever. Slowly, Lincoln got out and hoped she didn't see
the nerves smeared on his face.

"When you started following me, I wondered if you
were a stalker. Then I thought about it. You're too cute to
be a stalker."

There it was, that mesmerizing Hollywood smile.
When she flashed her pearly whites, Lincoln became
relaxed.

"I'm sorry about that. I didn't mean to freak you out."

"You didn't. It takes a lot to scare me. Now tell me,
what can I help you with?" Her head cocked innocently
to the side.

Lincoln stuffed his hands into his jeans pockets and
looked over her wardrobe. There was no mistaking she
was used to the finer things and had probably never worn
a pair of sweats in her life. He could tell she was the type
of woman who had a hair appointment every week and
never wore the same thing twice.

"Well, since you're asking, I would love to take you
out sometime."

Without Ms. Red Lipstick noticing, Lincoln held his
breath. His nerves increased, and he questioned whether
his pride could take another hit if she didn't agree to
go out with him. His ex-girlfriends had done enough
damage.

She dropped her arms at her sides and filled in the
space between them. The closer she got to Lincoln,
the more he smiled. The smell of her perfume, the sound
of her heels clicking against the concrete, and the sway of
her hips hypnotized him and tossed him in a trance. She
stood directly in front of him. Her breath smelled like
bubble gum.

"I would love to go out with you. Give me a pen and paper, and I'll give you my number."

Surprised yet ecstatic that she agreed to go out with him, Lincoln dug in his pocket for his smartphone and quickly handed it to her. He watched as she punched in her name and number. After Carmen stored her information inside the device, she slowly slid the phone back into his front pocket, her eyes never leaving his. Just before she walked back to her car, she patted his pants, ensuring the mobile device was where it needed to be. The sweet smell of her perfume lingered in the air. Lincoln cheesed like the Cheshire Cat as he watched her drive away.

When her vehicle was out of sight, he looked down at his smartphone. "Carmen," he read off the screen. "Nice to meet you."

Chapter 5

Murry missed one last room on the jet to boast about—the conference room. A sleek oval-shaped marble meeting table surrounded by eight chairs glowed underneath the skylight. A flat-screen television was tucked inside the wall a few feet away from a bar located in the corner of the room. Renee admired it all, delicately touching the table and chairs. She noticed the difference in quality in comparison to her home's conference room by the mere touch. Her girly flats lightly slapped against the tiled floors. Immediately, she looked down, hoping she didn't leave a scuff mark. Facing the bar, she observed decanters of various sizes beautified with specs of diamonds.

"Would you like a drink?"

A little startled by the meek and soft voice behind her, Renee turned around while attempting to relax her facial expression. Portraying a kind demeanor came easy when Renee faced a petite, doe-eyed girl who looked to be no older than 23. She wore the exact flight attendant outfit as the others who entertained the men on board. However, her clothing was more loose fitting and professionally appropriate.

Doe Eyes pointed to the bar as she made her way to it. "I can pour you whatever you like." She touched the top of two of the tallest decanters. "Here we have Pyrat and Legacy rums." The tips of her finger dropped to the wider and shorter decanters. "As for vodkas, we have Diva Premium, Belver Bears, Billionaire, and last but not least, Kors."

Renee was never one to buy items based on the price tag but solely on what she liked. These top brands and money she was fenced in by on this plane become a little overwhelming. The men she traveled with were at least twenty years her senior, yet their spending habits were coming across as flashy new money.

"Surprise me," Renee forced out.

Renee had forgotten which liquor was which. After she heard the names of the first two, she had mentally checked out. In the beginning, she was impressed by Jaxs's lifestyle. It was a different type of world. But now it was only coming across as show-off status, which resulted in Renee second-guessing whether these men could give her any real insight on life.

Doe Eyes poured Renee half a glass of the second rum introduced to her. "You seem like a rum woman." A friendly smile lit up her face as she handed Renee the glass.

"Far from it." Renee tasted the drink. Her face scrunched up, and she placed the glass down.

"You're the first one on this plane not to act like she liked anything offered to her." Doe Eyes chuckled intensely as she slapped her hand on her chest. Her flight attendant cap crept down the front of her head.

The vibe took over the atmosphere and eased the judgment Renee enclosed herself in. "Life's too short to be anything other than yourself."

"I heard that," the young girl agreed.

"You hiding back here or something? I haven't seen you up front," Renee questioned. There was nothing else she had left to do other than start a conversation while she waited for Neel.

The young girl poured the most expensive rum inside a new glass. "And I'm grateful for that. This is my post. My job description differs widely from what you see out there." She put down coasters, and at the head of the table, she placed a drink down on the coaster. "What's even better is being among a fellow female today."

"How can you be so sure I was born a woman?" Renee quizzed. The world had changed in so many ways that she found it harder and harder to read people. So instead of assuming answers, she asked questions.

"For starters, I can tell that you barely, if at all, are wearing makeup. I have nothing against transvestites, but I don't agree with how they conduct and parade themselves around these men. Whatever happened to self-respect and dignity?" Doe Eyes lightly shook her head.

"This lifestyle does something to you, whether you notice it or not," Renee offered.

"That's where I disagree, Ms. . . ."

"Jordan. You can call me Jordan."

"Ms. Jordan, I know what these men are into and all of the illegal activities they're submerged in, but when is enough enough? When do you get out and give yourself a new identity, a new start at life? I am a firm believer you will not live a life you don't want to."

Renee said nothing. She continued to listen to the thoughts of a woman who had a lot to say but no one to say it to.

"Even what I'm doing is wrong. I don't want to be around these men. They're risking their lives for the almighty dollar, and like a fool, I took the job for a piece of the pie. But I've decided to get out even if it means I'm just as poor as when I started. This will be the last time I work for Mr. Jaxs. He tried to talk me out of leaving, but I've made up my mind that I'm ready for the healthier, happier, less stressful chapter of my life."

The determination and seriousness in her tone resonated with Renee. Had she been just as sure as Doe Eyes in her decision to leave this life alone, she wouldn't be there. However, there was a small part that questioned whether leaving the life she'd known for over the past ten years was the right move. She wondered if all the glitz and glam was set up with hopes of leading her back inside the lion's den. Did she want to leave it all alone, or was it a thought that felt right only in the moment?

"The worst thing anyone can do is try to talk me out of a decision I've made. If you're not God or my parents, then you don't know what's right for me. I've learned over my short time on earth that people look out for themselves first. A lot of people only care about what you can do for them and only them." Doe Eyes wiped up the sprinkles of rum that missed the glass during her pouring session. "Everyone always thinks they know what's best for you. Have you ever noticed that?" She lifted her head from cleaning. Seeing an unresponsive Renee made her apologetic. "I am so sorry. Here I am throwing all of my issues on you when it's obvious you're here for a vacation with colleagues. I am being so unprofessional. Please forgive me. Act like I never opened my big mouth." Doe Eyes cleaned faster. "I'll be right out of your hair."

Renee didn't comment right away, but when she did, she kept her sight fixed on the corner of the jet decorated in gold. The gold-plated tree branches gave the illusion that they were growing within the airplane. "No, no, it's okay. Keep going."

"No, no, I've said enough, and I'm sure I've done enough damage."

"Please!" Renee cleared her throat. "I assure you all is well. Now please continue."

"I guess I'm tired of doing what I think is right for everyone else. I'm ready to put me first." Doe Eyes reverted to the soft-spoken kid who first approached Renee. "My whole life I've had a hand in this type of life. I'm ready to witness something else."

Neel made an appearance, and the conversation immediately came to a halt. "Renee, I'm sorry I've kept you waiting. Has Carmen been a good hostess?"

Renee placed her sight solely on the young woman she'd been conversing with for a short time. A hit of disgust struck her face. "Your name's Carmen?"

The woman smiled. "Yes, it is."

Renee forced a smile. "It's nice to meet you, Carmen. You've given me a lot to think about." As soon as she finished her comment, her smile disappeared.

"I hope that's a good thing," Neel intervened, unaware of their discussion. However, he felt entitled to give his input.

"Very much," Renee assured him.

"Have a good meeting," Carmen said, then vanished behind a door.

Walking farther inside, Neel extended his hand. "Have a seat."

Renee's behind was on the verge of sitting down when Neel stopped her. "Not there."

Hands planted flat on the table, and butt midair, Renee froze. She looked around in search of the issue.

"Heads of the meeting sit at the head of the table." He now stood in front of her, his eyes directing her to the seat at the left of where she intended to sit.

Their eyes met. Renee never broke their eye battle, and neither did Neel. One of the biggest mistakes made on Renee's behalf was never surrounding herself with people who were above her, other than Metro and Dane. She lacked the etiquette and respect necessary when participating in meetings she wasn't in control of.

"Understand, Renee, the meetings you'll have are not a power struggle but a learning experience." She released a steady, smooth breath of air while recollecting the piece of advice Metro bestowed on her before they stepped on the jet.

Standing erect, she nodded, held out her hand, and placed a smile on her face. "You're right. I apologize. It's a pleasure to officially meet you."

After the two engaged in a handshake, she redirected herself to where Neel instructed she sit. From his pocket, Neel pulled out a sky blue handkerchief and patted the sweat attempting to touch down on his nose. Without taking a break, he downed a majority of the liquor waiting for him.

"You're a fool," he blurted out after breaking away from his drink.

"Excuse me?"

"You want out before you've even reached your full potential. That's a dumb move."

Before finishing the drink, he grabbed one of the decanters from the bar. Renee was sure he hadn't a clue what he'd selected. "Tell me, why do you want out?" he asked while mixing the two drinks.

The brief silence brought to Renee's attention Neel's nonexistent accent. Metro mentioned him arriving in the

U.S. thirty years ago, yet she still envisioned she'd detect a speck of India. She'd hope to meet each man for who they were, the past included.

You stay in this lifestyle, and it wipes out every trace of you in its leave, creating a new you, Renee thought. "It's time."

Neel almost choked. His smirking while drinking resulted in the liquid going down the wrong pipe. "You've been reading the drug dealer's manual. 'It's time,'" he mimicked.

Air escaped from Renee's lungs, traveling throughout her chest and leaving her mouth. Her shoulders rose and fell, a weak effort of losing her nerves. She didn't like him.

"If the shoe fits," she responded.

"Is that so?" Neel leaned back in his chair. He situated his feet on top of the table and leaned to the left to have a clear view of Renee. "Why stop being who you are and become the average Joe?"

"Who said this"—Renee opened her arms outward—"was me?"

"Only those who are this, even a morsel of this, actually live it."

Renee turned away, the small saying sinking into her brain and forcing itself into a seat next to millions of other thoughts her cranium contained. "That fragment is dead. I want more. This," Renee said, dragging out the word, "has taken too much."

Neel spun his legs off the table. His lanky limbs slowed before they touched the floor as he stood. His large, anorexic palms rested on the table, plunging into the marble, while his chest caved in. The neckline on his "one size too large" tank top dropped and exposed his hairy brown chest. The thin, slick hairs jammed together by sweat caused her stomach to rumble and vomit to climb up her throat. Renee squeezed her eyes shut and turned away after she caught a glimpse of his nipple piercings.

"That's because you didn't give enough. You have to give everything you have, let go of all your wants and needs, and submit to this life in order to reap the benefits!"

By the end of his small speech, his right hand had balled into a fist, and he pounded on the marble two, maybe three times. His breathing turned uneven, what air escaped from his mouth sour and stale. Now closer than what they once were, Neel's nose grazed the side of Renee's cheek. He pulled away only to place his nose right back where it was. He slowly started rubbing it against the cheek he was introduced to moments prior.

Renee pulled away, her reaction swift and without hesitation. Tight faced, her freshly threaded eyebrows fell downward and created lines just above the bridge of her nose. Renee grabbed ahold of the chair's arms and stood. Neel pulled himself farther on top of the table, his stomach flat on the marble like a baby crawling on a play mat. Then he stretched his arms out until they reached his prey. Unable to move out of his reach fast enough, Neel's unnaturally limber hands wrapped around one of Renee's wrists and tugged her back down into the chair. Without giving it any thought, Renee swung her free hand, only for Neel to grab that wrist and secure her in place. Neel handled her like a rag doll and pulled her forward with as little strength as possible. Too close for comfort, Renee turned away, her neck a fragile and vulnerable piece of flesh that lingered in front of a bloodsucker. Neel deeply inhaled her scent. The fresh, high-fashion smell that New York women wished to bathe in seeped inside his nostrils.

"I've missed the smell of a natural woman," he whispered, inhaling once more before continuing to speak. "I love my trannies. Still, there's always something missing, something that can't be duplicated. I could never figure out what it was, but now I know. It's the scent. The natural, undeniable scent of a woman."

Renee fidgeted and stretched her neck as far from him as she could. That only made him tighten his grip on her more.

"You're not going anywhere. What would you say, and who would you say it to? Money rules everything, and power only secures the position."

Unsure of how she did it, Renee freed herself from his hold. The heat of her anger radiated from her skin. She pushed him. Although stronger and heavier than he appeared, Neel was caught off guard, and his basketball-player physique slid off the marble table and slammed back into his seat. Without thought or control of her actions, Renee pounced on the table and in two long strides was hovering over Neel. Squatting, she snatched a handful of his long, dyed blond, greasy hair. Her dry hands ate away at the lubricant that polished the cracks of her palms.

Spit from the lean spaces between Renee's teeth seeped out. "Don't you ever!"

"Let him go, Jordan." The innocent voice belonged to the young woman whose dreams were parallel to Renee's, and she pointed her gun at the head of an enraged, table-hopping Renee.

Renee looked up and met the eyes of the only soul on the plane she was deceived into believing was harmless and nothing more than a stewardess who served drinks and food to villains.

A loud, stretching sound of laughter flowed out of Neel, his body shaking and jumping during his fit of joy. "Money buys it all. It even buys the freedom of the guilty and protects them in the process."

Renee's hold constricted.

"Jordan, let him go."

Staring into the eyes of a happy-go-lucky Neel, who was given a temporary facelift, Renee let go. Carmen made her way across the room, tossed a small bag into Neel's lap, and pressed the muzzle of the gun to the side of Renee's head.

Frantic and with a lack of patience, Neel dug the long, mutated nail of his pinky finger inside the substance and brought it up to his nostrils. After a big sniff, he presented not a smile but a shrill look that drowned Renee from the inside out.

"If you leave, you will be just as you are now—powerless. You will be vulnerable and highly accessible to all of life's evils."

In need of seconds, he dipped into the powder and ate it with his nose, all while standing in front of a still-crouching Renee. Carmen jammed the gun harder against Renee's head, warning her to remain still and obedient. Neel sank his nail back inside the small bag. However, before pulling it out, he emptied it inside his opposite hand and dived his head into his makeshift bowl, inhaling maliciously. Content with his dosage, Neel lifted his powder-stained face and touched Renee's cheek with his hand covered in white residue.

"Power is what you make of it. Power gives back what you have given it. You let go now, and nothing will come of this decision except you going back to how you once were—a weak little girl violated by her stepfather."

Renee winced. Her hands balled into fists and her eyes lowered. Carmen pushed the firearm harder against her.

"Shhhhhh," Neel whispered. "I'm not trying to anger or disrespect you. Just trying to remind you of the benefits and peace a woman in your position retains. How does it feel for me to caress your hard yet ample cheek?"

With his thumb, he rubbed her.

"For me to touch you?"

Two of his fingers trailed down her face to her throat and stopped just above her breasts.

"A stranger, taking it upon himself to engage in such personal acts."

He forced a smirk, then took a look at her and the residue she was blotched with. His already-dilated pupils fell in love with the leftovers, and he licked them off of her. Renee breathed out harshly.

"I can feel your disgust through the goose bumps on your skin, yet there's nothing you can do but be a victim. Are you ready for that? Are you ready to go back where you came from, or worse, who you were?"

Chapter 6

Planted on the hefty table, Renee hung her legs off the edge. Back and forth they swung past one another and created a man-made wind. The longer she waited for her next meeting, the faster she tried to instruct her legs to move. Definitely after meeting with Neel, a situation she yearned to redo to be given the opportunity to release her anger, the expensive, valuable items settled on the aircraft had been given two faces. The first was luxurious and favorable, the face of what the world craved and chased whether by legal or illegal means. The poster of what Americans considered high quality and a comfy, cushioned essential when living a life of prosperity. It was all Renee had captured, with a few things not far out of reach. It's what had given her stability and the ability to be her own boss. She made her own schedule, hired her own employees, and created and deflated whatever rules during whatever times. It was empowering. It was the American Dream.

The second face was two-faced, a pact made with the devil, where everything you ever dreamed of was handed to you, wrapped in shiny paper with an oversized bow and all yours. That was, if you paid the piper when the time came. It was always thought the price would never be high, nor would favors be cashed in at any time, but that was never true, and the price was always higher than the reward. The top-shelf liquor and billion-dollar airplane were reminders of how much she'd have to put on the line in order to stay on top. This lifestyle came with a lot of give-and-take, risk Renee had always been able to handle as long as her past stayed in the past.

Her right leg kicked a little higher than she intended and gave her a clear view of a pair of flats she could honestly admit she spent way too much on. She remembered when she bought them. She was months into selling drugs when she walked by a shoe store. The display light hit them perfectly, and it gave them a personality and voice of their own. Decorated with nothing except soft rainbow colors and an even softer interior, they were perfect. She listened to the salesman give his best pitch. Renee's conscience told her not to buy them, and feet itched to walk away, but she couldn't. She wouldn't.

She had something to prove to herself. She had to confirm her old self was buried in the past. Had the old Renee still been around, and had she entertained her, her money would have stayed in her pocket, but she was no longer that person. Renee could no longer be that person, and wearing those girly flats rather than boots and sneakers would be her transformation. It was time to live for the future and let go of the past.

"Don't jump!" A loud roar of laughter trespassed inside the meeting room and snatched Renee's attention from her shoes. Seeing Murry amused with himself was no reason for her to look his way for more than a few seconds. She acknowledged his presence, only to quickly take that acknowledgment away.

"Did Neel come on too strong? Stir up some long-lost emotions you care not to speak on?"

Renee slid off the table, headed for the door. She passed Murry and purposely bumped his shoulder. Their clash moved him a little out of the way.

"Feisty. And here I am excited to finally talk to someone who isn't Spencer about retiring."

So close. Renee was so close to breathing in air that hadn't been corrupted by Neel's stone-cold reminders. Red-eyed, she turned around.

"I think you're doing the right thing. Get out while you can, while you still have a hint of humility left in you and while this still beats." He pounded his fist into his chest. He grabbed a decanter, took a swig, then placed it back down. His face scrunched up. "Even when I was still in that life, I never spent my money on this prissy shit. I put away my money, invested, and bought into a couple of businesses. Made my money work for me, you know?"

Renee never moved. Her mind still swirled over what transpired with Neel, and her anger was still high.

"Neel's an asshole. He was cool in the beginning, but this whole way of life and the shit he's putting up his nose is fucking with him. He's addicted to this shit. He lost himself a long time ago, and that's exactly why I got the fuck out." Murry moved over to the long couch on the side of the room, and he sank in the instant he sat down. "He's one fucked-up individual, but I'd be lying if I told you whatever he said to you was a lie."

"And how could you be so sure of that?" Renee challenged.

"He's many things, but ignorant and unintelligent he's not." He snickered, slapped his right foot on top of his knee, and continued. "Plus I'm sure everything he told me when I was thinking of getting out he told you. And everything he said was right. The moment I decided to leave, things changed for the worse. But it didn't last, because eventually, I came to the conclusion that nothing stays the same forever, not if you don't want it to."

"When you got out, what changed?" Still on edge, Renee made it possible to tone her emotions down slightly and do what she came to do: speak.

Murry huffed. "The respect. To a certain extent, you lose people's respect when they know you've bowed out. People then test you. They have some false idea you're untouchable when you're knee-deep in the game, but when you get out, they look at you like you've fallen from grace." He took a deep breath. "I had a lot of points to make, or at least I thought I did. I wanted people to know that with or without my position, I was not to be fucked with. But soon that shit got old. I wasn't in the business no more, yet I was still putting in work. Finally, I realized if I was going to let go of this life, I had to let go of that mentality. Motherfuckers are always going to be motherfuckers. It's their nature, so it was time I'd be me, a free man."

It was like talking to an entirely different person compared to earlier. Murry spoke from a serious and level-headed place. He left the jokes at the door and showed another side of himself.

More questions came out of Renee's mouth. "Why'd you leave? You mentioned earlier not wanting to lose yourself like Neel, but is that all? Is that the only reason?"

"Hell no! Unlike a lot of motherfuckers, I like myself and the dicks I suck. You can't suck dick if you're dead, and I've come close to death too many times to keep risking it all. That alone made me want to get out, but when I saw the shit Neel and Jaxs were getting themselves into and how much they changed, I knew it was time to go. I love those sons of bitches like they're my brothers, but they're going nowhere fast. I don't care how much money they have. There is such a thing as having enough. I value my life."

"Is that all? The main reason you walked out is to avoid death?"

"Is there a better reason?" Murry looked at her oddly, questioning.

Renee looked down and noticed a piece of glass on the floor. It was big and pointy. She almost bent down to touch it, in hopes it'd poke her and wake her from this nightmare. There were too many decisions to be made and questions in need of answers. She was now unsure of her decision, and her thoughts ran rampant. She wanted to agree 100 percent with Murry. She wanted to admit there was no other reason more important than staying alive after Page almost killed her. Life achieved a higher sense of value, along with attaining happiness and peace. However, after her encounter with Neel and the memories he brought back, Renee wasn't sure how she felt anymore, because going back to being vulnerable and dominated could not be an option.

Murry continued speaking. His truth opened him up and exposed the feelings he felt compelled to share, something he hadn't done enough of. "This shit will change you. It'll morph you into some fucking minion. You know why gangstas are always using the term 'soldiers'?"

Like a child who absorbed information from a parent, Renee listened intently and shook her head.

"Because you're expecting to live and die for this shit. You're nothing but a number, a damn shell of your former self." Murry scratched the side of his face.

Renee's eyes were larger than usual, and her breathing was slow and steady. "I didn't change," she softly responded.

"You ever kill before you got into this world or even do some real shiesty shit you regret?"

"No, not that I can recall," Renee admitted.

"Have you killed and done some fucked-up shit when you got in?"

Silence.

Murry folded his hands behind his head. "Then you changed. I know your kind. Your personal life is shit, so you play a hand in a game, only for you to turn out worse than you were before."

"What kind are you?" This was probably one of the most thought-provoking conversations Renee had ever had.

"One of the worst. The kind who had something to prove."

Renee wanted to him to elaborate. She wanted to inquire some more about his backstory, but she asked a different question instead. "Letting it all go, is it worth it?" Waiting for the answer caused Renee's nerves to stab and paralyze her.

Murry dropped his arms and then wiped a hand down his face. "How can I put this so you understand it so clearly you'd think you felt it yourself?" He paused and viewed this wording as severe as a cure for cancer. "It was the best decision I've ever made. I saved myself when I thought I didn't need saving."

Renee's legs wanted to give out from under her. She felt herself shake and hoped he didn't notice.

Murry smiled, happy with himself. "I still don't regret what I've gotten myself into, because had I not, I would not appreciate my life."

"I guess that means you'd do nothing differently."

"Not a damn thing," Murry boasted.

Renee leaned against the door and slid down until the floor broke her fall. "I have my own reasons why I'd like to get out." Renee rested her head against the door. "I'd like to be normal, ya know, start a family without worrying whether my identity has been discovered and if a fucking hit is on my head. I'd like to release all the stress that comes with the job, the paranoia and twenty-four-hour tough-girl act. I'd like to give myself the chance to let my guard down and actually *feel*." Renee pushed her upper body up and put both her fists in the air.

She slammed herself back against the door. "Then again, I can't go back to where I came from. This life gave me strength and power, everything I needed but didn't have in my past life. This life made it possible to get the revenge I deserved paired with stability. But . . ."

"But what?"

"Now you and your sick-ass friends just gave me more reasons to both leave and stay." She rubbed her eyes and let out a chuckle. "And where the hell did this insightful Murry come from? Outside this room, you're nothing but a carefree jackass."

Murry joined in Renee's laughter. His right hand made a journey south and stopped when half his hand was stuffed in the top of his pants. Before his eyelids shut, he tried to suck out the food wedged between his teeth. A loud sucking noise poked at the silence before he finally spoke. "I'm fucking bipolar. My mood swings have a bigger turnover rate than the *Love & Hip Hop* cast." He laughed harder, then closed his eyes in search of rest.

Renee shrugged her shoulders. "Makes sense."

Chapter 7

Due to mental and emotional exhaustion, Renee took a page from Murry's book and found herself sleeping on the floor, propped up by the door. The plan was to close her eyes while collecting her thoughts. However, her brain shut down, and a catnap took over.

In her dreams, she was on a nonstop roller coaster at an amusement park she and Julian visited from time to time during their teen years. That was, when she was able to escape the confines of her mother.

The ride started out like any other normal theme park adventure: slow, inching its way to the top, its pace and mechanical sounds adding to the excitement and apprehension lodged in the chest of all its riders. It was all routine until the control panels blew out and sent the roller coaster racing ahead at full speed. Alone and petrified, Renee clung to the metal bar securing her in place, and when she wasn't screaming, she was praying. Her head whipped from left to right, and the bun on the bottom of her head unraveled. Down far below, people were the size of ants, pointing up and screaming. Unsure of how she was able to decipher their cries from so high, she listened to crowds of people wail.

"Stop it! Make it stop!"

"There's someone on there!"

"Oh, my gosh, she's going to die."

While park patrons screamed, staff dispersed, all racing in various directions, determined to end the horror that parents hollered over and children cried about. Small, steady bumps in the tracks became vicious and unbearable. Their impact slammed Renee forward again and again, shooting pain crisscrossing up her spine.

"Renee! Renee!" Metro's voice called out to her from down below.

She tried to look down but couldn't. The roller coaster was going too fast. Renee was unable to stop her back and neck from jerking. The tears fell from her eyes, zipped backward, and landed in her hair.

"Metro!" she hollered. It was all she could do. Her voice was her only outlet. More strongly than before, her back caved in and rammed into the bar. She fell out of her seat and in the air, like a baby bird kicked from the nest. The fall was fast, and the wind cut into her face, surpassing her pain. The ground was approaching, the asphalt glistening and enlarging by the second. Her nose slammed into the ground.

Her eyes shot open.

"You two are in here sleeping?"

Light snores leaked out from Murry's parted lips. Renee fumbled around to stand, one hand erasing the drool from the corners of her mouth, the other pushing her body on her feet.

"We're landing?" a raspy-voiced Renee questioned.

"Not for another hour. Wipe the eye buggers out your eyes, and do what you came here for." Metro pulled out a packet of tissues from his pocket and handed it over. "Neel told me your meeting went well." Like any other time Metro tried reading Renee, he clasped his lips shut and lowered his head slightly.

Renee cleaned her eyes. "You told him about me." She crumbled the tissue with one hand and covered it with her fingers. Renee could see the uncomfortable tension emerge in Metro's face.

"If you want the best information, they have to know who they're dealing with. You don't deserve generic opinions."

"You shouldn't have told him that." The tissue Renee hung on to became a stress ball. She squeezed and released the smooth tissue that was rapidly disintegrating.

Metro swallowed the large knot lodged in his throat. "To a certain extent, I agree with his methods. Without crossing any boundaries, he's giving you a taste of what can possibly come. I need you to see the full picture and have a clear understanding of what can go right and wrong regardless of the decision you make."

Metro knew all about Renee's past. Everyone who was close to her did. They never actually sat down and discussed her sexual assault, but that wasn't Renee's choice. There always seemed to be an underlying discomfort when the subject of rape was brought up in front of Metro, and he only seemed to get more awkward when Renee's past was touched on. Some time ago, Renee decided to shine some light on the obvious.

"Rape is a touchy subject for your husband, huh?"

She and the married couple were watching a movie, and a rape scene came on the screen. Automatically, Metro left the room, giving a watered-down excuse of having to use the restroom.

"Yeah, you can say that," Dane confirmed.

"What's his deal?"

Dane didn't respond right away. Renee could feel the wheels spinning in her mentor's mind while she juggled

*what she should and should not say. "I can't get into
details, but what I will tell you is men forcing themselves
upon women traumatized him as a child. It's the only
thing that could ever make him feel helpless."*

*The more time that passed, the more Renee made it
her business to piece together whatever clues she could.
Metro ignored the topic of rape just like he ignored the
topic of his mother. That led Renee to notice that Metro's
stories about his childhood never went past the age of 13.*

Renee's comment came out almost in a whisper. "It's
not your story to tell."

Metro glanced at her quickly, yet slowly enough to
indicate he was listening. He sidestepped her, now closer
to the exit. "Come out. Jaxs and Spencer want to speak
with you together."

A piece of Renee didn't want to move, or couldn't
move. She closed her eyes, instructed herself to breathe,
and made her way out of the room.

Spencer's seat never changed. He remained in the
same seat he took when he first stepped aboard. Jaxs, on
the other hand, was feasting on what Renee perceived to
be a medium-rare T-bone steak flanked by a spinach-ar-
tichoke baked potato. A frosty mug filled with beer sat
beside his plate.

"You don't strike me as the freezer-mug type," Renee
told Jaxs before she took a seat beside Spencer.

"Not all cheap things are bad." Jaxs chuckled at his
own response. Renee didn't.

"Don't mind Jaxs. He's forgotten where he came from."
Spencer's facial expression was very dull. He possessed
the look of what many envisioned monotone people to
look like.

Jaxs used his knife and fork to break down his potato. "Can't forget what you never had." A forkful of starch and artichoke fell on his taste buds.

"You wore your brother's hand-me-downs until you were in high school and lived off food stamps after your father's accident," Spencer reminded him.

Jaxs swallowed. "You love throwing that shit in my face, don't you?" The heavy fork dropped and banged against the plate. He snatched up the bottle of steak sauce, and after one hard shake, oozed brown sauce all over the meat. A majority of the steak was drenched in sauce, while a small piece that hugged the edge of the bone barely received any flavor.

"Accept yourself and maybe you won't see it that way. Hell, I'm blind, and I don't see it the way you do."

"Okay, ladies, maybe you should have this discussion in private," Metro intervened. He gave his friends an annoyed glare.

Jaxs jammed the largest piece of fat into his mouth. Chewing it, he remained fixated on Spencer, whose curled, stiff lips were frozen in place mid-chew.

"Is he watching me? I feel like he's watching me."

"He's watching you, Spence." Metro nudged Jaxs, and his muscular arm broke his friend's staring spree.

Jaxs downed the last of his drink and continued stuffing himself with food. "What do you want to know, Renee?" He looked at her, and a drop of steak sauce sat on the corner of his mouth.

Renee turned to the transvestites sitting topless and enjoying a bottle of champagne. The taller of the two fumbled with her breasts, obsessed with ensuring their evenness and height. Metro followed her gaze. "Get out!" he howled. Glasses and champagne in hand, they jumped up, and oversized silicone breasts bounced in every direction during their departure.

"Let's go have fun with that Indian fruitcake in the back. It'll be fun waking him up." They hiked their skirts up farther and headed to the only bedroom on the plane. Their asses were shown, and right before they fully disappeared, Renee caught a glimpse of DR's hand stroking his penis.

"I like to have fun!" Jaxs hollered at the transvestites' backs. His broad smile gave everyone a view of his sauce-stained teeth.

Renee's voice heightened. "Besides that . . ." Once Jaxs placed his attention on her and focused on the task at hand, Renee's tone reverted to normal. "Why are you still doing this?"

Jaxs smiled. "I like the finer things in life. Because of Spencer, you already know my family wasn't the most financially stable, so I told myself the first day I was bullied for being an albino who wore the same clothing days at a time, I'd make up for our lack of wealth by any means necessary."

"You made up for it, Jaxs. Now what?" Spencer questioned.

Renee cared to know as well, so she asked, "Yeah, now what?"

There was no more meat left on the ivory, oval-shaped plate. The only sign that it once existed were strands of meat caught between Jaxs's teeth. He sucked the bone clean and continued to lubricate it with saliva even though all flavors had vanished. Giving the bone one last lick, he held it between his fingers. "I keep going until I become the richest man on earth. I was born a poor albino kid. There's not much given to me unless I take it." Jaxs eyes looked around the room. His leg shook, and eventually, he began to scratch his arms. Bad memories tended to grab Jaxs by the neck when conjured and fill him with anger and anxiety.

Metro nodded at his friend, encouraging him to say more. Jaxs nodded his head and tried to cease movement. It was refreshing yet odd for Renee to witness Metro in a light outside of husband and retired kingpin.

"Carmen!"

The not-so-innocent stewardess rushed in the room. Her short legs struggled to stand firm while one hand rested on her chest.

"I need a drink, something strong," Jaxs ordered. "I need a drink, something to help relax me," he went on to tell everyone in the room.

Carmen left and quickly reappeared, holding a short, fat glass filled with brown liquor.

"Thank you." Jaxs drank a little less than half, and his leg continued to bounce up and down. His left hand rested on his thigh, and whether he knew it or not, Renee could see his pointer finger tap relentlessly.

"The health issues that come along with being albino aren't easy for the poor. That's not including the bully-ing and constant wishing you looked like everyone else!" The volume in his voice increased. Everyone noticed but no one commented on it. Jaxs took another sip of his drink, actually a gulp. He covered his mouth with one hand, his lips sliding through his partially divided fin-gers, all while he tried to compose himself and stabilize his breathing. "This world acts like everything is divided in two. It makes you think it's either black or white when really it's nothing but a load of shit. Anything that is un-familiar and doesn't fit the American Dream mold is looked down on and belittled."

Jaxs's mouth opened, and his chest heaved up and down so much, Renee wondered if he was asthmatic. She and Metro held a conversation with their eyes.

Is he okay?

Yes. You're not the only one who can benefit from this conversation.

This is awkward.

This is life.

The hefty glass slammed down on the long, slim table. "Every day some ignorant son of a bitch asked me, 'What are you? Why are you so white? You can't be white. You have to be some sort of mutant. Does this hurt?' Some would pinch me and poke me like I was some sort of experiment. Things only got worse when I entered junior high. A lot of people hadn't even heard of an albino, so jokes were made about me, and I was fucked with every day." His hand wrapped around the glass again. Every second that passed, his fingers squeezed harder and harder. It was his release. It was what kept him in control when he felt incapable of keeping it together.

"Then I met Metro, and it all stopped, the laughing and the pointing." The grip on the glass seemed to loosen. This was evident to Renee because the red in Jaxs's knuckles lightened.

Jaxs appeared more flushed than he already was, and his bottom lip hung low. He didn't look Metro in the eye. His emotions prohibited him from doing so. However, he had to ask. Finally, after years, he mustered up the courage to ask the questions he hid from. "How did you do it, Met? How did you make it stop?"

"That's not important. What's important is that it stopped."

Jaxs nodded. Part of Renee questioned whether he understood what he had nodded to. Metro never dodged a question unless it was for one of two reasons: the timing wasn't right, or Jaxs couldn't handle the truth.

"I can't go back to being the weakling my mother gave birth to. Growing up, I was a burden, a thing. I was another reason for debt and for ignorant motherfuckers to feel more superior once they found out I was black. My father didn't have a great job from the beginning, but it was good enough and got us through. But when he got into a car accident, what little we had went out the window."

Renee's breath caught in her chest. Her eyes met Metro's. Neither moved nor spoke. However, both sets of eyes held sympathy for Jaxs.

"But now I'm rich and powerful and considered normal." Jaxs's face twisted a little. "People don't question me, and my parents don't have to worry about a damn thing. I'm who everyone wants to be."

Metro dropped his hand on his friend's shoulder.

"You're seeking a sort of undeniable, unrealistic sense of acceptance. I don't mean to be disrespectful, but I don't suffer from that. Why should I stay in this lifestyle? How can this possibly benefit me? We are not fighting the same battle." Renee looked from Jaxs to Metro.

Jaxs examined her. He took all of Renee in, from the crown of her head down to the tip of her toes. He sat up in his seat and leaned downward. "We're exactly the same. We're both running from something: our past. We hate . . . no, we despise our past selves, but in order for us to ignore and escape those memories, we indulge in what we're good at: destruction." Jaxs tried to smile, tried to lighten the emotions in his eyes. "Without the drugs, the money, the power, and our titles, we're nothing. And that's the worst thing we can ever be."

Renee turned to Spencer, and like magic, he turned in her direction. For some unexplained reason, he seemed to be the source of knowledge on this plane, and more than ever, Renee needed his knowledge.

"If I have any say in your decision whether you lay your crown down, it would be to superglue that shit on your head and hold on to it like it's air." Jaxs stood up. "You came into this life for a reason. Are you really ready to let it all go?"

Jaxs waited for an answer. Renee sought to give one. She instructed her voice box to respond, but nothing came out, at least not yet. She bit down on her lip. Renee really couldn't stand having the attention on her. For a second, she allowed her thoughts to get away from her to think less about life-altering topics. Sadly it didn't last long.

"Can you really let go of all the reasons you started doing this?" Jaxs repeated.

Renee stuffed her hands in her pockets and pinched herself in order to answer. "I have to."

"You don't have to do anything except be black and die!" Jaxs's lips trembled. Momentarily he tightened them, and after regaining his composure, he continued speaking where he left off. "There's no chance of you becoming ordinary. It's all an illusion."

"Yes, but not for the reasons you think," Spencer chimed in. "Her type of ordinary and yours are completely different. Her hardships have passed. She now has a clean slate to start out with. If she gets out now, it will stay that way."

"Her issues went away because of her resources. They paved the way for her happy ending."

"And I'm sure it all came at a price." Spencer aimed his comment more to Renee than Jaxs. "After a while, you get tired of the debt you accrue and the lives you mess up, and you want peace."

"No such thing." Jaxs held his glass up, signaling for a refill. "To live is to suffer, so you might as well suffer surrounded by the best." Carmen poured the refill into his glass. "What we do is not so bad." The liquor kissed Jaxs's top lip and gave him the mustache he always wanted but could never grow.

"It's more than bad," Spencer challenged. "It's evil. Because of my name and what I had, it cost me my sight and my family."

Metro and Jaxs shared a look. "We agreed not to bring that up, Spence," said Metro. Jaxs nodded in agreement with his junior high friend.

"We agreed to give Renee the chance to know all the pros and cons that evolved around her either staying or getting out of selling. That is top priority. That is why we're here, and my story is what I have to offer. Renee, come closer please."

Renee moved closer to Spencer, and her knee knocked against Metro's, hard. "I'm here, Spencer."

"Everyone next to you, including Metro, wants you to reconsider your decision because unlike us they've lost nothing. They will never fully comprehend what it is to have that gaping hole inside your chest widen to the point you think you'll die from misery. The person responsible for this," he said, pointing to his eyes, "and killing my wife and three kids—who were under the age of twelve, might I add—I've done nothing directly to. The only problem that individual had was he wanted what I had. He considered my position an inconvenience, blocking him from what he felt was his rightful place. Everything I had my hands in wasn't one hundred percent legal, so I should have seen it coming, but I didn't. My head became big, with the help of these guys." He paused and swallowed before he continued. "I started believing I was untouchable."

"I'm not reliving this shit." Jaxs got up, and his body shifted from side to side.

"Oh no, motherfucker, you're gonna listen, and you're gonna listen good!" Spencer's foot slapped down against the floor, his voice taking on a mind of its own. He sounded brutal, vengeful, and almost psychotic. "Until your ignorant, in-denial ass leaves this shit alone, you're going to listen to this story each and every time I feel like telling it!" The veins in his thin neck bulged out.

"Calm down, Spence," Metro advised. Jaxs stood in place, his arms folded across his chest while deliberating whether to ring Spencer's neck.

"Don't you tell me to calm down. You're the worst one here, trying to keep this poor girl in the snake pit. What kind of man are you?"

Metro kicked aside the chairs dividing him from Spencer and pulled him out of his seat by the collar of his shirt. "I would die for this girl! You can sit here and tell your story in hopes it will make a difference, but I made a difference by bringing her into the only thing I knew how to do right!" Metro shook Spencer. His head dipped backward, and his glasses threatened to fall. "Worse has happened to her before I came into her life—constant rape, mental and physical abuse—but that all stopped once I was around to protect her."

Jaxs pulled on Metro's shoulder. "Let him go, Met. I'd love to kick his ass too, but it ain't right."

Metro violently shrugged his friend's hand off of him. "I don't want her to go, because allowing her to go would give her too much room to maneuver in this world, and she's not ready!" Metro took in air. "It's easier to keep tabs on someone you put on when you know that all of their business comrades are your friends!"

"Let her go, Met. You can't protect her forever. If any danger does come her way, it would be worse coming from this type of environment, you know that." Spencer allowed his words to sink inside his friend's head.

Metro released Spencer. His collar was wrinkled and stretched out.

"I, too, thought Courtney and the kids were protected. No one could have told me shit. I was the main advocate for loving that life, but that all changed when they took my family and then my sight. Their deaths were the last things I saw and the last things I will ever see."

Metro marched out of the room. A gust of wind pushed into each of them when the door he escaped through opened. The room fell silent after Metro departed.

"I haven't experienced what you two have." Jaxs sat down. "Maybe that's what it would take for me to get out, but until then I'm staying put and reaping all the benefits." Next to Jaxs, Carmen stood with a decanter in her hands. He snatched it from her and attempted to pour himself another glass. A splash of liquor missed the glass, and Jaxs attempted to lap up with his tongue what clung to the side of the side of the glass. "I'm out."

He got up only to drop right back into his seat. Carmen gave him a hand and helped him up with the goal of him staying up.

"Help me to the bedroom, brown suga. This shit's too depressing for my blood. Let's go where the party's at."

Carmen's arm wrapped around his waist before leading him to their destination. Wobbling and off-balance, Jaxs threw his arms above his head, a failed attempt to boost his spirits. "How the fuck did I become drunk so fast?" Jaxs laughed at the question he knew the answer to.

Jaxs's and Metro's exits left Renee surrounded by silence. It gnawed at her spirit and wouldn't grant her peace. It kept telling her loud and clear that Metro didn't want her to stay in the game so he'd profit off her, but because he felt that was the best way he could protect her and he refused to leave her vulnerable to the world again.

All the stories that had been shared touched a spot in her heart: the good, the bad, and especially the ugly. Everything she'd heard she imagined to be true. However, to actually hear these experiences from those who'd lived and sat in this life for twice the amount of time she had was what touched her and made her decision ten times more significant.

Renee liked what the life supplied. She liked the money and power. She liked being the predator and no longer the victim. It made her strong where she was once weak, and it was the only thing keeping her inside this lifestyle. She needed to feel secure and strong. However, she yearned to be softer, nicer, happier. Although she knew what she wanted inside, a piece of her still fought to stay. It was that piece she owed it to, stepping on that plane and hearing everyone out. That piece that kept her sane and made her strong throughout the years. Could she see herself as a Jaxs, as a Spencer?

"It's not my intention to scare you into my way of life. I just feel you have the right to know a little more from those who paved the way," Spencer let out, deleting the silence.

Renee moved her head up and down, only to feel stupid seconds after when she remembered he was blind.

"My misfortunes may not be yours. I just happened to see more of the bad than any of the good, and what good I did see came with people I will never see again."

"Metro should have never told any of you my business, especially when he was so willing to withhold yours."

"Don't be mad at him. My loss is an extremely touchy subject, one that has gotten me committed. When I was released, people walked on eggshells around me. One mention of my past gives people the impression I'll lose it all over again."

"He still shouldn't have told," Renee pushed.

"I agree."

Confusion came over Renee. "Are you agreeing just to appease me?"

"Yup."

The sheer honesty amused Renee. "At least you're honest."

"We'll be landing soon, so if there's anything you want to know before we hit Bora-Bora and I step off this plane, ask now."

Renee clasped her hands together and leaned forward. Maybe getting on this plane just to appease Metro was a mistake. Maybe she wasn't ready to leave the world she dominated. Leaving this world entailed walking away from respect, and Renee knew all too well how it felt to be disrespected before entering this world. "Does it get better? The depression, the memories, the pain?" If anyone could identify with her most, Renee came to the conclusion that it would be Spencer.

"I don't know. I'll tell you when I get there."

The last forty-five minutes in the air was a time of peace and keeping from falling off the edge for everyone. Neel and Jaxs spent their time relieving themselves inside two of the transvestites, while Murry caught up on sleep. Renee and Spencer kept each other company by sitting beside one another in silence. Metro remained wherever he ventured off to after his encounter with Spencer and only showed his face when it was time to see his friends off.

"You have my number, Renee?"

"Yes. I also have Jaxs's and Murry's," she reassured Spencer. Renee felt as if she had adopted three uncles.

"You call me whenever, for whatever, okay?" Spencer grabbed hold of her wrist.

"I promise," Renee told him.

He let her go, lingering around her before placing a hand on each side of her face. Spencer asked, "May I?"

Renee didn't rush to respond. She was too busy trying to understand his question.

"He wants to touch your face and get an idea of how you look. You must be one of his new best friends." Neel held hands with Orchid, her free hand brushing through his hair.

Renee looked a little uncomfortable. "Never been asked that, but sure."

Spencer's hands closed in on both sides of her face. He began with her cheeks, then worked his way to her chin on up. Renee closed her eyes, and he brushed his fingers across them. The last place he felt on her face was her forehead before he ran his fingers through her hair, taking in the texture and length.

"You're gorgeous," he whispered. Once again, his hand brushed over her eyes and nose. "Your features resemble my wife's."

"That's who she looks like," Murry tried to whisper.

Spencer's lips fell inward followed by a teardrop that rushed down his cheek. Gently he tapped her cheek, then after filling the space between his thumb and pointer finger, pinched her cheek like a grandmother. "Let me know your decision."

"Will do." Renee gave up a smile. Although he couldn't see, she hoped he knew it was there.

Stepping off the aircraft with Spencer holding on to his elbow, Murry waved goodbye.

"See ya later, queenpin. When you retire, you have to travel with me. It's always a party in Murry's world!"

"I'm not sure I'm ready for that type of party," Renee admitted.

Jaxs walked in front of both Renee and Metro. "The jet will fly you right back to the States. Take care of my baby." Jaxs and Metro slapped hands, then pulled each other in and embraced.

With Renee in view, he shook his pale finger at her. "My instincts tell me you're a force to be reckoned with. It'll be a shame if you tap out so soon. "

Renee only listened, her lips stretched into a line.

"I'm going to sweeten the deal. If you decide to stay, I'll make sure you'll gain a piece of the drug trade, not only out of New York but overseas. Let me know what you decide. The offer always stands." He took her hand, and they shook.

The offer was superb, but Renee had gained lifelong headaches from New York alone. Did she really want to add to her stress? Had she decided for any reason to stay?

At that second, her answer was no. "Thank you. I'll keep that in mind."

Neel stepped where Jaxs once stood. "It was nice meeting with you, Ms. Renee." Renee's presence darkened. The light in her eyes and openness of her heart downsized. "I'm guessing that since we haven't exchanged numbers, you won't be notifying me on what you'll be doing."

Renee blinked one hard time.

"Okay, then." He faced his friend. "Metro, tell Dane hello, and remember to join us next month. We'll be heading to Vegas."

"I'm going to have to pass on that, Neel. Take care of yourself."

Renee and Metro made it to their seats. Not long after, Carmen stepped out with two plates of food on a tray surrounded by small cups of sauces and appetizers. No words were exchanged during the first three bites of the lemon-glazed chicken and fettuccine Alfredo. It was the perfect moment to satisfy their taste buds and shut up their stomachs. A strand of pasta slid off Renee's plate and colored a small spot on the white floor. As she bent down to clean it up, words fell out her mouth.

"I would have preferred my business not to be told, but I'll let it go." She picked the food up with a napkin and took a drink of water that Carmen delivered.

"Good," Metro pushed out. Renee watched as a knot of chicken made its way down Metro's throat.

Smacking sounds and a few slurping noises escaped every now and then. Renee gazed out the window. The clouds that slowly passed by were a pleasant distraction. Carmen returned with a tray of desserts. The platter offered pound cake, chocolate mousse, cookies, and miniature ice cream sundaes. She hadn't set the platter down before Metro and Renee each grabbed a sundae.

"You two are so cute." Carmen handed Renee a napkin.

Metro wiped away the whipped cream and chocolate sauce that dripped off his lips and made it down to his chin. "What are you talking about?"

Carmen refilled their glasses with a water pitcher, and the other hand balanced dirty dishes with ease. "You and your daughter. You're identical, from your attitudes down to how you eat. I could hear you both smacking all the way from the cockpit."

Renee felt herself preparing to smack. She forced her mouth shut and tried enjoying the dessert in silence.

"I thought everyone on this plane was friends, but the way you got in Spencer's face, I knew my first reaction of you two was right. Only a father shows his love like that when his parenting is disrespected."

Renee finished her sundae. She put her spoon down and pushed away the cup holding whipped cream and chocolate sauce residue.

Carmen continued to speak as she walked away. "You're lucky, Jordan, Renee, whatever your name is. It's obvious he wasn't around when you needed him most, but he came back and has dedicated his life to protecting you. You're blessed. Wish I could say the same about my deadbeat father."

Renee poked her lips out a little and slapped her legs with both palms, creating a rhythm of music anyone in an uncomfortable situation gravitated to. Metro drank his glass of water longer than needed and looked forward. Renee spotted the individual pieces of gray that bloomed on Metro's face. She also couldn't help but detect the wrinkles on his hands and neck. Not all of those signs of aging were around when she first met him. Now time had caught up with him, the bags under his eyes a confirmation that maybe, just maybe, he lost sleep due to keeping tabs on his "daughter." He retired years ago but kept open the lines of communication between him and his old business partners. Now she knew why.

Carmen walked back inside the room, and rubber gloves covered her hands. "Can I get you two anything before I start on the dishes?"

"No," Renee answered. She paused and then faced Metro. "Dad, you good?"

Metro gave his attention to Renee, and a smile swiped across his face. "No, I'm good."

Chapter 8

"I heard you met the crew." One leg crossed over the other, Dane leaned her back against the kitchen sink and cabinets. She stirred the honey into her piping hot tea, and heat danced from up top.

"You're fucked up. You do know that, right? Those are some sick fucks you and Metro call your friends."

Dane gravitated to the kitchen table and took a seat. "Yeah, but they're useful. We've known them for a long time, and never do they cease to amaze me."

"Can I really trust all they've said?"

Dane gave up stirring. "If you couldn't, we wouldn't have connected you with them."

Renee dunked her finger inside her mug. The steam attacked the tip of her finger, and when she withdrew it, tea dripped from her finger and on the placemat. She placed her finger inside her mouth and repeated the process all over again.

"You take anything away from your meetings?"

"Yup. We're part of some fucked-up shit with a shit-load of fucked-up people."

"I could have told you that." On the table, Dane's phone chimed. She picked it up and glanced at it before placing it right back down.

"Since when do you ignore your phone? It could be a job." She prepared to drop her finger back inside the mug. Dane reached over the table and slapped her finger away.

"Stop doing that and drink the damn tea. This shit ain't cheap. There's some real herbs and pure honey in there, and it's not a job. It's those damn Instagram and Facebook alerts. I gotta take those apps off my phone. I don't even go on social media."

"Since when do you have Instagram and Facebook? And when did you get into this health kick?"

"Heifer, I've always been into health. You don't stay looking like this without putting in some work." Dane stood and sipped what she'd made from scratch. She held the glass and twirled it in place. Almost spilling its contents all over the waxed floor, she put it down on the table. "And social media is needed for a couple of jobs. These new-age youngsters and their posting makes my job too easy." Her phone chimed and vibrated numerous times, back-to-back. "Do me a favor and turn my phone off."

On her way to turning off the phone, Renee peeked at Dane's screen saver. It was a picture of Dane and Metro hugged up in front of some tropical place with wildflowers and rainfall. Renee turned the phone off, the photograph trapped in her mind. There was nothing wrong with that photo, not one tidbit anyone could pick apart and down. It was perfect, from the beautiful background filled with nature and its colors to the smiles on Metro's and Dane's faces. There was no photo-editing software capable of creating those genuine grins. They were happy, really happy, something Renee wanted. Renee pushed Dane's phone away.

"Dane, how did you find out Metro was retiring?" When the word "retiring" left her mouth, Renee's chest stiffened a bit. No discussion with Dane about retiring ran smooth.

"Like you, he told me, 'I'm retiring. I'm out.' I knew he had his reasons, so I let it be."

"When he finally did, did your relationship change for the better?"

Dane slid in her seat. "Where are all these questions coming from?"

"I'm curious."

Dane knew bullshit when she heard it, but with this bullshit, she wanted to know where the smell was coming from. "It did. It gave us both a sense of relief. We became happier." That was all Dane could admit, the only information she could hand over when the truth wasn't given to her. Dane played with the heads of the salt and pepper shakers that rested in the middle of the octagon-shaped table. Grains stuck to the bottom of her fingers. With the points of her stiletto nails, she plucked them off.

Renee became taken over by the particles. She tried following where every tiny salt and pepper granule flew once it was separated from Dane's finger. Her vision went astray and landed on the finger that held Dane's wedding band and engagement ring. The picture she'd seen before of their wedding day was magical. Their smiles and auras were just as touching and emotional as the picture she couldn't get out of her head. That's what she wanted. She wanted the marriage, the ring, and the vacations that came with pictures others envied. She wanted true happiness.

"I've made up my mind," Renee announced. "Since Metro and I got back, I've given it more thought." Renee rushed and plunged her finger into the mug of tea, quicker each time so as to keep Dane from intervening.

Dane left the seasonings alone. Their smell radiated faintly from her fingers. "What's it going to be?"

"I'm out." She'd said it before. Only now that she'd said it again did it feel complete and steady.

Dane's eyes rolled, accompanied by her repeatedly slamming her mug down on the table. The homemade tea flew from the mug. Specks of liquid landing on her hand, arms, and face were tiny fires burning her. What landed on the table created small puddles.

"This is bullshit!" Standing from her seat, Dane's body bumped into the table and knocked her mug over. Automatically it broke into big and small pieces and was now nothing more than a mess on the floor. Dane stepped in the sharp shards, her sneakers breaking them down into smaller fragments. Leaning into Renee's face, she grabbed a handful of the custom-made tablecloth she purchased from Japan.

"Curious my ass. What the fuck were you doing, trying to soften me up?"

"Nah. I was trying to see the bigger picture," Renee answered with a straight face.

"What are you doing? Have you been listening to anything we've told you?"

"Have you? How many more clues do you need before you're convinced that it's time for me to get out? Your own friends told me to leave!"

"Not all of them! I know who said what!"

Renee slapped the table. "You should understand, fuck! Your own fucking husband got out!"

Dane freed the cloth from her grip. The force she put into pushing it aside caused every item on the table to shake. "Who will take things over for you?"

Renee rubbed the sides of her head with both pointer fingers. "Don't start, Dane. Don't start this shit again."

Dane clapped her hands together, her back hunched over. "Refresh my memory and tell me who will run our business, who will you be handing over everything we've built to, and who will be given access to all of our connections!" By now Dane's feet were stomping one after the other. They moved so rapidly and on beat that had she not been screaming, Renee would have mistaken her movements for dance steps. "Come on, tell me. Who the fuck will reap all the benefits? Because you've gone soft!"

"Watch it, Dane." Still in her seat, Renee's stern, unyielding tone made up for her height.

Dane ripped the mug Renee toyed with off the table and, with the arm of a baseball player, chucked it across the room. It collided against the frame of the kitchen's entrance and exploded. "Over my dead body!" Dane's skin was turning beet red.

"Why are you taking this so hard? Why are you being so closed-minded?" Renee knew she was asking too much during a time when Dane's head was unscrewing by the minute. However, the question was one of many in need of a voice.

"You're making a mistake, a big mistake." There was no stopping Dane from moving her head from left to right. "You're ruining it all."

Renee, too, was now out of her seat. Behind her chair, she was walking in circles. Her fingers bent while stabbing into her hair.

"You're psychotic! Giving it all to a stranger!" Dane pointed and then threw her hand in the air.

"I don't know how many times I have to tell you! She's my fuckin' sister, Dane, and your ass needs to accept that. Why do you want to keep me down in the slums so bad? What, you can't bear to see your top moneymaker go?" There were lots of feelings hovering inside Renee that constantly rose and exposed themselves with every disapproving act Dane showed whenever she mentioned getting out. "Or is it that you want me under your thumb forever?" Renee's finger pointed in Dane's face.

Dane's mouth balled. Her lips slipped inside her mouth and became invisible. The tension tightened in her jaw, pulsing and beating like a heart. "Don't insult me, little girl." Dane's tone was a hissing noise bubbling from the throat on out.

"It's the only explanation. I know better than anyone how much you like to be in control."

Dane filled in the small amount of space that separated them. She walked into Renee's finger, her finger hitting the bridge of her nose. "Because I know you have officially lost your mind and obviously no longer can decipher your head from your ass, I'm going to let that shit slide." She walked farther into Renee's finger before finally smacking it out of her face. "Get that shit the fuck outta my face," she spat. Dane gave Renee her back, and before fully stepping outside of the kitchen, she held on to the frame of the wall. "You're going to regret it, Renee, and you're going to regret it bad."

Renee leaned on the table, conscious to not place all of her weight on it. "Whatever happens, it'll be my mistake to make." Sliding down in a seat, Renee repositioned her feet, glass crunching beneath her shoes. She scraped her shoe back and forth, her goal to free herself from crunching noises.

"Then so be it."

Kicking away whatever glass was near, Renee looked up after completing her objective, only to see she was alone. It was just her and broken pieces of glasses stained by herbal honey tea.

Chapter 9

Dane and Renee didn't speak for the rest of the day. Although Dane's house was extremely large, both ladies found it hard to avoid one another. When one was out in the backyard taking in the fresh air and scenery, the other came with hopes of achieving the same goal. One would walk inside the kitchen in search of snacks, only to find the other's head jammed inside the fridge, arms filled with what the other belly craved. They kept bumping into one another. Both women thought they'd outsmart the other by making a quick getaway to the guesthouse, but as usual, that led to them only bumping into one another and evacuating the place immediately. They'd leave their destinations empty, which resulted in another high possibility that they'd meet again. The same actions played out until sunset when each one decided to retreat to their bedrooms for the night.

In bed, dressed in a white tank top and matching boy shorts, Dane ran the number of conversations she'd had with Renee concerning her leaving and continued documenting them in her journal. She'd never say it out loud, and she sure as hell would never say it to Renee, but she did understand why she wanted out. Her reasons were valid and a natural human desire. However, keeping the business in the family was of high importance to Dane. She and Metro had come such a long way and opened up not only their money but their hearts to Renee. She couldn't see someone else in her best friend's shoes. Knowing Renee as well as she did, Dane knew inside her gut that she'd go through with her life plan by any means necessary, leaving Dane to eventually accept her decision and let go of her wants. That's how it would go. They would all be happy and move on, except there was one problem. Dane could not and would not allow Carmen in their world.

Dane was a great judge of character. You had to be when you were part of life's horrid pieces, and that's what confused Dane about Renee. Like hers, Renee's intuition should have spoken to her and expressed loud and clear like an ongoing alarm clock that something wasn't right with Carmen. Dane could smell it on her, see it in her, and hear in her voice that she was an opportunist. Wanting family was one thing, but Dane felt Renee was diving into sisterhood headfirst without a helmet and safety gear. She was appearing desperate, not to mention irrational and impulsive.

Sitting up in bed, her legs bent and her back pressed against the headboard, in black ink Dane wrote in script, *This isn't going to end well.* She pressed down on the period and allowed the pen's ink to release itself on the page until it was nothing but a blotch of black sinking through to the next page. Besides that one sentence and the date posted in the corner of the page, nothing was written. She spent the entire time in her king-sized bed thinking of paragraphs and paragraphs to write, but no other writing marked this page.

"Hey, love." Metro closed the door behind him. He leaned down so that he was at his wife's level, and he kissed her lips. "What are you still doing up?" Metro unbuttoned his shirt. Underneath, a white tank top, which some called wife beaters, covered him.

"Renee's made her choice."

Metro had one arm out of his shirt.

"She's leaving," Dane spat out.

Metro took a deep breath and released it. "I can't say I'm surprised. Hell, the things the guys told her made me question why I didn't get out sooner."

"This is different, Metro. She wants to give what we've built to some model reject who hasn't been around for one good second. Fuck out of here," Dane spewed, her face twisted and covered with a look of disgust.

Metro's hands were digging inside his back pockets, preparing to empty their contents. Moving slower than usual, he picked out a quarter or two and dropped them on the dresser.

"What are you thinking, Metro?" Dane's tone was hard and annoyed.

"What are you talking about?"

"You're thinking about something, something I'm not going to like. It takes no one this long to empty their pockets."

Metro let out a sly smile. "You're right. You're not gonna like what I have to say."

Dane rolled her eyes. Her bra strap fell, and she left it where it landed.

"We weren't extremely close to Renee when we took her in."

Dane sucked in her cheeks, took deep breaths in and out, and advised herself to speak in a calm manner. "Are you comparing Renee to that girl?"

"Not Renee, the situation. You're locked on the fact that she's a stranger, so if you want to get technical, so was Renee."

"If you want to get technical, she was a stranger to you." Dane stretched out the word "you." She had to ensure that Metro got the hint.

From his hand, Metro poured two dollars' worth of quarters on the dresser, the sound of change click-clacking against the wood a welcome distraction from his wife's temper tantrum. "You're my wife. If someone's a friend to you, they're a friend to me. I don't have to sit up all night having girl talk so they're not considered a stranger. She's grown to be family."

"You know what I'm saying. At least one of us knew everything we had to know about Renee before welcoming her with open arms. We didn't just look at her and say, 'Oh, she's our friend. Let's give her everything we earned and go skipping down the Yellow Brick Road.'" Dane transformed her voice into a high-pitched, animated child's voice.

From Metro's second back pocket came nothing except a brand-new stick of gum and a candy wrapper. "You're overreacting." He reached inside his front pockets and pulled out Dane's phone. "Your phone was in the kitchen. No wonder you didn't return my text. It's off." He tossed it at his wife. She caught it and dropped it beside her.

Dane sat on her knees, then crawled over to her husband. "I don't like the bitch." Her eyes blinked rapidly.

Removing his pants, Metro sat down on the bed, contemplating how to respond to his wife. "I hear you. I really do, but I don't see Renee changing her mind for no one. If anything, her decision is now concrete."

Dane listened intently, waiting until Metro said something that demonstrated she was right and he was in agreement that she should officially shut down this whole thing with Carmen taking over.

"But I've never known your feelings to steer us wrong. Granted, I don't understand them half the time."

That comment caused Dane to smile.

"You always did come out right, so watch her and do what you have to do to protect your family."

Dane crawled into her husband's lap and kissed him. "Thank you."

He dropped his face into the nape of her neck and inhaled. Underneath the back of her shirt, his hand traveled upward and rubbed her back. The feel of her was the softest thing he'd ever touched since they'd first started dating. "I'll be back. I'm getting in the shower." With her wrapped in his arms, he rolled over and plopped her back where she came from.

Dane fell into her oversized pillows. She thought back to when she asked Renee to turn off her phone. She grabbed her device, turned it on, and scanned through all of the phone calls and text messages she'd missed. It wasn't much, which was no surprise. This month had been slow when it came to people putting out hits. The first text was from Renee.

Did you touch my bathing suit cover-up? Give me back my shit!

Dane's eyes darted over to her closet door, where the purple and white cover-up hung from off the knob.

I didn't touch your shit! Dane replied.

She added an emoji giving her the finger followed by a meme of a celebrity rolling her eyes. She sent it, chuckled to herself, and made a mental note to sneak the cover-up back to a place where it would be believable Renee had overlooked it.

The next text she opened was from one of her regular customers. He needed a hit done as soon as possible, so soon that he was willing to pay double what she normally charged. The last text was from Metro.

On my way home. Want me to bring back any-thing back?

If only she had seen that sooner. Renee had finished off all the snacks. Some she believed Renee didn't really want, but she didn't want Dane to have them, so she ate them all. A new text came in.

Damn liar. I want my shit.

Dane was not big on texting, but annoying Renee seemed like the most entertaining thing to do at the moment. She positioned her thumbs to reply when at the top of her smartphone a message dropped down, informing her that someone on her Facebook page replied to what she'd posted weeks ago on her dummy page. She swiped up and put it out of view when another notification appeared right behind the first.

Carmen's Winning sent you a friend request.

Dane opened her Facebook app. On her page, she was tagged in a number of posts and had approximately fifty friend requests. The majority were from people whose pages looked fake or who were nosy and made it their duty to try to figure out who the woman behind the stolen picture was. She looked at Carmen's Winning profile picture. Sure enough, it was the one woman Dane despised most on the planet. There Carmen was spread-eagled on a gray car, wearing a sheer black bikini and stilettos that were so pointy they could poke your eyes out. Clicking further in her profile, Dane crossed her fingers in hopes she could snoop without accepting her friend request. No luck. Like almost every other social media profile, it was private, and she was denied all the things worth looking into someone's profile for.

She accepted the friend request. Dane looked at Carmen's last post from ten hours prior. It was a meme of a crown-wearing woman. The caption read, Let Me Adjust My Crown and Get My Day Started. When she scrolled down, she noticed a bunch of sentences she had written along with hash tags:

#Bossbitch

The best thing I could have done was come to New York. Time to conquer this city. #winning #theworldismine

What they won't give to you, take.

#moneymoneymoneymoney

You don't have to like me. Money is all the friend I need.

There were hundreds of likes on every post Carmen made and even more comments, from men telling her to check her inbox to gold diggers confirming that they, too, were bad bitches and only cared to make money and not friends. The page disgusted Dane. It represented everything she stood against.

Clicking into Carmen's photos, Dane saw that each and every album held nothing but selfies and half-naked photos of Carmen. Men went crazy when given a visual. There was not enough time in the day for Dane to read half of the comments, and if there were, she wouldn't waste her time. The more Dane looked through the pictures, the more her blood boiled. Dane envisioned how'd she kill Carmen. It became the highlight of her day. While she clicked through photos, new comments rolled in, and a new message came into Dane's inbox. A bright red number one sat in front of the message icon, waiting to be opened and no longer be a mystery.

She tapped the message icon. On top of numerous junk messages, from people Dane only added to keep up appearances and who were selling stuff, was Carmen Winning on top of a car. Dane opened the message. She read it slowly, pronouncing each word perfectly in order not to misread or misinterpret a thing.

Who are you? I see we have a lot of mutual friends. Are you from Miami?

Oh, this is better than texting, Dane thought as she rubbed her hands together in an evildoer kind of way. What Dane already knew and could vouch for was that profile pictures and a gang of posts could be deceiving. If she wanted proof that this was the actual Carmen, it needed to come from the suspect's mouth along with substantial, unshakable evidence. *I'm liking social media a little more,* Dane thought before responding.

I used to, but now I'm in NY. I got family out here. #Brooklynmade

Shit, I must have caught the hashtag bug. Dane chuckled. She looked her sentence over once more, then read it out loud. *Yeah, sounds like someone her age would write.* She pressed the send button.

Carmen posted a shocked emoji face. **Me too! Just found out I have a sister. That's some crazy shit, right?**

"Bingo, ladies and gents. We have ourselves Renee's sister!" Dane posted a shocked emoji face alongside an emoji whose mind was being blown. **Shiiitttttt, good luck with that,** Dane sent.

Why do you say that?

Because if you fuck up, you're a dead woman.

Before she sent it, Dane read the sentence over and over again to herself. It was perfect. She sent off the message.

Immediately, the time stamp indicating that Carmen had read the message appeared. Dane proceeded to delete her Facebook account and any other social media accounts where she used the photo of one of her past victims. Paper trails were a no-no and being a sloppy social-media writer was a no-no, but damn it felt good to have her hand around Carmen's neck, even if it was virtually.

Dane clicked the necessary buttons and read the guidelines on how to deactivate and delete her account. Her night was looking better, and she loved it.

Dane's phone went off. Another text from Renee came across the screen.

I'm heading back to New York the day after tomorrow, sticky fingers. Time I go back to my surroundings. Your ass can make someone miss being in jail.

Dane rolled her eyes. My bags will be packed and ready to go, she responded.

Fuck no. You're not coming with me. I'm leaving to get away from you.

"Try and stop me," Dane mumbled. She wrote her last text to Renee that night swiftly.

Too fuckin' bad. I told you I'm going back with you, and I'm not leaving until you change your mind or Carmen's out of the picture, whichever comes first.

Renee sent an emoji of a middle finger.

Chapter 10

As soon as Renee entered her bedroom, she took off her shades, dropped her oversized purse on the chair next to the door, and closed her eyes for a second. She took a deep breath. As much as she enjoyed the peace and tranquility that Jamaica supplied her, she had to admit that there was no place like home. Slowly, she opened her eyes, and she was happy to see Julian sitting out on her terrace, playing a game of chess, alone. Jamaica was beautiful, but without Julian by her side, she found it to be lonely. She was happy to see her man. With a smile on her face, she walked and stood in the terrace's doorway, her shoulder leaned against the frame. Julian had not noticed her. He was too focused on the game.

Renee cleared her throat, and he looked up at her.

"What are you doing creeping up on me?" His smile seemed to light up the darkness that covered New York. The cool night caused goose bumps to form on Renee's arms, a reminder that summer was no more. She was happy to say goodbye to the heat and hello to fall. This change of seasons made it official. Renee was starting life from scratch.

"If I'm correct, you should have sensed me coming from a mile away. You're slipping." Renee didn't think it was humanly possible, but when she spoke to Julian, her smile grew, and her heart raced so much it hurt. For years, she had prohibited herself from feeling and showing any type of emotion. Now that she had thrown that type of living out the window, her love for Julian spilled all over the place, and she loved it. She walked over to him and sat on his lap, her arm wrapped around his neck.

"What are you doing back so early? I thought you needed to get away from here for a second," Julian inquired.

"I wanted to surprise you, plus I missed you." Renee stared deep into Julian's eyes. She told the truth, but those weren't the only reasons she returned home five days early.

"I can believe that, but your eyes are telling me another story. What's up?"

Renee turned away and looked at the huge building's lights. She didn't want to talk about her conversations with Dane while away, but she had no choice. She wanted to tell Julian what was wearing on her mind so that he could help ease the stress.

Without looking at him, Renee answered, "I was going to lose my mind if I had to spend one more second in Dane's presence. I liked it down there, but she ruined it all by constantly trying to talk me out of leaving the game. That woman needs to be in a mental institution for real."

Julian laughed. "Tell me something I don't already know."

Renee turned to face him. "I'm serious, Julian. She's obsessed with me staying, and she's convinced that Carmen's no good."

The sound of Carmen's name made Julian numb. The biggest mistake Julian ever made in life was sleeping with Renee's sister. Granted, he had no idea the stranger he encountered on a flight was Renee's father's illegitimate child, but it still constituted a stab in the heart. When the cat was out of the bag and Carmen's identity was revealed, Carmen's eyes, whenever she came around Renee and Julian, always told him, *I still remember, and I still want you.* She'd give off subtle hints when Renee's back was turned, which confirmed that what he assumed she felt was anything but a lie.

The night he and Renee sat in a hospital room distraught and crazed with emotions over her almost being killed by her youngest sister, Page, Renee finally decided to commit to their relationship. The couple opened up to each other about everything. However, Julian couldn't fix his mouth to tell her about Carmen. After being a witness to the love of his life getting banged up and expressing her feelings from a hospital bed, he realized that was no place to confess what he'd done. He couldn't add to the mayhem she called her life, and more importantly, he couldn't risk losing her since he had finally captured her. Yet things grew worse once the new-and-improved Renee strove to have a relationship with her sister and keep her around. All Julian wanted was for Carmen to go away. No Carmen would result in no risk of his secret being exposed. If Renee allowed Carmen to have the business, he'd bet his right arm she'd keep Carmen in close proximity, just as Dane and Metro had done with her to ensure her success.

"We went at it every day. She told me I was a fool for wanting to give this all up and a bigger fool for leaving it to someone she claims is a stranger and she doesn't trust. But she's not a stranger, Julian. She's my sister. I already lost one, so why not hold on to the one I have left?"

Julian was taken aback. He didn't know how to respond to Renee's comment. He was used to the cold-hearted, selfish Renee, not this woman whose heart had defrosted and who had done a complete turnaround the second she left the hospital. The last few months were like heaven on earth for Julian. Renee was the woman he dreamed of, but with this secret weighing heavy on his heart, he could not enjoy this change 100 percent. And now she was on his lap, welcoming Carmen into her life and heart with open arms. His stomach turned.

"You are not the same woman you were months ago, Renee, and I love that, but you're not out of the game yet. You have to remain sharp. You're still calling all the shots and selling. In order for you to be out, you have to hand it over to someone, but it can't be just anyone. We worked too hard on building this shit for it to crumble. The person you select must be right, because you'll have to introduce them to our contacts, which automatically requires them to be trustworthy. We can't have no clues that lead back to us. Then and only then can you wipe your hands clean of everything and be out."

"So what are you trying to say, Julian?"

Julian squeezed her a little. "She's your sister, I know that, and I know you desperately want a bond with the family you have left but—"

Renee cut in. "You don't trust her either. You think she has some kind of motive too? Out of everyone, I'd thought you'd want me to hurry and get out so we can finally have a real relationship. You never wanted this life. You only got involved to have my back and be my right hand."

"I want you out." Julian looked her straight in the eye. "You need to get out because I need for us to have a real

relationship, but you have to tie up all loose ends first."
And forget you've ever known Carmen and sever any con-
nection to her. "Dane still has family in this business. If
given to the wrong person, it can be mishandled and destroy them."

"What do you really think about Carmen?"

She'll tell you I slept with her and you'll leave me, all
because you can't get this bullshit idea out of your mind
that she can be family and you can continue where you
left off. Julian scratched the back of his head. He thought
carefully how he'd respond. "Something's not right
about her. It's in her eyes."

Renee turned away from Julian. Her mind replayed
everything he had just told her. She trusted him more
than anyone else in the world. Therefore, to hear him
piggyback off of what Dane had told her caused major
discomfort. She had let her guard down and officially
kicked Jordan out of her life because she wanted a
chance at being normal. She wanted a fresh start.

"I just want out. I don't care who takes over." Renee's
lip slightly quivered.

"But you have to." Julian rubbed her back, completely
aware that the seeds he tried so desperately to plant had
sunken in. "This not only affects you. We'll be out, but
Carmen's green. I don't give a shit who she fucked, one
fuckup and it will trickle to Dane's aunt and uncle and
ruin them. Do you want to take that risk?" Julian rubbed
her back slower. "What if she's not trustworthy? She can
trace so much back to us."

"I hear you. I don't want to disappoint anyone, but I
can't continue living like this. I have to get out by any
means necessary." Renee's hazel eyes sparkled in the
moonlight, and tears dropped down her cheeks. There it

was. She finally said out loud what she tried not to feel. She didn't want to let down the only people who loved her, but she couldn't sacrifice her happiness.

"Promise me something?" Julian asked.

Renee did not answer right away. "What?"

"Move smart."

Julian could have mentioned additional reasons why Carmen should not be her protégé. He could have continued to plant the doubt in her mind that he wished would help him in the long run. However, Renee's tears showed she'd had enough for the time being. Julian could only imagine the mental beating Dane put on her while in Jamaica, so he'd lay off for the night, especially now that he'd learned Dane too was not a fan of Carmen.

With Dane also in Renee's ear, it shouldn't be hard getting rid of Carmen. In the past, Julian and Dane engaged in discussions regarding putting a hit on Page in order to ensure Renee's protection after learning Page's ill intent. Julian didn't want to go back down that road, but if Renee didn't take the advice of those closest to her, he'd do what he had to do. He couldn't risk Carmen telling Renee about them. He couldn't lose the love of his life.

"I missed you." Julian turned Renee's face toward his and kissed her so passionately her body melted and turned hot. The stress of everyone talking Carmen down quickly subsided. One of the reasons Renee missed Julian so much was that she was horny. Being in paradise with no man and around a couple madly in love made her juices flow.

For a second, she pulled away, and she took her shirt off. She released her hair from its bow and allowed it to fall to her shoulders. Julian always loved her hair to be loose when they made love. Renee dove into his lips, and he lowered her bra's left cup. Her breast spilled out. Hungrily, he took her nipple into his mouth.

Renee's head fell back. The cool breeze was not enough to put her fire out. It only hardened her nipples more.

"I want you now," Julian whispered in her ear.

Renee looked at the tall buildings and pictured someone with a telescope watching them. The thought alone turned her on even more, so she got up from his lap and seductively peeled out of her jeans.

He watched as her jeans came off, then her panties and bra. He stood up and removed his shirt. In the middle of walking toward her, he stopped in his tracks when he heard banging on the bedroom door.

"Renee! I'm going out. I have to meet with a potential client!"

Julian looked at the door and thought he'd lost his mind. "Dane's here?"

Renee rolled her eyes. "I told you she doesn't trust Carmen. So she said she's staying with us until she's out of the picture."

Normally, Julian would be mad if someone dampened the mood on his sex session, but hearing that Dane took getting Carmen out of the picture as seriously as he did could not have made him happier. He bit his lower lip and grabbed Renee. Julian laid her down on the floor and had sex with her like never before.

Chapter 11

In a Queens apartment, takeout containers littered the living room floor, and darkness covered the entire room. The blinds and curtains were tightly shut. Occasionally, a breeze would enter the apartment, allowing fresh air to enter Jared's lungs. He sat paralyzed on the couch and was miserably quiet. Bags rested under his eyes, and his skin was pale, due to the neglect of sunlight for three months. Shirtless, Jared ran his hand over the scar that graced his stomach. The night Renee told him that they would never be, the night that followed him being a loyal worker of hers for years, which led to them having sex and him obsessing over her, was the night he was shot by a stranger who stood at Renee's front door, and was left to die.

In the foyer, Jared had lain bleeding on the floor and listening to the struggle taking place upstairs between Renee and Page. With all his might, he tried to get up and rescue Renee, but his body wouldn't allow him. The harder he tried to drag his way to the stairs, the weaker he became. Tears rushed from his eyes the moment he realized there was nothing he could do to save Renee's life. His hand was pressed against his wound as he tried to apply pressure to it. He refused to die. It wasn't his time. The second he balled up the bottom of his shirt and pressed it against his gunshot wound, he lost consciousness.

When Jared finally came to, he was in a hospital connected to machines and an IV. His stomach was bandaged
up, and he was alone in a big white room. Repeatedly, he
closed his eyes and opened them, trying to focus on his
surroundings. Before he could recollect the past events,
a middle-aged Spanish woman came into the room. She
looked at Jared and walked over to the side of his bed.

"How are you feeling? You're lucky to be alive, you
know."

Jared looked at the nurse as if she were crazy. He
hadn't any idea what she was talking about or the slightest clue where he was. "What are you talking about?
Where am I?" His eyes roamed around the room once
again. His body ached, freezing him in place.

"I'm nurse Moreno, and you're in the hospital, Mr.
Psych. You were shot in the stomach, and you would
have bled to death if you had gotten here ten minutes
later. Your surgery went well, no vital organs were hit,
and the bullet was removed. Thank God your friends got
you here when they did. Now take it easy. The doctor will
be here shortly to take a look at you." The nurse placed
her soft hand on top of Jared's and gave him a motherly
smile, assuring him that everything would be just fine.

When she left him alone with his thoughts, Jared struggled to remember what had happened. What friends?
Jared had none. The only friend he had, he had killed,
all for the love of a woman. He took a deep breath and
closed his eyes. Finally, it hit him: Fergus and Calloway.

Fergus and Calloway were Renee's cleanup crew.
They were very strange twin brothers who were the own-
ers of a funeral home and had no problem making bodies
disappear. They were tall, lanky, pale white men who
were both molested by their uncle as children. When they

turned fifteen, they killed their uncle, Pete, and disposed of the body so well that it was never discovered. To this day, everyone still wondered what happened to Uncle Pete while on his monthly fishing trip.

The twins were obsessed with death. They preferred the company of the deceased to that of the living. The molestation had demolished their psyches to the point of no return, so when they were presented with the opportunity to get rid of bodies for a living, the two jumped on it. The men's awkwardness and desire to live in isolation from the outside world were exactly what Renee had needed in a cleanup crew. They would never talk and never cross her, because if they did, she would take away what mattered most to them: death.

Jared remembered hearing Fergus's and Calloway's voices as he drifted in and out of consciousness.

"I thought Julian said they needed a cleanup. This one is not dead. I can hear a heartbeat a mile away." Calloway pointed at Jared, who was lying in a puddle of his own blood, unable to move or speak.

Fergus looked down at Jared, his eyebrows caving in. He took his foot and pushed him flat on his back so that he would be able to identify him. "What a shame. It's Jared," Fergus mumbled. The twins could hear movement upstairs. They knew it had to be Julian and Renee.

"We don't deal with the living. He said he needed a cleanup, so I say we either let him bleed out or we kill him now. We are not in the business of saving lives." Calloway looked down at Jared like he was dirt beneath his shoes. He could not stand the living. Neither could Fergus, but at least he could tolerate them. When grieving families would enter their funeral home to bury a loved one, Calloway never spoke with their clients. It was all Fergus. If it were up to Calloway, he would kill everyone he met. He had no soul, but Fergus had a pinch of one.

"No, Calloway. They probably think he's dead. Let's get him to the hospital before they know we're here."

Calloway looked at his brother like he had lost his mind. "Did you not hear me? We don't save lives. Let him die while we round up the bodies. I can tell he doesn't have much longer."

"Which is exactly why we must go now. We're taking him to the hospital. Help me pick him up."

While Fergus tried to get Jared up, Calloway watched with disgust written on every corner of his face. He knew the look his brother's eyes held. Fergus was crushing on Jared. Calloway took a deep breath and pushed to the back of his mind the idea that his brother was smitten over a man he barely knew. Finally, he leaned over and helped get Jared off the floor and out the door. Fergus was all Calloway had, and although he didn't agree with many things Fergus stood by, he was his brother, and he would always be there for him.

The twins quietly made their way out the door and drove Jared to the nearest hospital. They never told Julian and Renee that Jared was alive. When Julian brought Jared up to Fergus, he just told him that it had been taken care of. He had a feeling that telling Julian otherwise would be a big mistake. Julian had seen Jared unconscious that dreadful night and needed confirmation he was what he seemed to be: dead. He never liked Jared, so his death was the icing on the cake.

Now Jared sat alone in his stuffy apartment, reliving the memory of the night he could have died. He may have been on earth in the physical form, but mentally and emotionally, he had checked out. History was repeating itself, and Jared was a ticking time bomb, ready to go off. He had survived one heartbreak that took place many years ago, but now that Renee had broken what took years to repair, Jared didn't think that anything other than having her in his arms could repair his heart. He wanted to tear Renee's life apart. He wanted to take away what she held dear and close to her heart: Julian. That way, she would have no choice but to run into his arms and finally see that they were meant to be.

Jared stopped rubbing his scar and grabbed a pair of black silk panties from across the couch that he had stolen from Renee the night he watched her sleep, before their argument. He needed something of hers for every night that he would be without her. His thumb slowly rubbed over the material. He closed his eyes and thought back to the night they made love, the night when everything made sense. With both hands, he firmly held on to the panties, revisiting the moment that had changed his life forever.

With his eyes tightly shut, he could feel himself entering Renee. At that second, a tear danced down his cheek and landed on his hand. Jared's eyes shot open, the wet sensation yanking him out of his thoughts.

"I love you, Renee, and I'm coming for you," he whispered, his voice hoarse and menacing.

Chapter 12

It was surprisingly warm for an October evening. Mobs of people rushed home from their nine-to-fives, dressed in suits, frowns, and tired eyes. Renee and Carmen walked through the busy streets of New York, engaged in conversation. Renee's hair was pulled back into a tight ponytail, and knee-high Timberland boots graced her feet. Slowly, she walked with her hands folded behind her back and her eyes trained all around her. Carmen, on the other hand, looked high-end in her champagne-colored ankle boots, skinny jeans, and sheer multicolored blouse under a jean jacket. Her hair was bone straight and stunning due to her cutting it into layers. Both women received countless stares, but only Carmen reveled in the complimentary glazes. Renee remained focused on her surroundings and conversation.

"I hope you're listening to everything I'm saying. I hope you're taking this all in." This was Renee and Carmen's first meeting, and Renee had just dropped some important jewels of wisdom on her. Renee wanted to retire right away, and the only way she could do so was if she molded Carmen into her protégé as soon as posa sible. She had convinced herself during restless nights that Carmen's proper training was the key to her leaving in peace. It reassured her that she was making the right choice.

Carmen regained focus and continued to pay close attention to everything Renee said. She had to admit she had never heard such intelligence in all her life. Renee's breakdown of her operation and how she acted as a ghost in the streets of New York was pure genius. Carmen's ex, Benz, had nothing on Renee.

Carmen nodded her head, indicating she was indeed listening to everything she said.

"What do you think about what you've heard thus far?" Renee never looked at Carmen the entire time she spoke. She took in the streets she had been withdrawn from for so long.

"I think you're a genius," Carmen responded. She looked at Renee with much respect and admiration. She didn't like that she looked up to Renee, but she couldn't deny that she wanted to be just like her.

Renee smiled. "We all are when our freedom is at stake."

The women walked into an empty park and sat on a bench facing a basketball court. For two minutes, they sat in silence and watched a teenage boy doing drills up and down the empty court. He was in deep concentration and didn't notice the women staring at his every move.

"You see that?" Renee asked, with her eyes glued to the young boy. "You can never be so deep in thought that you fail to acknowledge your surroundings. All it takes is one second. One second for someone to catch you off guard and knock you off your throne."

Carmen saw the chilling stare Renee gave the teenager, and she knew that snatching her crown would not be as easy as she thought. She directed her attention toward the ball player and imagined he was Renee. Imagined she was on that huge court, all by her lonesome in this cold, cruel world, with no goons, no money, no power, no nothing. She imagined she was vulnerable and stripped of everything that acted as a barrier between her and the rest of the world. Carmen pictured herself approaching Renee, fear etched on her face while taking her life. After seeing herself as queen, she smirked and forced herself out of her imaginary world.

"So you're telling me you never, not once, overlooked the snakes in the grass?"

Renee's mind drifted back to Slice, a childhood friend who Renee trusted and who had worked for her, a disloyal fuck who tried to rape her. "Never," she lied.

Carmen nodded, internally smiling. *If that were true, I wouldn't be sitting here.*

After minutes of silence and both women building their thoughts, Renee finally broke the silence and blurted out, "You get your own crew. You can have my corner boys, but as for the lieutenants, cleanup crew, and all of the other valuable players on my team, they're off-limits."

Carmen tried not to show it, but she was pissed. Her eyes remained glued on the monkey bars, and she felt the color leave her face. When she said she wanted everything Renee had, she meant it. She wanted it all: the crew, the money, the power, the respect, and most importantly, the man.

"With all due respect, Renee, how do you expect me to survive in the game without your soldiers, the very reason you acquired longevity?"

The teenager focused on the rim and shot nothing but three-pointers. All that could be heard was the sound of a basketball splashing through the net.

"Never get greedy. Take what you can get. I am giving you my empire, my connect, and you want my soldiers, too? You don't know these men from a hole in the wall. How do you know you can trust them? How do you know they won't turn on you and try to take everything that I've earned from a new jack like you? I am giving you a chance to bring in your own allies and put on your people. The hard parts are already taken care of. Take it, Carmen, and be grateful."

Carmen's face tightened, and she concentrated harder on the playground. "So you'd rather have your men starve instead of work for me?"

For the first time during their whole conversation, Renee finally looked at Carmen. Her face was stone cold and vicious. She was offering Carmen the world, yet she wanted the universe. There was no way she was leaving behind Julian, Calloway, Fergus, and the few loyal lieutenants she had left on her team. They would all go with her as reassurance that her identity would forever be a secret, and that chapter of her life would be closed for good. Renee decided to move smart. Julian was right. Her decision not only affected her. However, there was one person she wanted to exit the game with her for personal reasons, and that was Lyfe.

Renee didn't have a father for long and had known nothing about Lyfe until recently. It hurt to discover her uncle had been a father figure to Carmen for all the years she'd suffered without family. Renee wanted to get to know him better, so to try to avoid the risk of losing another family member to death, he had to leave, yet Renee doubted this would be easy to achieve. Lyfe was an old-school gangster who'd run the streets until the end of time, and Renee questioned whether he'd leave Carmen alone to fend for herself. However, Lyfe had dedicated a large portion of his life taking care of Carmen. Now Renee wanted her chance at having a father figure.

Carmen's response to not having it all made Renee re-hash the disapproving statements from those closest to her about Carmen.

"There's something grimy about that girl."

"How can you want to give everything to someone you don't know, someone who acts so thirsty?"

"Something's not right about her."

"Carmen's green. I don't give a shit who she fucked."

Renee found herself irritated. "Not that it's any of your business, but my people will be taken care of. If I leave, they leave. I don't care who you are, I'm not leaving any-one behind with any real evidence on me to go down with you in case you fuck up. So get the thought of my top men being with you out of your fuckin' head."

Renee looked deep into Carmen's eyes, angry at the young female who seemed to have had the family that should have been hers. Carmen wanted her crew when she already had Lyfe and her empire. Why try to take it all?

For several moments, the women had a staring contest, and neither turned away. Then Carmen reminded herself that Renee's life of luxury was not yet hers, so she turned away, and threw up the white flag.

"I understand. It's just that I thought I would at least have Julian as my right-hand man or someone on your team who's just as loyal. You didn't do it alone, so I wanted the same people to throw some of that good luck my way." Carmen watched the ball player lean over. With one hand on his knee, he used the other to wipe the sweat off his face with his shirt.

Renee still looked at her. Like a pit bull, her eyes were locked on the side of Carmen's face. "Like I said, get it the fuck out of your head. Everyone else comes with me, especially Julian."

Carmen's eyes lowered and twitched just a little. The young man walked off the court and out of the park. Carmen wondered if she could play the game just as good as he had and would walk away without a scratch, walk away as a champion and the last woman standing. Whatever the outcome, Carmen would do it with Julian by her side. She didn't care what Renee said.

Carmen moved around a little on the bench. She tried to get comfortable. "I get it. Get my own crew. Consider it done."

Julian sat in Renee's office, which was now their office, staring at Tolstoy's *War and Peace* planted on the bookshelf. His eyes darted back and forth between the two words. His mind hoped for peace, but his gut told him war. Although he wished he and Renee could have a storybook ending, he knew this was only the calm before the storm. After almost losing Renee, Julian moved in with her immediately. He got rid of his place, and without Renee's knowledge, purchased a home on Long Island. Julian would never feel 100 percent at ease until they were out of the game. Until that happened, he would have a place tucked away that would act as their safe haven, just in case.

Living with Renee was not an issue. Having Carmen appear more and more each day was. Whenever their eyes met, he felt the storm brewing. He felt the intense tension between them. Julian was no fool. He read

Carmen like a book. Her eyes screamed lust, and her body whispered sex. The slithering smile displayed on her face when she saw him indicated it was only a matter of time until their skeletons fell out of the closet.

Julian's eyes landed on war and wouldn't move. He felt his blood run cold and heart rate slow. Over his dead body would he allow Carmen to tear down what he spent years building with Renee. He wanted the American Dream, the two kids and house with a white picket fence, and nothing would stop him from getting that. He had hesitated to bring Page down, but never again would he make the same mistake.

Since Dane's arrival, he hadn't been able to speak with her one-on-one. Either Renee was around, or Dane was nowhere to be found. Renee had been gone for hours, so Julian picked up the office phone and dialed Dane. She had been gone since he and Renee woke up, so he knew they weren't together. However, his stomach turned, because deep in his soul, he knew Renee was with Carmen.

"Dane," he spoke into the phone. "We need to talk."

Chapter 13

Carmen laughed harder than she ever had in her entire life. She peeked through her low eyelids at her date as tears slithered down her cheeks. Her beauty-pageant smile was on display, revealing the joy her soul was experiencing.

"You're a fool. You know that, right?" It felt so good for Carmen to laugh. It was a stress reliever from Renee's protégé training.

Lincoln smiled while Carmen laughed at his story. He examined every aspect of her face: the twinkle her eyes gave off, the way her dimples fell farther into her face, and the strands of hair that dropped due to her head whipping back and forth when she laughed. She was a work of art, *Mona Lisa* on display for people to gawk over and admire. It was only their first date, and already Lincoln was falling into a puddle of love. Little did he know, Carmen's love would soon turn him cold, eventually leaving him lost and alone in a world he once found happiness in.

"I've told you about my family, childhood, and my weird employment as a male secretary at a law firm. Now it's your turn to tell me something about you."

Carmen's eyes landed on the lasagna dinner that she had prepared and Lincoln had devoured in the dining room. All that was left were dishes, two empty bottles of wine, and tomato sauce staining the tablecloth. Her eyes maneuvered over to Lincoln, who sat next to her on her living room couch. He was a good guy who wasn't very familiar with the streets but was familiar with a broken heart. Carmen smirked. She didn't come from a naive fairy-tale background like Lincoln. She didn't have a legitimate job. She was training to take over New York and strip Renee of everything she was and ever would be. This question was comical, but before she answered, she eyed Lincoln for a minute.

"There's not much to say. 'Papa was a rolling stone. Wherever he laid his hat was his home. And when he died, all he left us was alone.'"

Lincoln gazed into her warm hazel eyes and didn't know how to take her comment. Was she joking? Pulling his chain? Or was she dead serious? He searched her eyes for answers but saw nothing. No clue that would give away the truth. When she looked back at him, it was almost as if she looked right through him, a breathing statue with no emotions.

"I'm my father's love child. He got with my mother while separated from his wife. He had a whole other family I knew nothing about until he died. The weird part about it is he was actually a good father. He made sure I had the best, no matter the cost. Maybe that's why I'm so materialistic now."

Carmen's eyes fell on her red bottom shoes nestled next to her love seat. She missed her father terribly and thought back to when he would spend days at a time with her and her mother. Being with him was better than being at Disney World. She didn't have the need to meet cartoon princesses, because in her world, she was a princess: Daddy's princess.

"As much as I love him, I am not blinded to the fact that he was a part-time father. He gave his all to his other family, while I only got bits and pieces. Some men just don't understand that money can't buy everything." There was an awkward silence when Carmen stopped speaking.

"I'm sorry," was all Lincoln could get out.

"Don't be," Carmen said, her dazzling smile lightening up the sad moment. "The past is the past, but the future, now that is what I'm looking forward to."

Carmen's bruised heart was short-lived when she thought of how her life would be once Renee was out of the picture. Renee would make up for having the full-time father who should have been Carmen's, by giving her everything. Everything Renee ever valued and worked hard for would no longer be in her possession.

Lincoln didn't know what he was feeling. It frightened him that his heart would either skip a beat or triple its pace every time he looked at Carmen. The only woman who had ever taken his breath away was Shelia, and here was Carmen, stealing his heart all in one date. Her model looks and lack of a father figure made him want to be her knight in shining armor. Finally, he had found someone who he believed was in search of the same thing he was: love.

Lincoln's hand inched toward Carmen's, both their eyes watching its movement. He felt his breath catch in his throat, and he prayed she wouldn't reject his sign of affection.

Carmen smiled. No man could resist her, and she loved her power over the opposite sex. It never failed. She grabbed his hand, a black widow wrapping her prey in her web of deceit. Her finger rubbed his knuckles, and her eyes melted his heart. A contract had just been signed, and a victim was born. Lincoln was hers, and whether he knew it or not, he was entering a game he didn't know the rules to.

Chapter 14

Dane's eyes followed Carmen as she walked through the dining room and into the kitchen. Her eyes shot daggers, and her blood drained from her body, leaving her cold, stiff, and homicidal. Her right hand balled into a fist and remained that way until her middle fingernail slit her palm and blood oozed down her hand. The moment the droplet landed on Renee's marble floor, Carmen walked out of the kitchen, and the two women locked eyes. Dane's catlike eyes were low and ice cold.

Slowly, Carmen walked past her, her eyes never going astray. The longer the two held on to their staring match, the deeper Dane's nails ripped into her palm. Finally, Carmen disappeared from Dane's sight, and her hand fell open. A wave of blood released from her grip and painted the floor burgundy.

Dinnertime crept around, and crystal plates full of salmon, mashed potatoes, and spinach sprinkled with garlic sat in front of Dane, Renee, and Julian. Goblets filled with red wine sat beside each plate, ready to chase down their meals. The room was silent while Renee and Julian ate. Dane sat as stiff as a log on the other side of the dining room table, staring at Renee. Not a pinch of her food was touched or a drop of her wine sipped.

Dane's hair was slicked back in a tight bun, which silently pulled at her almond-shaped eyes, which were

naturally light brown but were now dark brown due to
her bad mood. She sat erect against the gold-plated chair
with her hands neatly folded in her lap. They dined this
way for a total of twenty minutes, which was exactly how
long it took Renee to finish her meal, wipe her face with
a napkin, and finally address Dane.

"What's the problem now, Dane?"

It took Dane a solid minute to answer Renee, but
before she did, she stared in her eyes. It was her way of
letting Renee know that what she was about to say she
had better listen to. Dane was not much of a talker. Her
eyes told it all. One just had to listen.

"She's already a dead woman walking, yet you still
choose to have her in my presence. You must have
forgotten my credentials, so allow me to remind you."
Dane reached under her chair and retrieved a folder. She
slid it across the long table, and it stopped in front of
Renee's plate.

Renee closed her eyes and took a deep breath. She was
really in no mood for any of Dane's antics that night. But
she knew if she continued to ignore her, Dane's mood
would only worsen, so she reached in front of her and
opened the folder. Inside sat Dane's resume. Renee's eyes
glanced over her educational and professional experience.
Words such as "poison," "weaponry," "assassination,"
"strangulation," "psychological manipulation," and
"decapitation" jumped off the page. Dane was an assassin
and studied the art of death. Obviously, Renee must have
forgotten who she was trotting Carmen in front of.

Renee folded the paper into fours and tore it to shreds.
Dane had instilled in her never to leave behind an ounce
of evidence, so her going out of her way to write this up
meant she was not a happy camper, and she demanded

Renee's attention. Renee stood up from the table and walked over to the crackling fire. Roaring with rage, she threw in the pieces of paper along with the folder.

She sat back in her chair and looked at Dane. "What you're asking for me to do is irrational and reckless. You're jumping to conclusions based on thoughts and not proof."

Dane's skin went hot, and her blood pressure increased. In the beginning, Renee's decision to hand over everything to a complete stranger angered her, but now she was disgusted. Dane gave Renee countless chances to see the light, yet she chose to live in the dark. Never had she put up such a fight or questioned one thought of Dane's before, but now that she was, Dane was slowly losing any patience she had left in her. She and Metro had molded the perfect protégé, and now she wanted to demolish their legacy.

Dane slapped her hands together into her lap, restraining herself from leaping over the table. "Since when have my thoughts ever been wrong? Or my gut told a lie? I am being polite by asking you not to hand everything over to that little wench. But if you don't come to your senses, and soon, I'm going to tell you what you're going to do."

Renee lowered her head and grabbed globs of her hair into her fists like she was seconds away from ripping it out of her scalp. Dane was testing her, and Renee was milliseconds from going off on her. It was one thing for her to receive guidance, but to be spoken to like a child was unacceptable.

Julian placed his hand on her back, an indication for her to relax.

Renee released her hair and began talking. "I respect you, Dane. You've been more of a mother to me than my own, but you will not tell me what to do. If you wanted full say concerning this business, then Metro should have never left."

Renee stood up from the chair and leaned her hands on the table. "Don't make this more difficult than it has to be. Don't let a war break out because the old school won't convert to the new."

Renee was not thinking about any of the words that were leaving her mouth. For the first time in a long time, she was thinking with her heart. She wanted out of the game and into this thing called happiness. Because of Lyfe revealing his identity to her, introducing her to Carmen, and her not dying at the hands of her sister, Renee felt she was given a second chance at life. She wanted to take full advantage of it. She had turned off the light switch labeled "boss," and turned on her heart. Little did she know that by turning off her boss status, she had gotten rid of her common sense as well.

Renee didn't allow Dane to respond. She walked out of the dining room and headed straight for her bedroom.

Julian smirked at Dane. "You still want to do this alone? At this rate, a war will break out between you two just so that she can guarantee Carmen's safety."

Dane's top lip raised and she rolled her eyes. When Julian reached out to her with regard to the two of them working together to get Carmen out of the picture, Dane turned down the partnership and said that she flew solo on this mission. She had not forgotten about how Julian's failure to listen to her months prior had almost resulted in Renee's death. She didn't need anyone holding her back. She wanted Carmen's head more than she wanted air.

Dane rolled her eyes. She didn't want to admit it, but he was right. If Renee continued to go down the road she was on, she was sure to start a war between her and Dane. Renee had turned a blind eye and no longer cared about viewing each situation from every angle. Dane's thoughts jumped from place to place. She didn't want Julian involved in this mission because she did not need history repeating itself. Not long ago, she had wanted to take Page out ASAP while Julian dragged his feet because he considered Renee's feelings. Now that she and Renee were at odds, she needed Julian. If he could keep her calm, it could help prevent things going from bad to worse

Dane sneered. Never had she imagined she'd need anyone other than Metro. "I'll help you, but we do everything my way." She got up from her chair. She never gave Julian a second look when she walked out of the room.

Julian smiled. Things were starting to look up.

Chapter 15

Dressed in all black, Jared's baggy jeans, hoodie, and shades seemed to shield him from the world. His fresh construction Timberland boots stood tall on the concrete as he waited to drive his brand-new 2013 Altima off the lot. Everyone around Jared wore conformable winter jackets as the end of October neared November, but he stood tall with his hands stuffed in his hoodie pockets. After so many months of being bedridden, Jared wanted to feel the air. He welcomed life and everything it had to offer.

Eyeing his new toy, anger surged through him for waiting this long to get a new car. It wasn't his fault that he was unable to get a new car and apartment before now due to his wounds. But he still wished he had taken care of things sooner. His eyes watched his surroundings. He was dead to the world, and therefore, everything he owned had to disappear.

"Mr. Jared, your chariot awaits," the dealer sang as he held the keys out for Jared to take.

Jared stepped forward to retrieve them but was stopped in his tracks when a female whose hair was dyed pink walked between them so fast all he saw was her back. Jared snarled while watching her disappear into the dealership. Once the keys were dropped in his hand, Jared jumped in his car and made his way back home. He had to get out of that apartment and into a new one as soon as possible. It was by the grace of God that Renee hadn't sent people to verify his death, and instead took the word of Fergus and Calloway. Jared looked at the passenger seat, and its emptiness caused the already-dark cloud over his head to turn into charcoal.

Once upon a time, Waves occupied that seat, and not to see him there was a stab in the heart. Waves was Jared's only friend, and he sent him to his grave for the love of a woman who didn't love him back.

Driving through the streets of the Bronx, Jared struggled with his feelings. He missed his best friend, but it killed him because he knew that if he had to do it all over again, he wouldn't change a thing. He would still put the very same bullet that ended Waves's life into him. His fight for Renee was far from over. Therefore, in his mind, there was still a chance for her to love him and for them to live happily ever after. All he had to do was get rid of the brick wall that stood between them whose name was Julian.

Opting to take the streets, he ran into traffic, where he sat patiently waiting for the car in front of him to move up. He looked out the window and saw a teenage couple walking down the street, hand in hand. The innocence the two gave off sent Jared back in time to when he gave his heart to his teenage love, Amber. She was the definition of beauty, a tall, chocolate female with a pixie haircut and a body the shape of a Coke bottle. She captured his heart the second she looked his way, and she wouldn't let go. The two were a match made in heaven. There was no greater fit for Jared than Amber. What made this relationship ten times better was the fact that Amber was Waves's cousin. The three became inseparable and earned the name the Three Stooges in high school. Back then, Jared was a free spirit and had a lively personality that was revealed due to Amber's spontaneous and goofy character. She made him feel like a kid again and then led him into manhood when she took his virginity.

Amber made it possible for Jared to forget about his life and to look forward to the future. Like every other time when Jared's thoughts drifted to Amber, they were temporarily cut off. Whenever she came to mind, her memory took a back seat to the stories his mother told, the tales that explained how Jared was brought into this world.

Growing up was a constant battle after Jared's father abandoned him and his mother when Jared was the fresh age of 8. His mother's family had disowned her and turned their noses up when she chose to love and marry Meyer, Jared's father. Meyer was a con artist, a wolf dressed in sheep's clothing, who preyed on weak, wealthy women in search of love and happiness. He made it his duty to live off the money his so-called "love interests" were raking in. When he had drained them of all their cash and self-esteem, he moved on to the next victim whose way of life he hoped would be of greater interest and entertainment.

Women's emotions were nothing but a game he played until the bitter end, which resulted in two of his victims checking themselves into mental institutions, one committing suicide, four fleeing the country, and the rest filing for bankruptcy and trying to pick up the pieces of the lives they once took pride in. Destroying lives then leaving women to pick up the slack landed each one of his targets in a whirlwind of depression and regrets, including Jared's mother, Penelope.

Penelope took her family's warnings about Meyer lightly and only focused on how he made her feel. He charmed her into believing that her status as an heiress did not faze him and had absolutely nothing to do with him courting her. Everyone who knew of Meyer's doings whispered in her ear that he was using her and was only interested in the money her family had made creating computer programs used by the government to track down criminals. Penelope wouldn't listen. Men had come and gone in her 26 years of life, and she was sure she could point out a user at first glance. She pushed away everyone she'd once held dear to her heart, and she drowned herself in the lies and fakeness that Meyer dished out.

For one year, their life was a fairy tale that she refused to wake up from, but when Meyer proposed, she was pulled out of her dream. Her parents told her if she married him, they would cut her off and act as if she never existed. Crushed and startled by their harsh ultimatum, Penelope quickly lashed out and responded by saying that they could take their money and last name. She guaranteed that she and Meyer would produce much more money and respect than her parents ever had. With all the money she had left to her name and a brilliant business plan she'd drawn up, Penelope went into the contracting business, which took off like nothing she had ever seen. With the help of the few rich girlfriends she had left who actually believed in her and Meyer's love, life was better than when she was living in the shadow of the Whartons. However, all good things soon ended.

A year after they tied the knot, Penelope got pregnant and found herself unable to devote herself to the business she had started from the ground up. Carrying Jared proved to be difficult, and the doctor ordered her on bed rest when she was three months into her pregnancy. She needed her baby to be healthy, but she also needed her business to continue to flourish. Therefore, she did all she could do. She listened to the doctor and worked from home.

Working from her bed via telephone and computer resulted in sleepless nights, stress, and lack of appetite. Her health started to deteriorate, and her unborn child's health was in danger. Her determination to remain on top and prove she could survive without a penny from her parents led her down an unhealthy and dark road, which gave Meyer the green light to take everything that she had worked hard for with the snap of a finger.

"Baby, you can't do this anymore. You're putting yourself and our child in harm's way."

Penelope loved how Meyer referred to everything as "ours." He was so selfless and loving. "I know, and that's not what I'm trying to do. But with you still out of work, and me on bed rest, I need to guarantee our income. From the beginning, the stakes were high, and everyone was against us. I can't allow them to win."

"And you can't allow them to drive you crazy, either." Meyer took her hand into his, their fingers tangled together.

Penelope took a deep breath. Her mind drifted off to her wedding day when only twenty people witnessed the happiest day of her life. Her parents were not in attendance and didn't even allow themselves to be there for her in spirit. She would never admit it, but her soul missed them without boundaries.

Meyer shook her shoulders, bringing her back to reality. Their eyes met, and without words being exchanged, he knew exactly what occupied her thoughts.

"They won't, but we can't step down from our pedestal either."

Purposely, Meyer allowed silence to sweep over the room before he spoke. "Then allow me to run the business. Hand everything over to me, and you get some rest. Someone needs to be at the office to make sure everything is running smoothly. You can't do it all, Pen. You're not a superwoman, no matter how much you try to be."

The sound of a fax coming in disrupted their conversation. Penelope read the fax about a new client in need of her services, who her vice president, Bruno, thought they should take on.

"I have Bruno in the office. Everything's okay the way it is."

"Bruno is not the president, and Bruno's not your husband. I know the ins and outs. I helped you build all of this. Frankly, I take offense that you didn't even look to me to run things while you're pregnant. How fast you forget that I put the rest of the money down when you came up short, and not even your little rich friends could help."

"I didn't forget, Meyer. I just didn't think you wanted in. I didn't think you would want to run this type of business. You always talked about wanting to run your own restaurant."

"Well, that doesn't seem to be happening, now does it? I gave you everything I had, so that dream is down the drain. I need to support my family. So what's it gonna be?"

Meyer had never spoken to her that way. She had never seen the fire in his eyes that she was now viewing, and honestly, it frightened her. Feeling stuck, with no room to breathe, she did the only thing she felt she could, and that was give in. Jared kicked her. She was five months into her pregnancy and knew that once she gave birth, her attention had to go to him.

"Okay, for the sake of the baby, the business is yours. I need to be a mother to my child anyway. In the morning, I'll have everything put in your name."

Meyer beamed. He never thought that taking over Penelope's money would be so easy. He knew all those years of hanging in there would eventually pay off.

He leaned in and kissed her on her forehead. "Now that's my girl."

Only a few months after Penelope stepped away from the business world and into motherhood, her love-struck marriage turned into a controlling nightmare filled with abuse and anarchy. Meyer took their business to new heights and denied Penelope access to their money other than with his approval. She was given an allowance. Her home turned into a prison, and she never left without Meyer by her side. The ironic thing about it all was that Meyer was a great father. The spitting image of him, Jared was given the best of everything, including constant attention. Penelope was proud of her son's relationship with his father, but the black eyes and broken ribs were more than enough reason for her to despise Meyer.

Meyer stayed around longer than he planned. When it was confirmed that there was nothing left for him to rob his wife of, he divorced her and left town. Penelope was left without a penny to her name or control of her contracting business. Meyer never paid child support or alimony and, without a job, there were days she went without eating just to guarantee her son's belly was full. The few friends she had left turned their back on her. It was one thing for them to stand by her when she was in love but another to have a poor friend asking for hand-outs. It was limitless how many times Penelope picked up the phone to call her parents, but her pride always talked her out of it. She kept telling herself that if she pulled herself up by her bootstraps once, she could do it again, and she did.

For years, Penelope and Jared were on government assistance, but everything changed when Venice Harold came into their lives. He was a high-powered attorney with a kind heart and hefty bank account. He turned a lonely, scared, and hurt Penelope around and became the man she was in dire need of. She never imagined herself becoming a lawyer, but with Venice's help, she returned to school, passed the bar on her first try, and the two became an instant power couple. The money returned, but this time their home was filled with the real love Mary J. Blige sang about. Meyer was a distant memory, and the only man Jared had ever acknowledged as his father was Venice. He questioned Penelope about Meyer, and when he got his answers, he hoped he was somewhere dead in a gutter. The man who he was supposed to look up to had left him for dead, making it impossible for him to ever forgive his actions.

Honking horns and people yelling out of their windows for Jared to move with traffic yanked him from his mother's tales. The story of how he came into the world always sent him to another place and stuck with him like a bad rash, which was a constant reminder that he had yet to follow in Penelope's and Venice's footsteps. Starting in his teen years, Jared had set out to capture the love his parents displayed in front of him since the first day they met. In his mind, love was magical. It conquered all and made everything roses and daisies. It brought light into the dark and forced the negativity of their past, known as Meyer, in its corner. The day Venice stepped foot into their lives, everything was made okay. However, that positive scenery did nothing but create a monster.

At only 16, Jared was determined to mimic his parents' love and produce a relationship of his own. While normal teenagers dated, worried about fashion, and attended parties, Jared put his all into Amber. Her kind heart and bubbly personality drew him in and hugged his heart. There was a spark set off that he never wanted to burn out, so for the three months that he was with her, he nurtured this flame and tucked it deep away for no one to fiddle with. The first time they made love, Jared had an out-of-body experience. It was in his deck of cards for them to be together, and there was nothing he wouldn't do for her. His young mind had taken over and missed all the signs that indicated he was being used only so that Amber could get back at her ex-boyfriend, who had cheated on her with a girl from another school.

During that time, Jared was one of the most attractive, popular boys who attended their school. Most of the time, he kept to himself and barely gave any female the time of day. Amber made it her mission to woo him until she accomplished what she set out to do. She dated Jared for months with the objective to butcher her ex's emotions more then she already had. Although she did enjoy the time she spent with Jared, her feelings weren't real, and their time was only borrowed.

On the night of his birthday, she broke it off and came clean about her intentions. Jared bit down on his inner cheek so hard in an attempt to refrain from crying he drew blood. Unfortunately, his pain won, and tears still fell. The sweet, caring girl Jared grew accustomed to was really a selfish, deceiving gold digger who had no intent to find love.

Once the truth was out and Jared stopped crying, he temporarily saw red then blacked out. To this day, he couldn't recall how he managed to get Amber's body, wrapped in plastic, to fit into his duffle bag. But what he did know was that Waves helped him dispose of the corpse and never mentioned the incident to anyone, not even to his aunt, who obsessed over finding Waves's cousin's and her daughter's killer.

Amber was Jared's first teenage kill, but she wasn't his last. Brittani, the captain of the cheerleading squad and a straight A student, was his second victim. Her virginity was what lured Jared to her, and for six months, they were unbreakable. He fell hard for her and created an intense connection the night he took her virginity. Their world was unshakable, and they maintained a solid foundation until she cheated on him. Now sexually active, she went from a good girl to promiscuous. Her drastic change in lifestyle sent Jared over the edge, and he found himself abducting her, torturing her for hours, and then choking her to death.

How could he forget Daisy, the wild child known as the flower who had grown from concrete? He fell for her wit and rebellious nature and thought he could tame the beast. However, things didn't turn out that way. She broke his heart when Jared found out she had hit on Waves. Daisy was spontaneous, and in her world, anything went. Since she was so careless and did things spur of the moment, Jared carelessly and out of the blue pushed her into a lake, fully aware that she couldn't swim.

And then there was Janae, his most recent ex who saw her dead sister and tried to kill Renee because that's who she believed murdered her sister.

Out of traffic and far from the impatient drivers, Jared drove past the brownstone he once shared with Janae. His eyes never looked at the tower of bricks he abandoned days after killing her. It was easy for him to let go of material things, but never a woman. All he wanted out of life was love, but it seemed to pass him by each and every time he thought he saw it coming. When it came to Renee, he had an obsession he couldn't let go of. There was an emotion deep inside him that sucked his soul dry, and a temper that flared at the very thought of her. He was tired of being hurt, and he needed her to know that she could not and would not get away with rejecting him. Once his point was proven and her punishment delivered, they would live happily ever after.

A sinister smile came across Jared's face when J. Cole's "Power Trip" seeped through the speakers. He turned the music up until it could go no higher and sang along with the lyrics.

Would you believe me if I said I'm in love? Baby, I want you to want me
Would you believe me if I said I'm in love? Baby, I want ya

Chapter 16

Dressed in a waist-length mink coat, Carmen bypassed everyone waiting in line at the club and headed straight to the entrance. November was quickly approaching. Just yesterday, the weather was good enough to wear nothing but a sweater, but today in New York, one needed either a North Face jacket or a mink. With her hands stuffed in her pockets, Carmen waltzed past the bouncer, the club's red ropes already open to her.

When their eyes met, the six foot two inch muscle-bound man nodded his head then asked, "Friday night? My place, same time?"

Carmen didn't bother to respond. Instead, she made her grand entrance into the party room and nodded, indicating that their weekly fling was still on. The club was filled to capacity, and the dance floor was flooded. Sweat could be seen dripping off the partygoers' bodies and splashing off the buffed glass floors. Carmen's suede boots click-clacked as she walked on the floor to the center of the room. When there was nowhere else to go, she stopped to observe her surroundings. There wasn't a seat in sight, and Carmen's face slowly started to turn ugly. Her eyes lowered, and her mouth curled up in a snarl. Every woman knew that expensive, cute shoes were not to be danced in, but sat in and envied. Like a lion to its prey, her eyes zoomed in on an empty chair with a coat draped behind it.

Carmen waltzed over to the bar and took a seat. Happy to be off her feet, she crossed her legs and put in an order for a cosmopolitan with the bartender. While she waited for her drink, she looked at the coat behind her seat, a sign that the stool was taken and not to be touched. Carmen laughed and grabbed it off the chair to look at its tag. *Ralph Lauren, good taste.* She held on to the coat, then looked around the club until she found her victim.

Bingo!

Carmen shook off her mink and threw it over the barstool and then walked over to a table of women only a few feet away. Her eyes were locked on the cheapest looking of them all. Carmen was a human calculator when it came to estimating the price of clothes, and the outfit worn by the girl she had her sights on added up to no more than $100. It made her a perfect target.

"Hi, ladies. I'm sorry to interrupt you, but you forgot your coat." Carmen held out the coat she found to the woman whose weave ran down her back and whose shirt was two sizes too small. Carmen's beauty-pageant smile was on display and made the women at the table immediately insecure. Her appearance and self-confidence shined through, and the windows to her soul told the story of a woman who got everything she wanted. The woman's eyes were fixated on the coat, and her face was filled with confusion. She opened her mouth to speak, but Carmen interrupted.

"I saw you guys leave the bar and head over to this table once it became available, so I thought I would bring it to you. I am a lover of fine things myself, and I know I would just die if I lost this nice coat." Again Carmen smiled while putting on her good-girl act. Her manipulative, conniving ways mesmerized many and pulled in everyone she met.

The girl looked at the coat tag, which was nicely displayed, and when she saw it was Ralph Lauren, she changed her entire demeanor. "Yes, thank you! I can't believe I left it. Sometimes I can be a real dingbat." The young woman tried to emulate Carmen's charming smile, but Carmen and her friends saw right through her. Every woman Carmen came across wanted to be like her. They yearned for her image and special touch that captivated men around the world. Carmen found the imitation to be entertaining, so she played along.

"No worries. Take your Ralph, and hold on tight to it now, girl."

The young woman smiled even harder. This time her eyes held more twinkle and hope that she was just as alluring as Carmen. She took the coat out of her hands. Holding on to an item so expensive made her night.

"Thanks again, and by the way, love the shoes!" She looked at Carmen's shoes and instantly fell in love with her style. She quickly turned to her friends, her wrist rising while preparing to tell the time. "We have to be out, y'all. Rebecca's waiting on us."

The "owner" of the expensive coat quickly got up and held on to the fabric so tightly her hands were losing circulation. No one objected. Instead, they all rose and walked out of the club, each face plastered with a fake, insincere smile.

Carmen laughed loud enough for dancers to look her way once the women were out the door. Women would do anything to be the "it girl," including stealing. That was none of Carmen's concern, so she walked back over to her comfy seat, grabbed the drink from the bartender, and asked for another. She wanted to drink the night away and worry about nothing. Life was hard, and being Renee's sister, having everyone's expectations of her to live up to, was even harder. So just for tonight, she wanted to forget all about people's expectations and be the person she was in Miami. She wanted to be the woman who didn't need to claw herself to the top but had enough pull to take it without warning. She wanted the money, power, and respect her ex took from her. She wanted her status back.

After three sips, her cosmopolitan disappeared, and a woman drenched in diamonds and flawless threads approached her. "Excuse me, but you're sitting in my seat." Before Carmen got a chance to respond, she looked at the back of the barstool and immediately asked, "Where's my coat? It was right here. I left it so no one would sit here."

Immediately, Carmen's acting skills kicked in, and her tender and alluring voice emerged. "Coat? No coat was here."

"Yes, there was. It was a black Ralph Lauren coat. I placed it right here."

Carmen's eyes got big, but on the inside, she smiled hard and happily. "Oh, my goodness! When I walked in, a group of girls was leaving the bar. I assumed it was one of theirs, so I gave it to them. They said it was theirs and took it."

"What? That coat was five hundred dollars and they took it? You have to be kidding me! Who steals a coat?"

Carmen looked at the woman in shock and gave the illusion that she didn't know what to do when in reality, she wanted to spit in her face and tell her off.

"They just left. Hurry, I'm sure you can catch them! The one who took it had long hair and wore navy blue stilettos!"

The diamond-wearing female gave nothing Carmen said a second thought. She ran for the door, believing she would catch the bandits. A wicked smile spread across Carmen's face as she watched the coatless woman hunt for a piece of clothing her controlling boyfriend had bought for her. Carmen's manipulation game was top-notch. If only people would stop and think about what Carmen said, they would detect the lies. She swirled around on her barstool, not caring about the potential drama she had caused, and downed the drink the bartender left in front of her.

For the next hour, Carmen accepted drinks from men trying to woo her and let go of reality. Learning the ins and outs of Renee's organization was mentally draining and required her undivided attention. There were codes to be learned, verbal and written, behavioral training, gun training, and so much more. She spent many days and nights listening to her explain the game. It was as if she were in college all over again, listening to the professor speak nonstop in the lecture hall. She needed to get away, wanted to get away. It didn't help that Dane was out to get her. Carmen could sense it. Dane never spoke, and when she did, she only threw shade. On countless occasions, she'd overheard Dane and Renee exchange words whenever she showed up at Renee's place.

Lost in her warped little world, she felt strong hands wrap themselves around her waist. She jumped and then turned around, only to see an angelic smile beam off Lincoln's face.

She started to feel the effects of the drinks when Lincoln slid on the stool beside her.

"What are you doing here?" She smiled.

"Buying you a drink." Lincoln got the bartender's attention and asked him to give Carmen another of what she was drinking.

Carmen leaned over and, like a vacuum, sucked Lincoln's bottom lip right into her mouth.

"If this is what I get for buying you one drink, let's see what I get when I buy you three!" Lincoln's smile sparkled like the lights that surrounded a celebrity's name.

For a moment, Carmen chose to get lost in them, but never did she get comfortable. Lincoln was a good guy, the man you took home to meet Mom, and Carmen was who women around the world warned their sons and husbands about. She was the plague. However, when she briefly looked into his eyes, she wished she could become a good girl.

She leaned in and kissed him with such passion it drowned out the loud music and obscenities shouted by people in the club. She allowed herself to fall victim to her innocence.

Lincoln smiled so hard when she pulled away, Carmen could not fight off her own instincts. The bartender invaded their moment in paradise when he slammed Carmen's drink down and then rushed over to the other pushy club hoppers. Carmen turned away and stepped out of their perfect little world. She welcomed reality back into her life and took a sip of her drink. "Really, what brings you here? You don't strike me as the clubbing type."

Lincoln hesitated to answer, his gaze fixed elsewhere. Carmen waited for Lincoln to answer. He looked like someone had spit in his Cheerios. "Lincoln!" Carmen screamed, her loud voice grabbed him out of his trance.

Slowly he turned toward her. "Huh?"

"What's up with you?"

Lincoln looked back to the crowd, and his bottom lip curled up. "I see someone I unfortunately know."

Carmen broke her neck and tried to see who he was talking about. "Who?"

"You see that girl with the pink hair?"

"Yeah, with the mini dress?"

"Yeah, her," Lincoln confirmed.

"Okay. What's the problem?"

"Let's just say her mouth put some heat on a close friend of mine." Lincoln remembered Tina spilling the beans concerning Renee's true identity at a club a few months back. From his view, nothing about her seemed any different except her hair color.

Carmen looked at Tina and tried to see what Lincoln detested about her, but failed miserably. "So what, she has a big mouth or something?"

"A very big mouth. She knows too much for her own good and is nothing but an alcoholic who frequents clubs. And what's sad is people actually pay her for what she knows." Lincoln wished he had a drink. He felt his anger causing him to get dizzy, and he had the desire to punch a hole in a wall.

Lincoln looked at Tina once more and shook his head, no longer interested in the conversation. "Forget her. I haven't seen you in days. Let me show you how much I missed you."

The countless drinks in Carmen's system caused her to get aroused and led her to demand Lincoln's attention. His eyes met hers, and Tina became nothing but a memory. He leaned in, and their tongues danced as he lost himself in a state of bliss.

Chapter 17

Carmen thanked God that she kept sneakers in her car. Her shoes dangled from her hand as she walked up the stairs to her Brooklyn brownstone in her all-black Air Max sneakers. Her huge blackout shades decorated her face, hiding the bags that hung low under her eyes due to her night of partying and sexcapades with Lincoln.

All she had ever heard about New York was that it was the place that never slept, and after living there for approximately two months, she now agreed 100 percent with that old saying. Whenever she got the chance to step away from her learning sessions, she hit the clubs and let her hair down. Renee still ran everything and still held her crown. However, she required her and Carmen to be joined at the hip during training. In Carmen's eyes, life was a treasure chest waiting to be robbed, and she had her hand directly in the cookie jar.

Carmen pushed her door open, and the smell of cheese eggs, biscuits, turkey bacon, and grits invaded her nostrils. Her senses were stimulated, and she instantly fell under its spell. She slammed the door shut, dropped her shoes on the welcome mat, and followed the aroma. Only one person could prepare a meal that grabbed her by her taste buds and caused her mouth to water, and that was Lyfe. She turned the corner leading into the kitchen and saw him sitting at the kitchen table with *The New York Times* in front of his face.

"You're just getting in." Lyfe never took his eyeballs off the article relating to health insurance when he spoke.

"Yes." Extremely exhausted and running on empty, Carmen slightly wobbled back and forth as she made her way over to the table and sat down.

Lyfe finally took his eyes off the black-and-white page and looked up at Carmen from behind the paper. He folded the newspaper in two and gently placed it on the table. "I need you to answer something for me, Carmen."

With her glasses still pasted on her face, Carmen gave her uncle her undivided attention.

"Are you ready for what you're getting yourself into?"

Carmen's glasses faintly moved when her right eyebrow rose. "Yes. Why do you ask?"

"Because you're staying out all night and making yourself a target before you even take over the business."

"What? How am I making myself a target? I'm going out to have a couple of drinks and relax. What's wrong with that?"

Lyfe moved in his seat, uncomfortable that his niece even found it necessary to ask that question. "Carmen, one of the things that makes you qualified to take over Renee's business is the fact that you're not known. You can be the ghost of the streets, just like Renee has been. Instead, you're out here frequenting these clubs and putting yourself on the map. You're not from here, so you need to keep your identity to yourself. You need to start listening to what Renee has been telling you."

Carmen rolled her eyes, disgusted that Lyfe had told her to listen to her older sister as if they were some kind of family. "So I should move like her? Be everything that Renee is? Wouldn't you say that's living in her shadow?"

"I say it's being cautious and smart. There's a reason Renee never got caught up, so therefore you're going to do exactly what she did."

"And if I don't?" Carmen had never spoken so recklessly to her uncle, but she didn't like where this conversation was heading. She felt that Lyfe was telling her to bury herself and live as Renee part two. Yes, she wanted what Renee had, but in no way, shape, or form did she want to change who she was.

"Then you're not cut out for this, and it would be foolish for you to proceed."

Carmen stared at Lyfe, and he tried his best to find her eyes behind the darkened shades. Carmen grinned, surprised with the business side of Lyfe.

"Okay, Unc, you've asked me your question. Now let me ask you mine."

Lyfe didn't respond. Carmen wanting to ask him a question did nothing to ruffle his feathers. He was the last of a dying breed, a man who feared nothing.

"The way you're talking has my mind turning. So I need to know, if I choose not to move like Renee, would you still work with me? Help me dominate the streets?"

This conversation angered Carmen so much, her right eye twitched, and her legs shook. However, when Lyfe's eyes no longer met hers and instead held a conversation with the floor, it was confirmed that taking what Renee held dear to her heart would not be an easy task. Lyfe did not answer right away, and the longer he took to respond, the more Carmen thought she would fall out from a heart attack.

Lyfe's nieces were his only soft spots, and now that both demanded his attention at the same time, he felt like he would be torn in two from each woman pulling at his arms. Lyfe's eyes slowly traveled back up to Carmen's covered eyes.

"No decision has been made, but I'm considering leaving the game alone." As the words left his mouth, their taste and sound were foreign, even to himself. Never was leaving his life of crime an option, but after he was approached with the idea, it didn't sound so bad. Why put his life in danger anymore? Why not live it happily? He was lucky to have survived for as long as he had, and it was now time to bow out graciously and allow the curtains to close.

Carmen ripped the glasses off her face so fast they nearly broke in two. "What?" She wanted to scream, but her words came out in a low, harsh tone, spiked with repulsion and disbelief.

"I think it's time Renee gets the uncle you've had your whole life. She needs a father figure, and she fears that if I continue doing what I am, I'll be ripped away from her before an actual relationship is formed."

Carmen laughed. First it started out as a chuckle and then grew into a full-fledged monstrous laugh.

"So that's where this talk stems from, Renee?" Carmen's hands folded on the table, her manicured nails sparkling in the sunlight that penetrated the window. "So you're telling me you're throwing me to the wolves, forcing me to find my way?"

"I'm not forcing you to do anything, Carmen. You chose this path. You didn't have to take Renee up on her offer. There isn't anything she has that you don't. I still would have taken care of you. You don't need to do this."

Carmen's tired eyes came alive and shot daggers at the only man who had loved and accepted her for who she was, regardless of the fact that he truly didn't know who she was. Carmen fought back the urge, the intense pressure to tell him that she was not even 50 percent close to having everything Renee had. Renee had a man who loved her and didn't abandon her like Carmen's ex. She had money of her own and power without the world even knowing her real name. Lyfe and every man she entertained were the exact reason she wanted her own life and Renee's. She was tired of being controlled by the dollar and needed to be in power.

"I don't want to be taken care of. I been taken care of enough. I want to run New York."

The look in Carmen's eyes was unlike any look Lyfe had ever seen. Instantly, he became uncomfortable.

"Then do it alone, just like Renee." After witnessing firsthand the hell Renee went through and blaming himself for allowing her to live a life filled with chaos and turmoil, he now wanted to help her obtain tranquility. Carmen wanted this life. This was never Renee's goal. She only took on this lifestyle so the world would feel her pain.

Carmen stood up so fast that her chair flew across the room. The fire that needed to be ignited in her in order to take Renee's place was now sparked. She wanted to have Renee's possessions and not lose hers.

Her mind told her to curse her uncle out and tell him where he could go, but her heart was now injected with rage, and it spoke ever so quietly. It told her repeatedly that if he wanted her to do it alone, she would. Carmen promised herself she'd do it better than any other person who walked this earth. The pain on her face was evident and revealed the anarchy soon to come. For the first time in his life, Lyfe had chosen someone over her, and here she was thinking her uncle would guide and protect her in this concrete jungle. That he would hold her hand and do all the work while she did nothing but sit on her throne and look pretty. This was not going how Carmen envisioned. This had taken a turn for the worse, resulting in her heart breaking.

Carmen turned, preparing to make her exit, when Lyfe spoke one last time. "I am not choosing her over you. I'm choosing to give her what I never did."

Carmen soaked in his words and pitied him for actually believing in what he said. Instead of voicing her thoughts, she walked out of the kitchen and never turned back.

Chapter 18

Carmen stormed into her room and slammed the bedroom door with such force her whole room shook. She slammed her palms on her vanity table and inspected each part of the cream-colored dresser. She admired how each small grain of wood came together and created something bigger than itself.

Carmen lifted her head and looked at her reflection, her hair dangling in front of her eyes, with two or three strands stuck to her face due to her salty tears. Weakness was spray-painted across her face, and her uncle's voice echoed in her mind. *"I'm considering leaving the game alone."* Life was unfair, and Carmen was the butt of its joke. The eyes that looked back at her were weak and in no way ready to fill Renee's shoes. She balled up her fist and punched the mirror, watching the pieces of glass jump into the air then gracefully fall to their demise.

Never was Lyfe not being by her side a part of her master plan. Her whole vision of being in power revolved around everyone doing her dirty work while she did nothing but sit and look pretty. Carmen figured if she kept Renee's crew, they would do everything that needed to be done, but when Renee made it known that her crew left with her, she settled for Lyfe picking up the pieces to a life she knew nothing about. Now he was considering laying his lifestyle down, which left Carmen sinking into quicksand before she even started her first day of work. All she wanted was the world, but it wasn't giving itself up to her easily.

Carmen's knuckles oozed blood, and she watched it drizzle down her hand. She flopped down on her bed and slapped her face into her hands, blood applying itself to her cheeks like makeup.

What am I going to do? had been the only words running through her mind for the past five minutes. She was so close, yet so far from a life she drooled over. She knew she didn't have what it took to be a queenpin, but she would never admit it. The words would never leave her mouth. Coming to terms with the prospect of losing her dream, she finally gave in to temptation and broke down into a sea of tears. There was no way she could sustain what Renee was handing over to her. She needed help and would do just about anything to receive it. Lyfe could say what he wanted, but Carmen took his words and twisted them to the point where she believed he was abandoning her and putting Renee first. She was embarking on a new journey, and if he didn't walk with her, he was walking against her.

Carmen wiped the tears from her face and sat like a zombie without an ounce of a soul, glaring at the striped wallpaper. Ten minutes later, her phone rang, but she ignored it, figuring it was Lyfe. But after it rang back-to-back, Carmen's tolerance for her ringtone ran thin, and she answered it without looking at the caller ID.

"What?" she yelled, her lips and hands trembling from pure frustration.

"Is that how I taught you to answer the phone?"

Carmen's eyes widened with shock. She looked at what was once her mirror, and with her manicured nails, she pinched herself. She needed confirmation that she was hearing who she thought she was. "It can't be," she whispered more to herself than to the voice on the other end of the line.

"What did I tell you about doubting me?"

"Never to," Carmen answered like an obedient child. Even after he had left her without a dime to her name or a pot to piss in, Benz still had a hold over her. Through the phone, she could feel his hand wrap around her neck, depriving her of oxygen. Carmen never loved Benz and, once upon a time, was only with him for his money, but that didn't mean she didn't earn it. She did anything he wanted in return for living the glamorous life. When associating with Benz, everything had a price tag on it, and Carmen was no exception.

"What do you want?" she forced out of her voice box.

"You."

Chapter 19

From across the City Island restaurant's table, Dane watched as Lyfe avoided eye contact with everyone at the dinner table. For the last couple of days, Carmen had been missing. Although Dane and Julian were ecstatic that she was nowhere to be found, something in the back of their minds told them that something was wrong. Whenever someone was too quiet, that meant plotting was taking place. They were giving Carmen one more day to resurface, and if she didn't, they would search for her themselves. In the meantime, they enjoyed their break from her. But when it came to Lyfe, there was definitely a problem taking place that no one knew about.

"Lyfe, is Carmen still sick? Is it the flu or something?" Renee sipped her drink, waiting for Lyfe's response.

With his eyes glued to the floor, he pieced together his lie. "Yeah, that's what it looks like."

Dane giggled. Lyfe was laying a shit storm on Renee, but since she always came prepared with her own umbrella, she saw right through it.

"She's training to take over the business. Isn't it . . . unprofessional for her to be missing in action?" Dane questioned.

"Unprofessional" was the exact word digging its way into Lyfe's cranium. He had just spoken to Carmen about being responsible, and less than forty-eight hours later, she'd run off to God knows where, entirely dismissing everything he'd said. Lyfe wanted to explode. It disappointed him that a person from his bloodline could be so careless. Regardless of how much he wanted to scold her, he couldn't. All he could recall was the last time they spoke. She was furious with him and reacted like a toddler whose toys were taken away. He had driven his niece away, but there was no way he could tell Renee this.

"She's sick. Some things are uncontrollable."

"And some things are bullshit," Dane shot back.

Lyfe pried his eyes from the floor, and the two engaged in a battle of gazes. He respected Dane, but she was overstepping her boundaries and had no right entering into the section of his life labeled family.

"Where is Metro?"

Dane's face slightly lost its edge, but it didn't reveal the nerve he hit. "Excuse me?"

"Metro, where is he? Why isn't he here? You've been away from home for quite some time. Isn't it proper etiquette for him to be here with you?"

"Why he isn't here is none of your business."

"And what's going on in my family is yours?"

Dane squeezed the napkin in her lap. Metro was not to be talked about. The reason for him not being in the States was for her and only her to know. Lyfe was skating on thin ice with a pair of sneakers on. Apparently, he had failed to acknowledge that with just one push, he'd go crashing into the frosty water and, within a matter of seconds, lose his breath. "When her own uncle is playing her for a fool, then yes, it is my business."

Lyfe's neck stretched out farther in Dane's direction. What she said was true, but never would he admit it and allow the world to see him sweat. Lyfe stood up and placed his hands on the table. He was so close to Dane that only she could hear him speak, but instead of keeping the conversation private and murmuring, he spoke loud enough for the whole table to hear.

"Stick to what you know, because playing detective isn't your forte." He smiled the type of smile that made you want to jump up, snatch it off his face, and drop it in his glass of water.

Dane held her composure. If there was one thing she knew about Lyfe, it was when he was bluffing. He must have forgotten whom he'd worked for, for most of his career.

"You're funny." She giggled. "But we all know who will have the last laugh."

When silence fell over the table, Lyfe picked up his knife and fork and cut into his steak. He wasn't hungry. He just needed the distraction. He heavily chomped down on the meat, eating as if the conversation that had just taken place never existed. Lyfe deliberated about where Carmen could be and avoided looking at Renee. It was hard not telling her what happened between him and Carmen, but what would be harder was telling her that he wasn't going to retire.

Renee sat in her seat, eating her meal. She listened to the words flying across the table, and her fork picked at the string beans on her plate.

Julian's eyes moved with the utensil and watched it stab into Renee's least favorite vegetable. Occasionally, his eyes leaped over to the untouched shrimp that normally would have been devoured. Family was a beautiful thing, but when it left you empty, it was detrimental.

Chapter 20

The second Carmen's heels touched down on Miami soil, all her senses came alive, and life was breathed back into her. Her plan for achieving her dream life wasn't panning out how she thought it would, and constant thoughts of returning to Miami and starting over plagued her mind. However, with Benz reappearing and beckoning her back to her hometown, Carmen wondered if she'd still consider Miami her sanctuary.

Carmen dropped her dark sunglasses over her eyes. Carmen diverted her attention to the subject at hand: meeting up with the man who she watched have a hand in the drug world, the man she'd been a trophy girlfriend to and was then discarded and proved was replaceable.

The all-black tinted Lincoln that Benz had sent to pick Carmen up from the airport pulled up to a modest, average-sized two-family home. When the car stopped and the driver didn't bother to speak, Carmen knew she had reached her destination. Her eyes met the driver's in the rearview mirror, and she smirked. They never liked each other, and she knew he was happy to see her kicked to the curb by Benz, but now that Benz had beckoned her, she knew his insides boiled with rage.

Carmen stepped out of the car and strutted up the walkway. The closer she got to the front door, the more of the property and home she took in. *So this is how he's living now?* Carmen laughed at the sight of his new home. Benz had definitely downgraded from living the life of the rich and famous to living the life of the average Joe, and Carmen would bet her two favorite handbags it was all for the comfort of her replacement.

Carmen rang the doorbell, and while she waited to be granted admission, she continued to observe her surroundings. "You're not in Kansas anymore," she told herself. The neighborhood was dry and appeared to be overly prim and proper. Carmen was sure each home she laid eyes on was occupied with homebound senior citizens or uptight middle-aged bores. As she was lost in her view of the neighborhood, the door opened, and two tall, stocky men filled the doorway.

"Come in, hold your arms out, and spread your legs," the shorter of the two ordered.

Carmen found it amusing how each man she encountered had worked for her at some point in time and now could not give her a simple hello. Although it was humorous, she shook it off because she knew where she stood. The past was the past, and once placed behind you, it was nothing but a memory. She did what she was told, all while keeping a straight face. Renee always told her it was human nature for people to try to read you, so give them nothing to go off. She was glad that her shades hid her eyes. It was one less thing she had to worry about giving her away.

After being patted down, Carmen dropped her arms and was told by the short guard who searched her to follow him. Walking to the back of the house, Carmen bypassed warm-colored furniture and pictures of Benz and the woman he left her for. She had never seen her, but

Carmen knew it was she. *He had me come to the home he shares with this wench. He done lost his damn mind.*

The squeaky sound of a door opening pulled Carmen out of her thoughts, and she entered the basement stairwell behind the guard. With her head held high, she walked down the stairs and tried to channel her inner Renee. She needed the business-savvy, tough girl to come through.

They reached a slim door at the bottom of the stairs. The guard opened the door and allowed Carmen to take the lead. Her eyes landed on Benz sitting comfortably on a couch with the remote control to the sixty-inch flat screen in his hand. He never looked Carmen's way, even after hearing her enter. The short guard headed back to his post, and Carmen stood glaring at the man who had abandoned her. The anger she remembered taking her over when he kicked her out resurfaced. The Benz who left her looked stressed and scruffy. This Benz was a lot more put together, and that made her want to scream. He had moved on and appeared to be doing better. Benz glanced at her, then turned back toward the television.

Carmen chuckled. "This bastard," she mumbled.

"Sit down," he instructed.

Carmen looked around the room for a place to sit other than beside him. Her eyes fell on the love seat across from where he sat, and she took a seat, her facial expression just as serious as it has been upstairs.

"Welcome. How was your flight?"

Silence.

"I know you don't like flying coach, so I made sure to fly you first class. Did they have the champagne you like?"

Carmen took a page from Benz's book and didn't acknowledge him or his questions right away. Plus his questions were meaningless and a waste of time. Her darkened shades made it difficult for him to know where she looked.

"The last time I flew with that airline, they had no liquor. That shit irked me, so I made them reimburse me. Now whenever I fly with them, I have a stocked bar strictly for me."

"What the fuck did you call me here for?" Carmen snapped.

Never while in a relationship with him had she spoken to him in that tone of voice. But looking at pictures of the woman who replaced her forced her to accept that she was a has-been. She felt irrelevant, and it burned her insides.

Benz laughed. "New York toughened you up," he commented with his eyes still locked on the television. Minutes passed before he spoke again. "Shortly after I left you, I went legit and got married."

Carmen's eyelids blew up, and she fought the urge to rip her shades off her face. She maintained her composure. She had begged Benz to marry her when they were together, because she knew that with a ring, she would own half of everything he had. Her mouth was agape, but she slowly closed it, deciding not to mumble a peep.

"It didn't take me long to figure out that going legit wasn't for me, so I reverted to what I knew."

Seconds passed, and the two sat in silence, Benz piecing together what he would reveal next.

"But my wife has no place in this life. She has no street smarts, no swag. She's . . ." Benz struggled to find the proper word to describe her.

"Boring," Carmen interjected.

Benz looked Carmen's way and into the shades where he imagined her eyes would be. "Exactly."

With the remote, he turned the TV off, and he leaned over. His hands folded while his elbows rested on his knees. "That's where you come in. I love my wife to death. She is the innocence in my corrupted world, but she's not enough. I need someone I can relate to. I need a mistress."

Carmen jumped out of her seat and headed for the door. There was no way she would come second place to anyone.

Benz didn't move. Instead, he called out for his tallest worker and waited for the fireworks to erupt.

Carmen flung the basement door open and was so enraged she didn't see the guard standing in front of her, and she ran right into his chest. She stumbled backward, and her glasses crashed to the floor. The lenses popped out.

"What the fuck!"

The guard stood in front of her with his arms folded over his chest, blocking the exit.

"Sit down," Benz demanded.

Carmen was so frustrated she wanted to throw herself on the floor and have a tantrum. She flashed back to when she felt defenseless against Renee. The first time they met, she had no choice but to take the disrespect. It was then that she wished she had Benz's protection, but the thing she wanted was no longer on her side. Carmen felt backed in a corner, so she did all she could. She fought.

"Fuck you!" she barked. "You want me to play second fiddle! How about you go get some damn counseling to fix your marital problems, because I'm not your solution!" Carmen turned around and hoped the huge guard had disappeared, but still, he blocked the doorway. "Get the fuck out of my way!"

The goon laughed in her face. In his eyes, there was nothing more amusing than a woman throwing a fit. The laughter pushed Carmen over the edge, and with all her might, she pulled him toward her and kneed him in the groin. Instantly, he dropped to his knees and let out a roar.

Carmen stepped over the guard, but before she made it fully over to the other side, she heard Benz say, "That's why I need you around. My wife would have never found her way out of an awkward situation. Instead, she would have been obedient and done as she was told. I need balance in my life."

Carmen froze, gawking at the stairs that would lead her away from the nonsense.

"You owe me," he said.

Carmen looked at him. "What?"

"You owe me. I put a lot into you, and you gave me nothing. Now it's time for you to pay me back, and you will give me what's due."

Benz's eyes were stationed on hers. She looked on the floor at the man curled up in the fetal position and moaning, then back up the flight of stairs. Even if she left, Benz would never leave her alone until he got what he wanted. Carmen took a deep breath and stepped over the guard and back into the basement.

He was right. She gave him nothing, not love, support, nothing. While they were together, all she did was take and act as the perfect trophy girlfriend. Once again, she looked back down at the goon and back up at Benz, a smile forming on her face. Nothing in life was free, so if

Benz was going to put her back against the wall and force her to do something she didn't want to do, then they were going to do it on her terms.

"Fine, but under one condition."

Benz waited for her to continue.

"Give me control of your team."

Chapter 21

A number of days had passed, and Lincoln hadn't seen or spoken to Carmen. His calls went directly to voicemail, and his home visits went unanswered. History was repeating itself, and depression swept over him. Women he cared for were falling off the earth and leaving him all by his lonesome. He wondered what he'd done that forced her to walk out of his life without saying a word, but he came up blank.

The strip club's neon lights danced across the room and colored Lincoln's face blue. His eyes lay low, and his shoulders were hunched so far down that only the bar kept him from tipping over. The faster the songs played, the faster the lights flashed. Lincoln watched half-naked women dance and live up to their stripper names. The burning sensation from the vodka rushed down his throat and took him to a world of misery and anger. His eyes were locked on a female who belly danced for a Chinese man. He allowed himself to fall victim to her rhythm.

"You like what you see?"

Slowly, Lincoln planted his attention on a slender, brown-skinned woman. Her eyelashes were long and looked like tiny fans on her eyes, while her hair was an ocean of waves crashing down on her neck.

"No," Lincoln slurred. He turned away and focused on the pretty colors.

"I bet your attitude is why she left you." Curly shook her head and motioned for the bartender. After placing her order, she looked back, only to see Lincoln's eyes burning holes into her face.

"You know nothing about me or my woman. So get back on that damn pole where you belong."

Ever since Carmen's disappearance, Lincoln's whole demeanor had changed. He drank like a fish, and whenever a drop of liquor touched his taste buds, he transformed into a mean drunk who no one recognized. Love was turning his heart black, and his good nature was quickly leaking down the drain.

Curly grinned. That little jab Lincoln threw at her was nothing. She was used to being disrespected because of her occupation.

"Thank you, Jim," she told the bartender. She kicked back her shot and took a sip of her martini.

"Save your breath. I know your story: good guy done fell for the wrong chick. You're too squeaky clean. You're too"—Curly looked him up and down—"innocent."

"Just a second ago you said my attitude is what ran her off, so what the hell are you talking about I'm squeaky clean?"

Curly drank the clear liquor until the glass was half empty. "The word 'attitude' can be used in a positive context as well. You're not her style. Even in a place like this, where you're fucked up and staring at ass, you still stick out like a sore thumb and have the words 'good guy' stamped on your forehead." She grabbed a pinch of his shirt and dropped it. "Not even your wardrobe can mask who you are."

Lincoln was at a loss for words, so he opted to stare at the stranger who had read him like a book.

"You'll never satisfy her, and if you do, it's only because you placed yourself into her world and proved yourself in the ultimate way."

Curly was once a good girl who was on the path to becoming a counselor, but she took a wrong turn in life and became stuck in the world of stripping. Reading people was her specialty, so when she spotted Lincoln, she thought she'd tell him about himself. She looked over at him once more and smirked. Reality was a bust, and she pitied him for having to live in it. She grabbed two small white pills from her booty shorts' miniature pockets and popped them into her mouth. She finished her drink and estimated how long it would take her to enter the world of ecstasy.

"Good luck," she told him and walked away from the bar.

The club's lights faded as the DJ announced the dancer known as Misery to the stage. Within minutes, Curly was on the stage dancing like never before.

Chapter 22

"My money, this house, and this lifestyle are yours. But my crew and this business are mine."

Carmen had been in Miami for three days, and it wasn't until today that she had discovered Benz had never gotten rid of the home they'd once shared. Back under the roof where she'd spent years of her life spending Benz's money, Carmen was unsure whether she was happy or disgusted to be back in the same house she was forced to leave. It brought back many memories, some good and some bad.

For the last hour, Benz and Carmen had stood in the middle of the huge living room going back and forth over Carmen having control of his crew. Days had passed, and Benz still wouldn't agree to give Carmen partial control of his troops. When he picked up the phone to summon her to Miami, he didn't expect a stronger and more powerful woman to stand before him. The last time he saw Carmen, she was this gold-digging doormat spiked with spunk, but she bowed down to his every demand. Now she was this woman with pull. The concrete jungle had molded her into a hardened soul that fit perfectly into his world.

Carmen walked over to the bar and poured herself a glass of vodka. She didn't answer right away. Instead, she sipped on the vodka.

"Benz, when she hands everything over to me, I won't need any of those things. You think I'm lying when I tell you her money is ten times longer than yours. Within a year, she would have been a billionaire, but she wants out, and it will all be mine. All I need is my own army."

Benz's chest heaved up and down. Hearing that Carmen would soon be worth more than him rubbed him the wrong way. When he felt his right hand ball into a fist, he quickly folded his arms across his chest to hide his frustration. "You're not getting my men, Carmen."

Carmen grinned, finished off her drink, and left her empty glass on the bar without a coaster. "Then how about this? The second I'm in control, I'll start supplying you with weight. She gets her stuff straight off the boat, the purest shit you'll ever come across. None of that shit that's been stepped on multiple times that you're pushing." The minute the words left her mouth, it was checkmate.

Benz had only been out of the game for a few months, but when he returned, there were new players in the game with better product. His head was just above water, and on a daily basis, he wondered how he would make it back on top. His breathing became heavier. He gave his small mansion a once-over, and it was that very second he was happy he didn't sell the home like he told his wife he had. From this day forward, it would be his and Carmen's home just like before. And the small, modest, cozy home he recently met with Carmen in would forever belong to him and his wife.

Nothing about the home he once shared with Carmen had changed. The glass stairs and ceiling with skylights indicated the life of the rich and famous, and if Benz didn't make some sort of move, and soon, he would be back living amid the average. With his arms still folded and his face screwed up, his piercing eyes stared right into Carmen's.

"I don't care how pure it is, I pay you not a dime more than I'm paying my current connect."

Smiling, Carmen walked over to Benz and stopped right in front of his face. "You can have whatever you like. Just say that your crew is mine."

Benz had done business with many crooks in his day, but doing business with Carmen made him feel like he has just made a deal with the devil. Against his better judgment, he held out his hand, waiting to feel Carmen's hand against his. When she shook it and sealed the deal, all he thought while looking in her smiling face was that he had just signed his life away, and he had no idea if he'd ever get it back.

Chapter 23

Two Days Later

Tucked away in a dark corner far from where Renee sat, Dane watched her and Carmen go back and forth. Renee asked multiple questions regarding where she'd been, and Carmen answered each one so quickly Dane was sure she'd been coached. Her responses were well thought out, and her facial expression was stern. Dane's heart raced, and her mind fell in shambles. She sat there confused, pondering if she was angry because Carmen was conning or because Renee believed every word that rolled off her tongue. Dane visualized the text sent to her from Calloway almost two weeks ago that read, She's going to the airport.

She had ordered the twins to find Carmen, and they found themselves flying to Miami, where they hoped to discover something incriminating but came out empty-handed. Dane wanted to blow a fuse when it was reported to her that they had nothing on Carmen, but she remained calm when Calloway told her there were head-scratching discoveries that he needed to look into before throwing up the white flag.

Julian was infuriated by the lack of evidence and wanted proof that Carmen was a snake in the most impatient, drastic kind of way. He lived for her card to be pulled.

As Dane watched him from her secluded corner, she noticed the uncomfortable look covering his face. She couldn't help but wonder if there was more than his bad feeling driving his desire to get Carmen away.

Renee seemed to be falling for everything Carmen fed her. She told her that she took her advice and flew back to Miami to build her own crew, and she stressed how much taking over her business meant to her. Stress shaped Renee's face, and deep, long bags hung under her eyes. Dane couldn't help but wonder what was going on in her head. For the past few weeks, Dane had kept her distance from Renee, determined to avoid any confrontation that could push her further into Carmen's arms. However, on many occasions, Dane's heart cried out because she couldn't stop wondering how Renee could question her judgment and dismiss her warnings. Fear plagued her because the hardened female she had molded into stone was crumbling right before her eyes, and she didn't know if she could ever be pieced back together. Drowned in this situation, that made Dane question whether she'd chosen the wrong protégé. On countless occasions since Carmen's appearance, she had asked herself if Calloway would have been a better fit.

Approximately ten years ago, when the twins were teenagers, she met them in the most unconventional way. Dane had found Calloway and Fergus, clumsy and full of fear, trying to bury the body of their 300-pound child-molesting uncle. Drenched in sweat, they tried to get rid of the corpse without being seen by anyone, but from afar, Dane watched everything. She didn't know what got into her that day, or why her feet carried her to the unbalanced teens, but they did. When she made her presence known, she taught them how to dispose of a body so that it would never resurface. The twins were in too deep to question her intentions, and they just wanted the body to disappear, so without giving it a second thought, they listened to everything she taught them. They took to her directions like a fish takes to water, and Dane sat back and watched the boys dismantle the body with ease and precision. She looked each child in his eyes and saw that the identical twins were anything but the same.

Fergus had the skill to kill, but deep down, there was still a hint of sanity and hope dwelling within his heart. When she looked closely, she saw a piece of his soul left in his rotting body. Because of this, Dane envied Fergus. His uncle took his body, yet he still fought to achieve some type of normalcy, and she couldn't help but wonder why her heart had failed to do the same. Angry at what her eyes revealed, she turned to Calloway, and peace washed over her.

Calloway was nothing like his brother. Like a savage, he tore the body apart. For him, killing was a sport, a game he longed to win. During the entire butchering, his smile never left his face. He was in his element. Calloway looked up at Dane, and when their eyes met, the words "I love you" slipped from his mouth. A chill surged through Dane's body. His eyes held not one ounce of emotion, regret, or good of any kind, yet he still forced the most powerful words known to man to escape his mouth. Calloway was a savage who only deserved to be in a cage. However, Dane smiled. She understood his insanity, understood that he was confusing love with her accepting who they were and showing them how to better their skill.

"No, my dear," she answered. "You love the kill. You feel for nothing but death. It makes you feel alive."

He was covered in blood. Her words slowly penetrated his brain, and when he looked at her and nodded his head, it was confirmed that was exactly what he felt. He had found himself and anarchy had officially broken loose. Dane knew that one day Metro would let go of being a kingpin, so she set her sights on Calloway being his protégé, but then Renee came into the picture.

She was an intelligent young female whose presence demanded respect and whose coldness gave frostbite to anyone who came into her space. Her thoroughness and thought process made Calloway appear unpredictable. Dane imagined that if Calloway took over, the streets would be flooded with blood, and she and Metro would spend most of their time cleaning up after him.

Unable to let him go after he had shown nothing but loyalty, she gave him his funeral home. When death was not in the air, Calloway seemed withdrawn and drained of life, so she gave him the gift of death and put a cherry on the top when she made them Renee's cleanup crew. The day the twins mutilated their dead uncle's body and handed the pieces over to a crooked butcher who owned a mom-and-pop meat market was the beginning of a deadly relationship. Now Dane questioned if Renee's charm had blindsided her and left her to do nothing but watch as everything her husband built fell.

Dane snapped back to the present when the room became deadly silent. Julian looked furious, and life seemed to have been poured into Carmen.

"Are you serious? That's all that needs to be done, no more training?" Carmen asked Renee, her voice bleached with happiness.

"It's always good to have a native around, so get at least one New Yorker on your team, and the keys to the city are yours."

Carmen jumped out of her seat, ran around the table to her sister, and kissed her roughly on her cheek. Her eyes landed on Julian, and a smile emerged across her face. Thoughts of making love to him invaded her mind and sent her on cloud nine.

Julian became enraged. His chest heaved up and down, and his hands shook.

"Thank you, Renee! You won't regret this!" She ran out of the dining room with plans to celebrate the end of her murderous training.

Julian took a deep breath in hopes of calming his nerves, but when he realized there was nothing he could do to relax, he laughed and thought, *fuck it*. He turned in Renee's direction, and nothing but honesty saturated his voice when he told her, "You must have lost your damn mind."

Dane's mouth dropped and took the form of the letter O. In all the years she had known the couple, Julian had never spoken so rudely to Renee. She froze and speculated if they remembered she was still in the huge room.

"Excuse me?" Renee's face scrunched up, and her eyebrow rose.

"You heard me. You lost your fucking mind if you think that bitch is coming in our circle."

As if they were connected at the hip, Renee's and Dane's breath caught in their throats at the same time.

A piercing pain stabbed Renee in her chest, and she pinched herself under the table, hoping to wake herself up from this dream. "Then commit me now, because she is."

Renee stood up to leave. She had a lot on her mind and didn't need the drama. She didn't know what had gotten into Julian, but if he wanted to argue, he was going to argue with himself. Renee turned to leave but was stopped by Julian's huge hand, which grabbed her by the elbow.

He stood up and looked down at her, his eyes darkening and his shoulders broad. "I been nothing but patient with you. I told myself that you were going through some fucking phase, but now I see that you're not. She's not taking over nothing. We'll let this shit burn down to the ground before that happens."

Julian saw red. He really thought that if he was patient with Renee and left her alone with her thoughts instead of flooding her head with his own, she would come to her senses. Obviously, she hadn't. The smile that Carmen gave him was confirmation that in due time, his secret would be out and his life with Renee ruined.

Renee didn't know what to say or how to react. All she could concentrate on was that Julian wouldn't let go of her arm and that his eyes screamed murder. She tried to pull away, but that only caused him to tighten his grip.

"You do this, and you lose everything," he said, his words cracking with weakness. But what he really wanted to tell her was that they would lose one another. His nerves and distrust in Carmen led him to believe that with a secret this big, and with Carmen in such close proximity, he wouldn't be able to avoid chaos forever.

Renee pushed the pain in her arm out of her head and allowed herself to get lost in the eyes of the man of her dreams. She searched for what he wouldn't tell her and tried to open herself up to honesty, but Julian was closed off, and he gave her nothing.

"Tell her you made a mistake," he hissed and released her arm. He regretted her seeing him weak, even for just a second, because now she sensed there was more going on than what met the eye. So just like Renee had done on many occasions, he jumped from one emotion to another and turned back cold. He looked at Renee as if she disgusted him and walked out.

With her mind and heart left in shambles, Renee flopped down in the nearest chair and, without her knowing, shared a cry with Dane.

Chapter 24

Carmen strolled into the club with a brand-new outlook on life. Things were falling exactly into place and couldn't be better. All Carmen needed was to recruit some native New Yorkers and the throne would be hers. It wasn't easy getting Benz to grant her partnership, but he did. After a few months of gaining his workers' loyalty, she would get rid of him and have complete control over his share of Miami. He was a fool for thinking she'd ever take him back without some form of punishment. He thought money was enough to appease her, but after he left her, she had grown to crave power and desired never to be taken care of by another man again.

The bouncer granted Carmen access, and she gave him a flirtatious grin. Their sexual escapade the night before would go down in history. As usual, the club was crowded and in full swing. Everyone came out to celebrate the end of the week and to let their hair down. Carmen had taken Lyfe's advice and slowed down when it came to clubbing. The last thing she wanted was to be placed on someone's radar and lose everything she worked hard to steal. She even went so far as to cut her hair into a short bob. She wanted her past actions to be a figment of everyone's imagination, and from this point forward, she would be a completely new woman.

Looking at the intoxicated people and feeling the rhythm of the music taking over, Carmen felt herself slipping into temptation and no longer wanting to take care of business. However, as if Lyfe stood right beside her, she heard him tell her, *"Take care of your business."*

Immediately she felt like she had something to prove and shook off wanting to go into party mode. She kept her eyes on the prize. In order not to look out of place, she ordered a Long Island Iced Tea and sat at the bar, searching the crowd for her prey. After seconds of hunting, her eyes zeroed in on Tina. She was pissy drunk and dancing between two guys who didn't look a day over 18. Carmen was pleased that she was a creature of habit and, like clockwork, remained drunk and club-hopping, just as Lincoln said.

The song Tina was dancing to ended, and she stumbled over to the bar, empty glass in hand. She parked herself beside Carmen and began waving her glass in the air, trying to get the bartender's attention while screaming, "I need a refill, Russell!"

Angry that Russell didn't look her way, she waved her glass in the air faster and harder while jumping on her tiptoes. Then, unexpectedly, she tumbled over and fell right into Carmen's lap.

"Oh, shit!" she screamed. Tina struggled to get on her feet but failed miserably. The room was spinning, and the lights blinded her.

Carmen smiled at Tina's foolishness. Everything was falling directly into her lap, and the joy on her face could not be wiped off. She helped Tina to her feet, and after she placed her glass on the bar and held on to it for support, she apologized for invading Carmen's space.

"I'm sorry, girl, but Russell knows how to make the hell out of a drink!"

At the mention of Russell's name, Tina instantly looked for him and tried to get his attention again. From the corner of his eye, Russell saw Tina trying to get his attention, but he ignored her. He dreaded Tina being in the club while he was on shift. Not only was she loud, but she was also a sloppy drunk. Russell believed in cutting off a partygoer who had one too many, but not his boss. His motto was, "As long as the money flows, so do the drinks." Russell feared that one day one of his drinks would lead to Tina's demise. He tried his best to ignore her, but when Carmen waved him down, he had no choice but to head over to them.

"What can I get for you?" he asked, his eyes glued on Carmen.

"Get my girl what she last had."

Russell looked over at Tina, whose eyes were only slightly open, and then looked back at Carmen. "Don't you think she had enough?"

Carmen dug into her purse, pulled out a $50 bill, and held it out to him. "As long as the money is flowing, so are the drinks, am I correct?" Carmen nodded toward the back of the club, and Russell's eyes followed. His boss stood against a wall, watching the entire interaction. Russell shook his head and went to make Tina another Long Island Iced Tea.

"Thanks! I don't know what the problem is. He acts like he don't wanna serve me. My money's green just like everyone else's!" Tina yelled, determined to cause a scene.

Carmen laughed. "You really should slow up on the drinks. You already look faded."

Tina rolled her eyes. "So what, you gonna judge me after only meeting me for what, ten minutes?" she said, looking down at her wristwatch. "You don't know me, so go on with all that."

Russell put the Long Island Iced Tea down in front of Tina. He grabbed the money neatly laid out on the bar and scurried over to other waiting alcoholics.

Tina snatched her drink and turned to walk away, her pink hair wildly flying in the air.

"All right, I guess you too good to make some money then, huh?" Carmen blurted out before she was out of earshot. At the sound of the word "money," Tina froze and turned back around with a smile so long she looked like the Joker.

"I'm sorry about that, girl. You know how it is. Motherfuckers hate so much, you can never tell who's real and who's not. I'm Tina, and you are?" She held her hand out, and Carmen accepted.

"I'm Carmen, and I hear what you're saying. But are you sober enough to give up some info, or should I catch you at a later time?"

Tina looked around, kicked her drink back, and then grabbed Carmen by her wrist. Carmen hopped off her stool and followed Tina out of the club. They walked far from the club's entrance and went over to the side of the building.

"Keep it down. I don't need everyone knowing that I got the juice. So what you need to know? And be aware, my info doesn't come cheap."

"Do I look cheap?" Carmen placed her hand on her hip, inviting Tina to give her jewelry and custom-made dress a once-over. Obviously, the cat caught Tina's tongue, and Tina got down to business.

"I need names of some of New York's thoroughbreds. Dudes who aren't afraid to put in work."

Tina chuckled. "Good luck with that. All the best work for Jordan and deal with no one, and the ones who would were killed months ago."

Carmen felt her chest getting tight. Even when Renee gave her the green light, she still stood in her way. "That's not what I want to hear. You need to dig deep in that memory bank of yours."

Tina could see that if she messed this up, she would be missing major money, so she did what she was told and dug deep into her memory. She pulled a name from her bag of tricks, one she never thought would leave her mouth again. "There's one, but I wouldn't recommend him."

"Lucky thing I'm not paying you for your recommendations."

Tina looked into Carmen's eyes, and an uncomfortable feeling washed over her. "His name is Jared."

Carmen felt the wind being knocked out of her, and she almost lost her balance. "You're a comedian now? Everyone knows he's dead."

"Everyone thinks he's dead. But I have connections in hospitals who say he's breathing." Nurse Moreno was a close friend of Tina's mother and was quick to inform them of their deceased love one Waves's best friend's condition. The news caused fear to travel up Tina's spine and around her waist. After hearing her brother was with Jared the night he passed, her gut told her Jared was responsible. Therefore, when she heard he was in the hospital, she prayed for his death, but her prayers weren't answered. She convinced herself that Moreno was mistaken and he died in the hospital that night, but when she walked past him while heading to a car dealership, she knew not even in her mind could she escape the truth.

Carmen didn't know this girl from a hole in the wall, but for some reason, she believed her. "Where can I find him?"

"I'm assuming his apartment, but I'm really not sure if he's still there." Tina scribbled his address down on a piece of paper and handed it over to Carmen. "I wouldn't trust him, but he'll get the work done," Tina admitted. Her thoughts were far away, with her brother whom she hadn't mourned because she was too busy enjoying the money he had left her.

Holding the address in her hand, Carmen felt like she had just won the golden ticket. She reached in her purse and laced Tina's palms with $400.

Thoughts of Waves quickly left Tina's mind, and greed took their place. "It was nice doing business with you." Tina hoped Carmen would be her new Page. Page had gone missing, and Tina missed her cash.

"Ditto," Carmen replied.

The two then went their separate ways: Carmen to her car, and Tina back into the club to get wasted.

Chapter 25

Carmen was happy with her progress. She could literally taste the power that would soon come her way. She would be lying if she said she had no idea how she'd get Jared over on her side. From day one, she knew his animalistic ways would benefit her whenever needed. However, when Renee made it known that her last encounter with him wasn't a pleasant one, Carmen couldn't help but think that she was better off without him. Thoughts such as those were easy to come by when you thought someone was dead, but when the dead came back to life, everything changed, and Carmen could no longer see her crew without him.

That no one knew Jared was still among the living led Carmen to believe that he wanted to stay dead. When someone wanted to remain undetected, they were not very quick to work with anyone. Yet deep in her soul, Carmen knew she would have to sway him by any means necessary, because without him, her reign would be short-lived.

One thing that irked her about New York was the parking. There never seemed to be enough. She walked up the block in her new high boots, the cold nipping away at the flesh her deep-V-neck dress revealed through her coat. Only a few feet away from her home, Carmen saw a figure sitting on her steps. Her pace slowed down, and multiple thoughts stampeded through her mind. Did Jared find out that she knew he was alive and come for her? It was times like this when Carmen wished Lyfe were with her. But she was a big girl, and if she wanted to be in this game, she had to play by its rules.

Her heartbeat sped up, and her mind took her back to when Jared didn't hesitate to kill the intruder in Renee's home months prior. She wanted to turn around and run, but her legs kept walking forward. After her seconds of fear, the headlights from a passing car hit the figure sitting on the stairs and revealed Lincoln's identity. Carmen's nerves withered away in the breeze, and calmness took over.

"Isn't this a pleasant surprise?" Carmen happily asked, filling in the gap between them. However, when she looked at Lincoln, she saw he was anything but happy. He looked drained, tired, and appeared to have lost weight.

"Where were you?" Lincoln's voice was dry and weak.

"Aw, you missed me?" She sat beside him, her hand on his knee.

"I'm serious, where were you? And why haven't I heard from you?"

Carmen withdrew her hand and stuffed them both in her pockets. She liked Lincoln. He just wasn't for her. If she would have ever chosen to change her life around, he would be the man for her, but stepping outside of herself would never and could never happen. Deeply, she inhaled and exhaled.

"Lincoln, you're a good guy, a real good guy, but you're just not my kind of guy."

"Why don't I believe you?"

A weak smile came to her face. He didn't believe her, because until her trip to Miami, the two had been inseparable. She had let her hair down and exposed her innocence, but that moment had passed.

"Don't take this the wrong way, Lincoln, but it really doesn't matter what you believe. What matters is what is."

Lincoln turned away from her and planted his attention on cars that passed. His mouth opened. No words came out at first, and when they did, his voice cracked. "What do I have to do?"

Carmen's face scrunched up. "What?"

"What do I have to do to make you want me?" He never looked at her while talking.

"There's nothing that you can do. We're from two different worlds. Trust me, you want no part of mine."

"Then let me determine that."

After the words left his mouth, Carmen didn't know how to take it. He was fighting for her. One part of her liked it. However, another part of her wanted to warn him and encourage him to run far, far away from her.

"Don't say I didn't warn you." Carmen didn't know what she was saying, but she found his determination to be a turn-on and wanted to experience more.

"Consider me warned. Now school me. Where were you?" His hand landed on her thigh, a clear indication that he could handle whatever she threw at him.

Carmen took a deep breath. *He asked for it,* was all she thought. "I was in Miami visiting my ex."

Lincoln nodded his head. "Are you back together?"

"In his mind, we are. Some time ago, we were in a serious relationship. We lived together and played house, but he refused to get married. So time passed, and I accepted it, figuring that as long as he supported my materialistic needs, all was well. He was a drug dealer and a damn good one. We lived the typical illegal, wealthy life you see on TV and read about in books. Everything was fine until I noticed him becoming withdrawn, and then months later, he left me. He told me he was leaving not just me but the game overall. He met someone who talked him into going legit and wanted nothing to do with me. He kicked me out of our home and never looked back. That is, until a couple of weeks ago."

Carmen paused, searching for some type of reaction from Lincoln, but she got none.

"Out of the blue, he called me and told me that he wanted to see me, so I made my way to Miami. He told me that he wanted me to be his mistress. His goody-goody wife is no longer doing it for him, and going legit was only a phase, so he jumped right back into what he knew." Carmen became so lost in her storytelling that the cold no longer bothered her.

"His wife? He married the woman he cheated with?"

"Yup, but he doesn't want to let go of her. He wants to have his cake and eat it, too. By day, he plays the perfect citizen and husband, but by night, he's a dope-slinging adulterer. In his mind, he's king of his castle, but I have something for that ass."

Carmen was now in a trance. She no longer felt Lincoln's reassuring touch or remembered that he sat beside her. All she cared about was getting revenge.

"I'm not over the fact that he left me out to dry. He's a selfish son of a bitch, and he lost his damn mind if he thinks I'll ever play by his rules. So I constructed the perfect plan. Within a few days, I will be in charge of New York's drug supply. I needed a team, so I talked him into handing over his men. His greed will be his downfall, because after I told him I'd give him a better price on them things, he took the bait and gave me power over his organization. But after I learn his ins and outs and gain the trust of his men, I will be the one kicking people to the curb."

Carmen's eyes were lifeless and far away from the steps they sat on. Yet they let Lincoln know that Carmen planned to do something much worse than dumping her ex. Minutes passed, and both of them sat lost in their thoughts until Lincoln broke the silence.

"I want in," he mumbled.

Stuck between reality and her own world, Carmen asked him, "What?"

"I said I want in. I want to be a part of your world."

Carmen laughed with her eyes half closed. "And what exactly would you do?" she asked him.

"I'll take care of whoever you want taken care of. No one will ever suspect the squeaky-clean dude."

Lincoln had never let go of the words given to him by Misery: "You'll never satisfy her." They haunted him, and the only way he saw himself escaping the truth was to immerse himself in Carmen's world and hold on to a love that was anything but that.

Carmen wanted to dismiss his offer and laugh in his face, but Lincoln had a point. No one would expect the innocent one.

"Let me prove myself to you. I can make this work," he begged.

Both of Carmen's hands were in Lincoln's, and his eyes were wide with hope. This was exactly why Carmen wanted to keep Lincoln at arm's length. She knew eventually she would ruin him. Now that he knew her ways and couldn't care less, she no longer cared where her life took him. "You're serious about this?"

"As a heart attack."

"Fine, there's just been a change of plans. I want you to make my ex suffer. Make him feel the pain I felt when he threw me out like yesterday's trash. I want you to kill his wife."

Chapter 26

Deep within her soul, Renee could feel herself transforming. Her heart beat rapidly, and her mind was all over the place. Sharp pains entered her chest, but she did nothing to escape them. Instead, she welcomed and became one with the agony, which made it hard for her to breathe. Her anger over the past day's events was at an all-time high and was sure to put her health in jeopardy if she didn't calm down.

Julian had left Renee's home the day Renee announced Carmen was officially taking over, and she hadn't heard a thing from him since. Today made three days since he walked out in need of time for himself. History was repeating itself, because once again, Renee stood on her balcony looking over New York and wondering where he was. Thoughts plagued her mind as to why Julian would be so against the idea of Carmen being her protégé that he would allow it to destroy their relationship. What bothered Renee more was that Lyfe had once again chosen Carmen over her.

Renee's eyes danced over the night sky, her hand shaking as it moved her drinking glass toward her mouth. She downed the remainder of her Pinnacle, and slowly, the vodka washed over her pain and caused it to temporarily subside. Renee knew Lyfe was avoiding her. He'd always find a way out of the conversation when she mentioned him leaving the game and was hardly, if ever, around anymore. She was not amused with his antics and allowed it to occur only because she knew hearing the truth would hurt. The truth was that he wasn't retiring and was staying in the game all for his beloved Carmen. Lyfe didn't have to tell Renee. She already knew. It left her feeling foolish that she actually thought he would pick her over Carmen. She felt ridiculous for believing she had a chance at obtaining a father figure.

She refilled her glass and drank it so quickly the liquid escaped out of the corners of her mouth. The tears that washed down her face burned, just like the liquor invading her body. All Renee wanted was to be normal and live a life of happiness, which included letting go of the past. With Julian and Dane constantly on her back about Carmen and Lyfe ignoring her pleas for a chance at having a father figure, it was clear as day that she wasn't meant to be normal. The writing was on the wall. Renee could be nothing more than she already was: ruthless. Since life had her pinned in a corner, she was going to do what she did best: fight. But this time, the blood would be redder than ever.

In the corner of his bedroom, Lyfe sat in a wooden chair with two photos in his hands. Light from the street lamps peeked through his wooden blinds and shined down on the photos just enough for him to see the faces of Renee and Carmen. He stared at them when they were children and thought of everything he knew about them both. He had a list a mile long based on facts he knew about Carmen and only a handful of things he knew about Renee. A tear escaped his eye when he looked at his eldest niece. He knew nothing about the little girl turned woman, yet he still chose to be there for Carmen. Lyfe knew he was making a big mistake and was doing Renee more harm than good if he didn't retire with her and get to know her better, but deep down, he knew Carmen couldn't do things alone.

Renee was thrown into this crazy world and was given two options: to either swim or sink. With no one in her corner, she taught herself how to survive and needed no one. Carmen, on the other hand, was a princess, a female who wanted and needed for nothing. Yes, she dabbled in the street life, but she was no warrior. She was a wannabe, and Lyfe saw that from the beginning. He needed to be there for her, because if not, the streets would eat her alive. He battled with whether he could live with his decision, but there was no way around it. If he left Carmen's side, Renee would want to take full advantage of life's joys, and on countless occasions have him travel with her and be happy. She even mentioned moving to Jamaica and him coming along, but Lyfe couldn't do that. Lyfe couldn't leave Carmen swimming with sharks, no matter how strong her team was. Carmen proved she would sink when thrown into the world with her constant clubbing and careless acts. The morning she stumbled into her home, Lyfe knew any hope of getting to know Renee was thrown out the window due to his dependent niece. He avoided Renee and conversations based on the topic, and it killed him, but he just didn't have the guts to tell her no.

The sound of the doorbell ringing pulled Lyfe out of his misery. He placed the pictures back into his night table and headed for the front door. Through the peephole, he saw Renee standing in all black, shivering in the winter's cold. He wondered why she didn't use her key, but he quickly remembered that if someone were dodging him, he wouldn't want to come in and invade their space either. Lyfe opened the door, and although he felt like the worst uncle known to man, he smiled at the sight of her. When he looked at Renee, he saw his brother, and the sight of her made him feel closer to the sibling he lost.

"Come in. It's freezing out there."

Without speaking, Renee walked into the house. Her construction boots banged against the hardwood floors. Her eyes roamed around Lyfe's small one-family home, one of his many places of refuge. She was happy he was here and not elsewhere, because if he were in his apartment, a lot of blood would have been spilled. Her eyes landed on a picture of her, Lyfe, and Carmen taken weeks ago in Las Vegas.

"You answered the door. Can I assume you're done dodging me?"

Uncomfortable that Renee chose to hold nothing back, he walked into the living room and had a seat. "I don't know why I ever thought you wouldn't notice." Lyfe took in the fact that Renee was standing on the other side of the room, a huge gap between them.

"What I want to know is why can't you let Carmen be a woman and stand on her own two feet? Why do you find it necessary to watch over her? She asked for this life and got it, so leave well enough alone."

Lyfe wished life were that easy. "What makes you think that if I chose to stay, it's because of her?"

Renee's face scrunched up. "If? Don't play games with me, Lyfe. Your mind is made up. You're not going anywhere, and you made me aware of your decision when you chose to act like a little bitch and avoid me.

You couldn't have been more obvious while at City Island. So tell me, why does she win this time? She's had you play her father figure for years, so what's wrong with me that I'm not allowed that also?"

Tears ran down Renee's cheeks. She told herself she wouldn't cry, but just thinking that she wasn't wanted killed her. She didn't bother to wipe the waterworks away. Her life was full of pain, so it was time she got used to it.

Lyfe dropped his head and fought back tears of his own. He was doing everything he knew his brother didn't want, and that was abandoning his niece.

"Nothing's wrong with you, Renee. Nothing ever was. But Carmen, she . . . she needs me. She can't survive in this game alone. Yes, you trained her, but she's no you. I give her a year, only a year, before the streets take her down."

"And how long would you give me before I self-destruct?"

Renee's face was a puddle of tears, and at that moment, his heart broke in two. He didn't know what to say. He just sat there and wished he could be there for her, but he knew he couldn't. The defeated look on Lyfe's face made Renee officially understand that a fairy-tale ending was not in her cards, and that the love of a family member had died with her father.

She nodded her head and finally spoke. "You're free, Lyfe. Free of your uncle duties."

Renee turned around and went for the door, not waiting for Lyfe to see her out. Seconds after entering the cold, she heard the doors being locked and saw the lights in Lyfe's living room go out. Slowly, she walked down the walkway and stopped, her eyes focusing on the house's dark corner.

"Torch it," she ordered.

Before entering Lyfe's home, Renee had given Fergus and Calloway the instructions to circle Lyfe's home with gasoline if she didn't come out within five minutes. Since no one wanted Renee's life to change for the better, she would change for the worse. The silence from the darkness let Renee know that she was understood.

As her heavy boots carried her away from the home, she suddenly stopped again and said, "And if he makes it out, kill him."

Nothing would ever be the same. Renee tried to live, tried to open her heart to life's riches, but no one would allow her to. No one would grant her desperately needed wish. As the saying goes, what goes around comes around. Since no one would allow her happiness, she would take away everyone else's, and that included Carmen's dream of being queen.

Chapter 27

I'm on my way, Dane texted her sister.

The driver who had been sent to pick her up from the airport drove down the streets of Miami in silence. After witnessing Julian's blowup and Renee's depression, Dane thought it would be best to give her some space. She never thought her and Julian's constant nagging pertaining to getting rid of Carmen affected Renee, but that night, it became clear that even Renee had her breaking point. So for four days and four days only, Dane would leave their world behind and fall back into a life that was normal.

It had been years since Dane had seen her sister. The last time she saw her was at Reagan's graduation when she received her bachelor's in psychology. Reagan was on the right path. She lived a life of innocence and knew nothing about her family's illegal activity. All she knew was that her uncle Ray and aunt Laura gained custody of her and her younger brother when they were children because their parents were murdered in a robbery done wrong. In her eyes, Dane had never quit medical school. Her family led her to believe that she had achieved her calling and still practiced medicine to this day. She never knew that she and her brother were the reason Dane stepped over into the dark side. Never knew that her aunt was a drug dealer who refused to leave the game alone. She had no idea that while they lived with her aunt, Dane saw it as her duty to protect them against their enemies and get revenge on their parents' killers.

Dane wanted to preserve Reagan's and her brother's innocence. She wanted to give them what was taken away from her, and that was happiness. Dane had no kids, so in her soul, she was their mother. Time passed, and Reagan decided that she wanted to move to Miami, where she would work toward her master's degree. It was her little sister's dream to become a psychologist and one day run her own practice. Therefore, with Reagan out chasing her dream, and Dane living her life in the fast lane with Metro, days became months and months became years since the two had last seen each other.

Dane watched as the city's palm trees raced past her window. She wondered how life would have been if her parents had never died. She looked down at her beautiful hands that had done such ugly things and knew that had they never passed, she would not have one drop of blood on them. Lately, Renee had been questioning her about when she would retire, and now that she was on the road to see her sister, the thought of retiring didn't seem like such a bad idea. She had accomplished what she set out to do when becoming a hit woman a long time ago, and now that she thought long and hard about it, what more was there for her to do in this business that she hadn't done already?

Dane felt the car slow down then come to a complete stop. She looked at the small, comfortable home that her sister occupied and placed her sunglasses over her eyes. The driver opened her door, and Dane's long legs came into view. Before she made her way to the house, she observed the neighborhood her sister chose to live in. It was quiet, too quiet in Dane's opinion. She looked around, searching for a sign of life. She saw no kids playing outside, elderly people taking a walk around the block, or hardworking parents coming home after a hard day's work. Dane didn't know why, but she didn't like it there, and whenever her feelings spoke to her, she listened.

Uncomfortable and on guard, Dane walked up to Reagan's door, and magically it flew open. The sight of her baby sister caused her to draw a blank. Looking at Reagan was like looking at her mother. Her hair was styled in loose waterfall curls that dropped down her back, and her bronze skin sparkled against the Miami sunrays.

"Dane!" Reagan squealed. She fell into her sister's arms, and Dane held on to her for dear life. She knew people changed, but looking at Reagan was like looking at their mother. While they hugged, Dane could feel their mother's presence. A cooling breeze surrounded the sisters, and Dane buried her face into Reagan's hair. Their mother was hugging them.

"I'm sorry about that," Reagan apologized. She forced herself out of Dane's arms. "I know you're tired. You just got off a plane, and here I am bombarding you with hugs."

Reagan had such a carefree, childlike smile. It was the type that made people rewind time to when they were a kid, and paying bills and going to work didn't exist.

"Never apologize for hugging me." Dane smiled. She could no longer contain her happiness. She was ecstatic to see her sister.

Reagan's smile got bigger, and she grabbed her sister's wrist. "Come in. Let me show you around."

It didn't take Reagan long to show her around her well-decorated, intimate home. Looking in each room,

Dane felt like the walls were closing in on her. She was used to huge spaces, like her home in Jamaica, and wondered what Reagan had seen in this tiny home. Then it hit her: Reagan wasn't her. Material things didn't better her mood or lighten up the dark days she spent stained in blood. Reagan didn't hold on to the anger that pumped through her veins, and that was all because she was normal.

The two ladies sank into the white couch from Ashley Furniture and sipped on white wine. Dane asked, "Tell me, how has life been treating you?"

Reagan's eyes sparkled and seemed to get bigger with every second that passed. "In a couple of months, I will have my master's and will be able to open my own practice. So I started looking around for office space. I just can't decide. Everything I see, I want." Reagan giggled, and Dane flashed back to all the times she tickled her as a kid, and she let out that same sound.

"When you get your degree and are ready to make a decision, let me know. It will be my graduation gift to you."

"Are you serious? Are you sure? Can you afford it?" The questions seemed to roll off Reagan's tongue.

"If I couldn't, I wouldn't offer."

"Oh, yeah, I forgot. My sis is a big-time doctor! You putting people back together and whatnot!"

In need of an escape from her lies, Dane poured herself more wine. The alcohol had reached the brim of her glass when she caught a glimpse of her sister's wedding band.

"Will I be meeting the mister tonight?" Dane nodded at her ring.

Reagan's smiled dimmed and then looked forced. "Yeah, he'll be home in a couple of hours," Reagan answered softly.

Not too long after Reagan made her move to Miami, she met her husband and wound up getting hitched. No one knew that she had vowed to love, honor, and obey this man until she made a call home after their honeymoon. Dane was the last to know her sister had jumped the broom. Reagan was scared her older sister would be disappointed in her for her spur-of-the-moment decision and for not allowing the family to help her plan and attend the wedding of her dreams. However, after she met Malcolm, she didn't want to wait to marry him. The faster she could take his last name, the better. Everyone was angry with her, but with time, all was forgiven but never forgotten.

"That's not the tone of a newlywed."

Reagan was silent. Her eyes landed everywhere except on Dane. She thought about her woman's intuition that kept knocking on her door. Almost a minute ran by, and Dane waited for her sister to speak, but no words were given.

"Are you going to just sit there, or are you going to tell me what's on your mind?"

Reagan's eyes were stationed on her glass, her mind playing a game of volleyball with her thoughts. "I think he's cheating," she blurted out.

Dane's body froze, and her blood stopped in her veins. "Why do you think that?"

"Out of the blue, he started coming home late, keeping more to himself, and it's nearly impossible to get in touch with him when he's out. Either it's that, or he's back to . . ."

Instantly, Reagan stopped talking. She looked at her sister and knew if she said what was about to come out of her mouth, she wouldn't approve.

"'It's either that or he is back . . .' Finish your sentence," Dane pushed.

It didn't matter that Reagan was in her twenties and hadn't seen her sister in years. She still couldn't hide things from her. She needed a woman to confide in, so she decided to come clean.

"It's either that or he's selling drugs again."

Dane's chest caved in. "What are you talking about?" Dane didn't raise her siblings to engage in that lifestyle. She did all she could to shield them from it, and now that Reagan was telling her that she had dealings in drugs, Dane beat herself up for being absent for so many years.

Reagan took a deep breath. "When I met him, he was a drug dealer. He made good money and was pretty deep into it. But after months of being with him, I couldn't do it anymore. That's not how I was raised, and I began to feel like I was betraying the family or something. And let's not mention how afraid I was that something may happen to him. The fear alone made me want to be with him twenty-four seven, just to guarantee his safety. So when he proposed, I didn't answer right away. Instead, I told him how I felt about him being a drug dealer. And just like that, he gave it all up. We were going to move out of Miami and start fresh, but I couldn't tear myself away from my school, so we stayed. Once he cut off all ties with his illegal lifestyle, we got hitched and moved into this house. He always wanted to open a business, so he washed his money and opened a restaurant." Reagan searched Dane's eyes for her thoughts but saw nothing.

"What now?" Dane finally asked.

"I don't know," Reagan answered truthfully, her eyes a puddle of tears. "But I know I can't live like this, and I definitely won't stand for infidelity. I just don't know what to do or where to start."

"I know what to do."

Reagan looked at her sister with hope in her eyes. "What? Tell me."

Dane thought visiting her sister would place her in a normal environment and remind her of a life she had left behind a long time ago, but obviously, her current ways followed her. Hearing that her sister's husband was possibly cheating on her enraged Dane, but to know that he was a drug dealer sent her over the edge. Dane was a hypocrite because she denied her siblings everything she indulged in on a regular basis, but that was only because she knew the dangers that came with the territory.

"You're going to let me handle things. You're going to tell him that I had to cancel and never showed. Then you will show me an up-close picture of him, tell me the type of car he drives and his license plate, and give me a list of all the places he frequents. Starting tomorrow, I will follow him the second he leaves in the morning. I will be waiting up the block for him to pull off at five a.m. However, I will have to leave here soon. I know the owner of a car rental company a few minutes from here that will give me a car right now if I give him the word."

Dane pulled out her Apple phone and shot a text to the man she was speaking of. Reagan was amazed with how her sister ran Operation Catch Malcolm down in just a matter of seconds. She didn't think she wanted her sister involved in her marital affairs, but how could she tell her no? Dane had a plan, a plan that she didn't doubt would work. Without further delay, Reagan gave her approval.

"You have my full permission to do what you have to do."

Dane looked up from her phone and at her baby sister. She wished she hadn't just spoken those words, because without her knowing it, she had possibly signed off on her husband's death warrant. Her phone vibrated in her hands, snatching her out of her deadly thoughts.

Calloway: The men Carmen recruited work for a Miami drug dealer by the name of Malcolm Maylin a.k.a. Benz. They seem to have an on-again, off-again relationship, but after meeting up a couple of weeks ago, they are now back on. Malcolm is dirty, Dane. Having him this close to us will be nothing but trouble, just like before. I suggest we exterminate him immediately.

Dane looked at her sister. Everything she assumed about her husband was nothing but the truth, and even though her intuition didn't steer her wrong, Dane still knew she would take the truth hard. She no longer needed to investigate Benz, but she would let her sister believe she was.

"Reagan, try to get through to your husband and tell him I didn't show, and then get me all the information I'll need."

Reagan stood up from the couch and made her way to the kitchen to retrieve the cordless phone. Dane was in the middle of stuffing her phone into her pocket when another text came in.

Metro: Lyfe's house burned down, and he was in it.

Chapter 28

Standing in the apartment building's elevator, Carmen's legs felt weak, and her bottom lip quivered. When the doors opened, her entire body went numb, and all she could do was stare at the wall on the other side. She was having second thoughts and wondering if bringing Jared back from the dead was a good idea. Her right hand balled up into a fist, and anger surged through her because she could not will her legs to move forward. The doors closed, and the elevator took her right back down to the lobby.

Alone, Carmen began to kick and punch the walls. She knew this behavior would never keep her on top, and she was now highly frustrated with how she was handling the situation. When the elevator doors reached the lobby and opened, Carmen was relieved no one was there. The last thing she wanted was to try to pull herself together for the sake of strangers.

She took a deep breath and pressed the button for the floor Jared lived on. She closed her eyes, and her head hung low as she waited for a second chance to exit the huge metal box. When the doors opened, Carmen's ears rang, and her eyes shot open. She bit the inside of her cheek and slowly walked into the hallway. She memorized his apartment number and searched for the signs that pointed in the direction of the B apartments. With her heart seconds away from breaking out of her chest, she turned the corner and immediately felt like she walking to the electric chair when she saw Jared's apartment at the end of the hall. She felt for her gun in her purse. She'd never used one before, but if she needed to, she would fill Jared with lead. Jared was a killer who never hesitated to take a life, and by her even going to talk to him, it put her in harm's way.

Standing in front of the cream-colored door with a shiny yellow knob, Carmen proceeded to knock, but the second her knuckles grazed the door, it opened. Carmen was met with emptiness, and cautiously she stepped into the apartment and looked around. It was completely empty and so quiet she was sure someone would jump out. Although Carmen was sure she was at the correct address, she jammed her hand into her back pocket and looked at the address again.

This is the right place. Then, like a light switch being turned on, Carmen's mood changed, and her body temperature rose.

She lied to me, was all she could think. Pissed that she actually believed everything Tina had told her, she crumpled the small piece of paper with the address on it and threw it on the floor. With fury surrounding her, Carmen turned around and made her way to the door. Her right foot had just touched the glossy hallway floor when she was yanked back into the house by her neck. Her breathing decreased, and before she could come to terms with what was taking place, a gun was held to her head.

"It's not polite to come to someone's home unannounced," Jared whispered in her ear.

Carmen's legs buckled, and her body ran cold. Her eyes zoomed in on her purse, which contained her gun, but there was no way she could get to it before being killed. She wished she had magical powers so that she could make the gun float out of the bag and into her hands. Then, within seconds of wishing, her purse appeared to be getting smaller, and her feet were no longer touching the floor.

Jared placed his gun back in his pants, and with one hand he held her in midair by the neck, squeezing the life out of her. "What do you want?" he growled.

Carmen was seeing black and was seconds away from blacking out. With the little bit of energy she had left, she kicked her feet and clawed at his hands. "I can't breaaaatthhhhhe," she fought to say.

Hearing Carmen struggle for air brought Jared joy, so he smiled and squeezed her neck harder. It wasn't until her body stopped moving and her eyes closed did he release his hold on her. Carmen's body landed on the floor with a loud thud, and she coughed uncontrollably. Her body shook while welcoming oxygen, but the second her breathing pattern got back on course, Jared was on his knees with his hand around her neck once again.

"How did you know where I lived?"

It was torture to have air enter her lungs and have it taken away all in the same breath. Carmen looked into Jared's eyes and saw that she should never have come. She should never have tried to speak with a lunatic.

"I really don't repeat myself, Carmen, so I suggest you talk, and fast!" His hands squeezed tighter, and this time, heavier, brighter bruises formed on her neck.

"I . . . I just knew," she spit out.

"Wrong answer." Jared grabbed a glob of her hair with his free hand and banged her head against the floor.

It was initiation time. Carmen had never sat back and thought about the danger she was putting herself in when replacing Renee. She never thought about the consequences that would take place if her enemies ever got their hands on her, but now she was learning. Now she was seeing firsthand that everything that glitters isn't gold, and she was scared to death.

"Okay! Okay!" she forced out. "Tina! A girl named Tina told me!"

Jared released her neck and hair. Still bending down, he smiled. "I knew you didn't have the brains to find me on your own. Now, what the fuck do you want?"

When Carmen was sure he would not choke her out again, she backpedaled against the wall and held on to her neck, thinking how much of a nutcase Jared really was. Before she got a chance to say a word, she heard a door open in the hallway. A fragile old woman peeked her head out of her house and straight into Jared's.

Jared stood up and looked directly at her. "Ms. Ross, we spoke about this. You stay in your house and mind your business, and I don't break your son's neck. Remember that talk?"

Ms. Ross nodded her head up and down.

"Now I have good news for you. I'm moving, so go back into your house, and I guarantee you won't see me again. But if you open your mouth, your son will see me very soon. Do we have an understanding?"

Again she nodded her head, then quickly went back into her home.

"I am going to ask you one more time, what do you want?" Jared asked, his attention solemnly on Carmen.

Her eyes could not come off the hallway. The door remained open, and she hoped someone not scared of Jared would come out.

He read her thoughts and responded by saying, "If you were any of them, would you help or call the police?"

Carmen knew that she wouldn't, so she took her eyes off the door and placed them on him. He waited to hear why she was in his presence, and she tried to speak but lost her voice. The look on Jared's face told her that she didn't have long to answer, so she forced the words out of her mouth.

"I want you on my team."

Jared placed his hand under his chin while looking at her. She sat on the floor without moving an inch, her hand still rubbing her neck with fear dripping from her face while saying she wanted him on her team. After replaying what she had just told him, he let out a laugh so hard it had to be pushed out from his gut. The laugh was so loud it echoed throughout the empty apartment and boomed out into the hallway.

"No, really, why are you here?"

Carmen sat up straight. It was now or never. If she was going to sit there and do nothing, then she might as well complete her mission and say her piece.

"I want you on my team. Renee is retiring, and I'm taking over." Slowly Carmen stood. She needed to be a woman and on his level, not on the floor being looked down on. "You're the thing I'm missing that will make me untouchable."

Jared never wiped the smile off his face. This was too entertaining to be true, so he stood there wondering if he should shatter her dreams by physically attacking her or by verbally humiliating her. He chose the latter.

"I will never work for another female. And if I were to, it sure as hell wouldn't be for you. You're a snake. I knew that the second you were in Renee's bedroom snooping around." Jared paused and then continued. "You're out of your league, little girl. I suggest you step aside and leave it to us adults."

It wasn't until he walked into the living room and preceded to pick up his luggage did Carmen notice it.

As he made his way toward the door, anger seeped out of her pores. She could not allow herself to be belittled by him. "No, you're out of your league. You need to stop trying to be Julian, accept that Renee doesn't want your ass, and get this paper with me!"

Jared froze, and like a statue, he became stiff and cold. He dropped his luggage beside him and turned his head to the side just enough to see her out of the corner of his eye. "You're not in Miami where there's palm trees and shit. You're in the concrete jungle where only the strong survive, so I suggest you watch your fucking mouth."

Carmen took a deep breath and walked closer to Jared. "Listen, I didn't come here for any trouble, but I need the muscle. If you work for me, I promise to make the money Renee was giving you look like pennies."

"If you had the slightest bit of a brain in your head, you would know I don't want the money. I want Renee. So go sell someone else your dream."

Once again, Jared grabbed his belongings and headed out the door. The farther he made his way into the hallway, the more nervous she became. There was no way she would survive in the game without a beast like Jared by her side. She was hoping he would take the place of her uncle, and watching Jared leave sent Carmen into a panic.

Before she knew what she was doing, she yelled out, "I can get you Renee!"

Jared threw his luggage, and the items crashed into the wall. With fury in each of his footsteps, he walked back to the apartment. He'd had enough of her mouth and would teach her when to shut up.

Carmen backed up. Her breath caught in her throat when she saw him pull the gun out and aim it right at her. Jared made it into the apartment, grabbed her by the neck, and pointed the gun to her head.

Instantly, her eyes closed, and she swallowed what felt like a brick. However, she wanted this life, so now she had to live it. "I can get you Renee," she whispered.

Jared didn't answer. The sound of his breathing in the silent apartment told her that she had minutes left to live.

"If you want Renee, you got Renee. She trusts me. Why else would she be handing everything over to me? But to tell you the truth, I despise that bitch. So if you don't do what I'm about to suggest, I'm bodying her the moment I get the chance, and then you'll never have her." Carmen was done being a little girl in a grown man's game and having people control her actions. From now on, she would be in command.

"You can't kill someone when you're dead." Jared pushed the gun harder against her skull.

"Who says there's not someone out there to carry it out for me? We all know messages can still be sent from the grave."

It was a game of chess, and with one move, Carmen silently screamed, *checkmate!* Jared had been missing in action for quite some time, and because of this, he had no idea what kind of power Carmen had earned. He was too angry to respond, so he remained quiet and allowed her to continue.

"You're quiet, so I assume you're giving me the green light to speak."

Silence.

"If you don't want to work for me permanently, then fine, but you will work long enough for me to make my mark. Once that's done, I will hand Renee over to you on a silver platter, and you two will then leave New York and never come back. I'll lure her somewhere for you to snatch her. Heck, I'll chain her ass up somewhere for you, if I have to."

A smile slid across Jared's face. He liked what he was hearing but didn't like who he was hearing it from. "I don't trust you. How do I know you won't screw me over and let her know I'm alive?"

"I told you I don't like her, and I need you. Besides, how else can I guarantee you'll give me what I want? I have to keep my mouth shut."

Jared allowed her words to float around in his mind. He wanted Renee more than he wanted air, and if he could get her without going to war, he was going to do just that. He lowered his gun and looked into her eyes. Jared trusted no one who couldn't look him in the eyes.

"I'll work for you for two months, and two months only."

"Two months? How can I possibly make my mark in—"

Jared cut her off. "Or I can kill you where you stand and exterminate everyone associated with you. Your choice."

Carmen didn't answer. She took what she could get and was happy that her team was now complete.

As he walked out of the apartment for the last time, Carmen asked, "How can I get in contact with you?"

"You won't. I'll get in contact with you."

With that said, Jared slammed the door, his boots stomping against the building's buffed floors.

Carmen was far from queen-pin status, but she felt like she was well on her way. On a mission to get out of the cold and into her home, she locked the doors of her car and walked across the street in the direction of her brownstone. Standing at her doorstep were two men, dressed in black trench coats, knocking repeatedly on her door. Their backs were turned toward her when she approached them.

"May I help you?"

The two men quickly turned, startled by her appearance. One said, "I'm Officer Reynolds, and this is my partner, Officer Rivera. We're looking for a Ms. Hunt."

"I am she." Carmen didn't know why, but she instantly became horribly uncomfortable.

"We're sorry to have to tell you this, Ms. Hunt, but your uncle Leon Bennett's home caught on fire last night. I'm saddened to tell you that he didn't make it."

Carmen's heart pounded against her chest so hard she could hear it in her ears. The world came to a halt, and her stomach began doing somersaults. She grabbed her stomach and ran down the stairs to the side of the brownstone, where she threw up in the bushes. After getting everything out of her system, she leaned against a parked car, her body sliding down to the ground while her conscience replayed the tragic news Reynolds had just delivered.

The officers bent down to her level, trying to help her up, but when Reynolds grabbed her elbow and attempted to pull her up, Carmen let out a heart-wrenching, ear-piercing cry. Witnessing the torment escaping her mouth, Reynolds and Rivera chose to leave her alone and instead keep her company. They never said a word. They just stood quietly and allowed all of New York to listen to her pain.

Chapter 29

Reagan ran into the house, the door slamming behind her. Her heart was beating out of her chest, and her face was hurting from her constant smiles. Her cream purse slid off her shoulder until she snatched it off and flung it on the couch. She patted herself down in search of her cell phone, and when she remembered it was in her purse, she smiled even harder at her excitement and jumped on the couch, knees first. Her hands rummaged through her purse like the Tasmanian Devil.

After class, her Realtor had contacted her, informing her that she had a place she believed would be perfect to start her practice. The minute Reagan laid eyes on the all-glass two-story office space with a garden and glass stairs, her heart came to a halt and her eyes to a shimmer. This place was like a dream, and Reagan wanted to be there forever. She was far from materialistic, but this screamed class and money. She looked outside at the people walking down the streets of South Beach and smiled back at those gawking at her. Their minds wondered if this breathtaking woman would purchase this space and open another store so they could fill their already-jam-packed closets with more accessories and clothing. Some even gave their bodies a once-over and hoped she was a plastic surgeon in search of a new location.

"I know this is expensive, so shatter my dreams now and tell me the amount."

Her Realtor parked herself beside Reagan and smiled. "Have some hope. If you tell me you want this right now, I can have ten thousand dollars knocked right off."

Reagan's eyes blew up. "Ten thousand? Are you see-ing what I'm seeing, Raquel? We're in South Beach. Why in the world would I get such a great deal?"

The middle-aged woman chuckled. "I got connections, Reagan. Now, are you in?"

Reagan would be a fool if she didn't take the offer, so she signed on the dotted line and raced back home to tell her sister that not only did she find the office of her dreams, but she got it for pennies. She told herself to call the second she stepped outside, but she held back. She wanted to be in the comfort of her home where she could act a fool and scream like she had no sense.

"You've reached Dane. Leave a message."

Happiness falling from her voice, Reagan screamed into the phone, her body nearly shaking. "Dane! I found the office that I want. This is the one, Dane! This is the one! It's beautiful and located smack dab in the middle of South Beach! And you won't believe how much it's sell-ing for!"

Reagan was pitching the numbers to Dane when her doorbell forced her to jump off the couch. "Hold on, someone's at my door," she explained to the answering machine.

Without missing a beat, she opened the door, her smile still etched on her face. "Hi, I can I help you?" she cheer-fully asked.

Boom!

Reagan's body fell backward, and her cell phone slid out of her hand. It bounced off the floor until it finally settled in its resting place. Reagan's face was blown off, the beauty of her smile permanently erased and thrown out into the universe, where positivity would sprinkle itself over others.

Tucking his hat low over his eyes, Lincoln jogged back to his car, his boots pounding against the pavement and setting off an echo into the neighborhood where no one's presence was felt.

Three Hours Later

The room was pitch-black, and the sounds of Benz's heavy breathing filled the room. Carmen sat straight up with her legs pushed against her chest and her arms tightly wrapped around them. Her normally neat and put-together hair was in shambles, and her head gently sat on her knees. Tears plummeted from her eyes onto the sheets. She felt lost, and her heart was vacant. Attending Lyfe's funeral was the hardest thing she ever had to do. Her feet were planted to the ground and refused to move when the casket lowered and everyone exited the burial site. Not even the rain soaking her clothes and her hair sticking to her face made her seek shelter. Instead, she just stood there, watching the hole.

Carmen had no idea what took place the night Lyfe was murdered. The police had confirmed that this was no accident, and whoever set his home on fire intended to. Carmen's head was spinning. Lyfe had so many enemies she didn't know where to begin or whose name to place a check or X next to. All she knew was that it was a sloppy job. No one with experience would have allowed his murder to be so evident. She imagined they would have at least made it look like an accident just to keep it from turning into an investigation. However, the person didn't want it that way. They wanted the world to know their sin and to send a message.

Deep in slumber, Benz turned onto his side. Carmen sank her eyes into his back. She fought to see in the dark. She came to Miami that same day, hours after Lyfe's funeral, in search of peace. She didn't expect Benz to be there. He constantly stressed that Fridays were dedicated to his wife and his wife only, so Carmen saw his absence as a chance to reconnect with herself. But that was short-lived and ended two hours later when he walked into their once-happy home and found his way between her legs in search of gold. Sex was the last thing she wanted, but if she wanted to relax, she had to give him what he wanted, which in the end would send him into a deep slumber.

Carmen never got the chance to tell Lyfe that she had formed her own troops and was on her way to reigning over New York. The thought alone forced additional salty teardrops to tumble down her cheeks. The reality that Lyfe actually gave his loyalty to Renee ate her alive. At the burial, Renee was stiffer and more disconnected than the corpse that rested below their feet. She had missed everything, except for the burial, and had shown absolutely no interest in paying her last respects. Her entire entourage was there, and Carmen despised each of them except for Julian. Their eyes met, and her heart jumped. She believed Julian's eyes held such innocence, and she longed for the day when he'd be hers. However, her ignorance blinded her from looking closer into his soul, because if she had, she would have noticed the faint look of death drenching his existence.

For what seemed like the twentieth time, Benz's cell phone vibrated and Carmen ignored it. She imagined it was his wife. She thought about answering it and letting the cat out of the bag. Buzz after buzz, it finally stopped and went straight to voicemail. Carmen hoped the phone's continuous vibrating remained unheard by a sleeping Benz. She needed her moment of solitude to not be disturbed.

She continued to cry and release all of the wishes that would never come true along with the pain she never thought she'd feel. After a half hour of tears, Carmen cried herself to sleep.

After what felt like only minutes of sleep, Carmen was woken by the doorbell ringing frantically accompanied by brutal banging. She sat up and saw Benz walking around the bed and out of the room.

"The fuck? I'm trying to sleep!" he yelled when outside the room.

Carmen slid out of the bed and poked her head outside the bedroom door. She fought to hear the words being exchanged between Benz and another male. However, nothing made sense. Their conversation was too muffled. The front door slammed, and Carmen tiptoed back into bed. Benz reappeared shortly, the color drained from his face.

"My wife, she's dead," spilled out of his mouth.

Carmen had never seen him so devastated, and because of that, her pain temporarily escaped her soul and made her strong. She showed no type of remorse and instead allowed a smile to appear across her face. The woman who had taken everything away was officially out of the picture. Why would she hurt and try to mourn her life?

Benz took a deep breath. He knew who he was dealing with, and chastised himself for even sharing the news with her. "Sorry to burst your bubble, but my men, your crew, are dead too."

As quickly as victory was declared hers, it was taken away. All Carmen wanted to do was turn back the hands of time and cry all over again.

Chapter 30

"I don't care who she is. When I see her, I am going to rip her throat out and feed her intestines to wild dogs!"

Dane's eyes were bloodshot, and her mouth shivered. It was amazing that she was able to stand without crumbling out of pure rage. Ever since hearing her sister's murder over her voicemail two weeks ago, her world had been without purpose, and her heart had been left in the morgue. Her mind couldn't come to terms with the fact that it was just weeks ago she was in Reagan's presence. Her sister's spirit sang, and her positivity radiated out of her. She gave the world more happiness. Now the person who Dane would have fought the world for, the person she had fought for the world for, was gone, and all she could do was blame herself. She knew the sharks that surrounded Reagan and didn't rid her waters of them soon enough. Now all she could do was think treacherous thoughts and tussle over which kill would best fit Carmen's demise.

Renee sat quietly. There was no need to fight a losing battle. She stood up for Carmen and saw the best in her when the rest of the world had seen nothing but the truth. Her eyes looked straight past Dane and into the wall. If only she could turn back the hands of time, none of this would have transpired.

With a face full of tears, Dane leaned in so close to Renee, Renee felt her breath against her cheek. "She's dead, and if you stand in my way, be prepared to lie next to her," Dane threatened.

For a long time, Dane didn't move. She needed her point to be made and her words to sink in. She buried her sister the day before, and there was nothing anyone could do to keep her off Carmen's ass. For years, Dane had lived within darkness, but the death of Reagan forced her into the darkest pit of her soul, a place she never knew existed.

Renee reached for her cranberry and vodka and took a long sip. She didn't respond until the glass was back on the table and her mind at ease. "You really think I'm going to stand in your way? Did I utter a word when you two went on a murdering spree, taking out Carmen's newly established crew?" Renee paused for a second. She allowed her words to sink into both Dane's and Julian's crania. "No. Instead, I pretended I knew nothing and allowed you two to take care of it." Renee focused on Julian, who sat at the far end of the table, staring at her. "I found it cute that you both thought I was so far gone that I knew absolutely nothing that was going on in my own camp."

Renee grabbed the bottle of vodka and poured herself another glass. "I've decided that Carmen will remain who she's always been to me: a stranger. But before I told her things were off, I wanted to eliminate the men she'd recruited, just a little insurance that if she took things badly, she would have no way of retaliating. So I called on the twins to find out who her men were, and you won't believe what they told me."

She downed the entire glass of vodka in one gulp. "They told me that they already knew who was on her team and everything else worth knowing about her because you two already sent out the order."

Renee spoke so slowly it was almost as if her warped little mind was in the process of piecing together a master plan.

"At first I was angry, because once again, you two took it upon yourselves to hide valuable information from me and take action on your own. It's that Page shit all over again."

"What I do is my business!" Dane screamed. She was so infuriated her chest heaved in and out, and drool trickled down the corner of her mouth like a rabid dog. The scream came from the pit of her stomach. She needed to let out all the aggression, all of the heartache, and what better person to lay it on than the sister of the person who killed Reagan?

Renee turned in Dane's direction, their noses nearly touching. "Calm down." Renee gave her a supportive smile. "I'm not going anywhere. We'll get her." Renee recognized the rage and the random outburst, along with being a slave to your own emotions with nowhere to go. She took Lyfe's death harder with every passing day. Understanding the emotions Dane was experiencing, she would not feed into her anger but feed into the solution.

Dane's breathing became heavier and faster. She was prepared to engage in a battle of words. Not be understood, not be cared for. "You want Carmen dead. I'm all in."

Dane grabbed a liquor bottle and threw it into the roaring fire. The flames jumped up, and the heat tickled the back of Renee's neck. Dane's heart was low, and her pride wounded.

"You're the only sister I have left," Dane let out. "Promise we'll get her and we'll get her good." Dane needed to feed off of Renee's coldness.

"Let's play a game." Renee smiled after she said a line from Dane's favorite movie. "And, Dane, one more thing," Renee yelled out. "If you want Carmen, you better move fast because if I get to her first, that ass is mine!"

Dane gave her undivided attention.

"Let's see who could get to Carmen first," said Renee. "Let's have a good old-fashioned rat race. Winner kills her!"

Dane tried not to smile, but she did.

"Show me what you got, old head. You may have the skill in killing, but I have the speed."

Dane stood in front of Renee, her hand held out to her. Only those close to Dane knew the best present to give Dane was the gift of death. "May the best woman win, young'un."

They shook on it. "Touché, old head, touché."

Chapter 31

Tina's hand maneuvered its way out of the shower curtain and into the sink. She felt around until she grabbed her glass of brandy and brought it back into her personal rainstorm. With a shower cap on her head and the music from her computer blasting, she danced to the music of Rihanna and gulped down the alcoholic beverage that consisted of 95 percent liquor and 5 percent soda. Drinking had always been Tina's favorite pastime, but after her brother passed, it seemed to become her livelihood and a way to block out how much of a failure she was. To her, life was nothing but a party, and if she died tomorrow, she'd have nothing to show for it.

Two months ago, she lost her job at the library, and a month after that, she was kicked out of school. Unwilling to face reality, her club-hopping doubled, and her one-night stands tripled. One of the life's hardships in the form of syphilis caught up with her. Her careless ways landed her in her gynecologist's office with bags under her eyes and her nails damn near bitten down to the cuticle over not knowing what her body was telling her. While on medication, she made false promises to herself that she'd change her life and do right. Her STD temporarily scared her. Sadly, not even a month after she was cured and the disease was out of her system, she started dabbling in Ecstasy. Bills and loneliness quickly came

back and haunted Tina. When life got hard, she was willing to do anything to avoid life's struggles, even if it
meant killing herself slowly.

She emptied her glass, and when the room started
to spin, she leaned her head against the tiled walls and
mumbled to herself, "Now it's time to hit the club."

When Rihanna sang her last "Pour it up," Tina felt her
vagina burn. The uneasy, unfortunately common feeling
was an indication a medical appointment was needed.

Dammit, that shithead told me he was clean.

In the silence of her bathroom, Tina turned off the fau-
cets. She cursed last week's one-night stand in her head,
pushed the shower curtain back, and stepped one leg out
of the tub when she was brutally forced back into the
shower. Her back and head banged against the wall so
hard the tiles above her collapsed. Dizzy and discom-
bobulated, Tina forced her eyes open and shut, fighting
to clear her vision. When the stars disappeared, she was
grabbed by her hair and dragged out of the bathroom.
The rug ate away at her legs, and skin particles beaded
the carpet as she was pulled. She moved so fast she was
unable to see the culprit's face but had a picture-perfect
view of his Timberland boots. Her mouth dropped open,
and her legs kicked wildly as her mind instantly became
aware of whom she was up against.

"Get off of me! Get off me!"

Her bedroom door creaked opened, and her body was
swung on the bed. The sound of her hair being ripped out
of her scalp echoed in the air.

"Is this how you speak to your brother from another
mother?"

Terrified, Tina frantically searched around the room
for something to protect herself with. Her eyes zoomed

in on the knife laid out on the empty plate that once held chicken Parmesan. With the speed of a cat, she raced over to the nightstand. Just as her fingers grazed the handle of her would-be weapon, she was pulled back and punched in her face with Jared's closed fist. Tina's head snapped back, and once again, she was sent into a daze. Her eyes rolled into the back of her head, and her legs dangled off the bed. Tina's right eye began to close, and her busted lip dripped blood.

"What's wrong, Tina? Cat got your tongue?"

Nothing would have made Jared happier than to send Tina to her grave. He should have never left it up to Julian to put her in the ground when they found out she revealed Renee's identity. Tina was like the plague that had spread into his world and made his presence on this earth known, but before he made her extinct, he needed her to run her mouth one more time.

"What did I do?"

For the first time ever, Tina wished she weren't intoxicated. The liquor made it twice as hard for her to snap out of it.

"You ran your mouth. How did you know I was alive?"

Jared watched as a drop of blood emerged from Tina's lip and traveled down her collarbone to her breast. With her one good eye, Tina followed Jared's stare. She watched as his eyes trailed the blood. After it surpassed her breast, his eyes remained locked on her C cups. His eyelids lowered, and she thought he smiled with his eyes. Tina let out a small whimper.

"Please don't," she begged. She knew that look. She'd been a victim to that sinful look, and it frightened her to the pit of her soul. She trembled and covered her breasts with her hands.

Blood mixed with tears stained her face. Jared grabbed her hair, wrapped it once around his hand, and pulled her face close to his. His tone was repulsed and devoid of respect when he told her, "You reek of alcohol, look like you're forty when you're only twenty-two, and I can smell the discharge leaking from you." Jared gave Tina's body a once-over. She had yet to notice it, but the partying, drugs, and drinking had taken a toll on her appearance. "And you have the nerve to think I would want you?" Jared was no rapist, and for her to insinuate such a thing infuriated him.

He pushed her head away and blew up in a fit of laughter. As Jared walked away from the bed, Tina clasped her legs shut, her tears ceased, and she wondered if she should be insulted that she disgusted him or embarrassed.

Composing himself, Jared rifled through her belongings. Purposely, he kept his back turned long enough for Tina to throw on some clothes and trap that horrific smell in her clothing. As quickly as she could, Tina fought against the pain and put on booty shorts and a T-shirt from the floor. She sat on her footlocker, ready to tell Jared everything he wanted to know.

"I saw you at the dealership, but before then, I knew you were alive because a friend of the family works at the hospital you were cared for at." For the first time in years, Tina was giving out information free.

Jared turned around with his arms folded and leaned against her bookshelf. "What exactly did you tell Carmen?"

"What she asked. She wanted to know the names of killers, and I told her yours. I told her I didn't recommend you, but she insisted on knowing."

Jared wanted to ask how she knew he was a killer, but then he remembered to whom he was speaking. "What do you know about Carmen?"

Out of habit, Tina replied, "Whatever I do or don't know will cost you."

Jared dove across the bed and grabbed her by the back of her shirt. Forcing her to look in his direction, he backhanded her. "Do you want to die tonight?"

Tina's body shivered, and she began crying hysterically. Quickly she was beginning to see that her mouth was getting her into more and more trouble. "Nooo."

"Then answer the damn question," Jared demanded, shaking her with one hand.

"I don't know anything about her. I've never seen or heard about her until I met her at the club and she approached me."

Jared searched for an indication that she was lying, but the fear in her face confirmed the truth. "Then I have a job for you. Since you brought her to my doorstep, I want to know everything there is to know about her." Jared knew that Carmen was Renee's long-lost sister, but for her to hate a woman whose business she was inheriting proved there was more to her than just being a sibling. He wanted to know exactly what that was. "And I need all of this information in a week."

Short of breath and teeth chattering, Tina forced herself to answer. "A week? You want me to learn all there is to know about this woman in just a week? That's impossible. I don't even know her last name."

"But you're Tina, New York's walking information machine, so get to work!" As he mocked her, saliva flew from Jared's mouth and landed on her cheek.

Tina sat there, bloody and full of pain. She had no idea how she was going to complete this mission, but looking at Jared with his crooked smile, she knew she had no choice but to find a way. Scared, Tina broke into a new round of sobs, which ricocheted off the walls and fell on deaf ears.

"You tell no one else I'm alive."

Frantically, Tina nodded her head.

"Now do me a favor, Tina."

"Whhhaaattttttttttt?" she cried out.

"Shut up."

Jared pulled her more toward him, and with all his might, he punched her in the face. Finally, he released her, and Tina fell back, unconscious.

Chapter 32

They lived in the same house, yet all Julian felt was distance. The only reason he had come back home was to pay his condolences at Lyfe's funeral and support Renee. However, the only thing he seemed to succeed at was attending the funeral. He and Renee were not on the best of terms, and both refused to speak or apologize to the other. They slept in separate rooms and ate dinner at different times. The house was officially divided, and a line had been drawn.

Julian was in another world. The room he had been sleeping in, he didn't even remember it being in the house. No room deserved to be occupied if it didn't contain Renee. On his back, he stared up at the ceiling and could feel Renee's presence radiating from across the hall. He imagined her sprawled out in bed, her hair scooped up in a bun while shorter strands dropped alongside her face. He missed holding her in his arms and making love to her during all hours of the night, but that wasn't enough to make him be the one to smooth things over.

Julian felt betrayed and disrespected. On countless occasions, he had made it known that allowing Carmen into their circle was nothing but a mistake, but all Renee did was take his warnings with a grain of salt and do what she wanted. He was tired of her picking and choosing what happened. How did they have a partnership when she took the lead the entire time? Julian would be lying if he said his outburst didn't cross the line, but he would be lying twice as much if he said this wasn't taking place because he was afraid his secret would come out. He knew that he should be happy that Renee finally came around to seeing things his and Dane's way, but he couldn't help but wonder why. In the pit of his stomach, he felt that hell was about to break loose.

These continuous thoughts invaded Julian's mind and forced the sandman to come early. His eyes felt like a bag of bricks and dropped within seconds. A half hour into his dream, a warm body curled up under the sheets against his body, and palms gripped his chest. Julian forced his eyes open and looked behind him to see Renee, her head nestled into his back. No one spoke. Instead, they lay there trying to make up for the nights they missed being in bed together.

"I missed you. Did you miss me?" Renee's voice was below a whisper and laced with emotion. She was angry about her current situation, but her love for Julian trumped all of her problems, and she found herself invading his space.

Julian didn't respond right away. Instead, he listened to the soft sound of her tone and took in the scent of her honeydew breath. "Is the sky blue?"

Renee rubbed her thumb against his cheek. "I have to tell you something."

Julian took a deep breath. Any news that came out of Renee's mouth was never good. He sat up, his back leaning against the headboard, and Renee laid her head in his lap.

"I killed Lyfe."

The words ran out of her mouth so fast she couldn't take them back even if she wanted to. Julian waited for her to say it was joke, but the longer the silence lingered, the more it proved to be true. Julian struggled to grab hold of his emotions. One second he felt confused, the next alarmed, then in denial and saddened.

"Shit, Renee, do I want to know why?"

"He chose to stay in the game because of Carmen. He wasn't willing to retire and build a relationship with me, and I wasn't willing to understand his reasoning, so I decided to hurt him as much as he hurt me."

A piece of Renee died when Lyfe rejected her, one of the last of the few pieces that allowed her to feel, so it was only fair he felt the same pain. Julian wanted to voice why he did and didn't agree with her decision. That he, too, thought Lyfe deserved to suffer. He was tired of the loads of her grief her family placed on her. Then again, he wanted Renee to know he believed that had she given him more time, he would have come around.

He let go of the thought of voicing his opinions as quickly as he created them. The deed was already done, so there was no going back. The sound of the ticking clock pounded in their ears and darkened the darkness. Renee's hazel eyes glowed in the light-absent room and pulled Julian into a world he felt most comfortable in.

"Is that why you want her dead?"

"Wouldn't you?" Renee's fingers danced across his lips. "At first, I was just going to tell her that owning my business was a no go, but after hearing who she associates with, it left me no choice. She's sleeping with the enemy."

Carmen being Benz's mistress gave Renee a legitimate reason to wipe her off the face of the earth. Killing

Lyfe was one thing, but to do the same to Carmen for the very same reason would make her look insane. There was bad blood between Renee and Benz dating back to when she first entered the game. Hearing that he and Carmen had history made her blame Lyfe for allowing the relationship. The more she found out about the past, the more it was proven that she never truly had a family.

"Do it fast."

Renee nodded her head. She couldn't agree more that Carmen should be taken out as soon as possible. After seconds of watching the hands on the clock move in slow motion, she asked the question that had eaten away at her for days. "Where did you go when you left?"

Julian didn't want to answer, but he didn't want to lie either. "I have a house on Long Island, a place I wanted to keep a secret in case we needed to get away one day."

Renee sat up, her hair dangling over her shoulders as she looked him in the eye. "You leave again, don't come back."

Julian wished he could explain to Renee that men dealt with things differently from women. He wished he could make her understand that when a man walked out, it wasn't always for the bad but to get his mind together and mend his heart. But as John Gray wrote, men are from Mars, women are from Venus. She would never understand. Instead, he agreed that it would be best to talk things out and not walk out from this point forward.

Passionately, Renee kissed Julian and their lips meshed. An electric shock raced through each of their bodies. He took her into his arms, and they sank into each other, becoming one. The feel of her skin caused guilt to raid Julian's soul. This woman was putting her heart, soul, and mind out in the open for him to have and share with her. All he could think about was months ago indulging in her sister. Julian pulled away, preparing to tell her what he should have months ago.

"Renee, I—"

Renee's phone started to ring, and it stole her attention away from Julian. "Hold on." Renee tried to grab the phone, which lay on their nightstand, but Julian held her firmly in place, his hands refusing to let go of her arms.

"Let it ring. The first time I left, I—"

"It's Dane. Maybe she's got Carmen." Completely ignoring the words coming out of his mouth, Renee paid attention to Dane's name flashing across the screen. The light from the phone held her attention. She shook Julian off her and grabbed the phone. Sitting on the side of the bed, her shoulders became stiff, and her back hunched over.

Hours ago, Julian would have loved to hear that Carmen was a memory, but his conscience couldn't have cared less now that he needed to tell Renee the truth.

She ended the call, and without turning in his direction, she parted her lips. Her voice was dry as sandpaper. "Dane has Lincoln. He's the one who killed Reagan."

Chapter 33

It is truly incredible what the human body can endure, because after being beaten for over two hours straight, Lincoln was still among the living. He stood erect with his legs tied up. Calloway held his arms behind his back and forced him to stand in place. The sounds of Dane's brass knuckles landing against his jaw bounced off the shaky walls of the abandoned Jersey home. Lincoln's entire body went numb, and he wished death would come sooner rather than later. He lost hearing in one ear and suffered from a broken nose and collarbone. Blood from the stab wounds Dane inflicted dripped on the plastic and covered the basement floor. He fell into and out of consciousness, and his body tried to maintain strength.

"Get his ribs, Dane. Crack his fuckin' ribs!"

"I'm trying!"

With everything Dane had in her, she landed blow after blow, her mind set on breaking his ribs. All she could see was her sister lying in that casket, an innocent woman killed for something she had no control over.

"Try harder!" Calloway screamed. He had seen the pain Reagan's death brought upon Dane, and he wanted Lincoln to pay for each tear that fell from her eyes.

Sweat dripped from Dane's head, and like a madwoman, she moved with the speed and intensity of a professional boxer. She threw out multiple combinations and allowed her mind to go off to another place, a place where anger dwelled and only the strong survived.

Lincoln cried out in pain. He could feel the cold metal from the brass knuckles connect to the white meat exposed from his wounds. He tried to speak and beg for his life, but the rag in his mouth denied him that privilege. After several more punches, a loud, crackling sound filled the room. Lincoln's swollen eyes slightly opened, and tears skidded down his cheeks. His breathing slowed, and saliva started to saturate the rag stuffed in his mouth. Never in his life had he felt such pain. He placed all his weight into Calloway's arms and sobbed.

Dane threw her fist in the air. A champion was declared. In the middle of her doing her victory dance, Renee and Julian walked into the basement. Renee's heart fell to her stomach. She hadn't seen Lincoln in years, and now he was saturated in blood and seconds away from death.

"Welcome to the party!" Dane yelled. Mentally, she had officially checked out and was drowning in a sea of misery.

"What's going on?" Slowly, Renee walked closer to Lincoln. The answer was obvious, but it was all she could think to say.

"We're getting justice," Dane snarled. She removed the brass knuckles and threw them on the floor. She dug into her sweats and pulled out a miniature bottle of gin. She inhaled it in one gulp and felt rejuvenated and less depressed.

Renee stood in front of Lincoln. His head swayed back and forth, and then his chin met his collarbone. He was unconscious.

"Drop him," Renee told Calloway. Her eyes were fixated on Lincoln.

With a thud, Lincoln's body dropped. His head crashed against the floor, and his eyes tried to open. Renee removed the rag from his mouth, and Lincoln coughed uncontrollably. He spit blood out on the plastic and moaned. With what little strength he could muster to fight against the pain, he forced himself up, low on his elbows. The simple act of allowing oxygen into his lungs became unbearable and brutal. He struggled to focus on the figure in front of him, and once he had, his pupils took in Renee, who was bent down beside him.

Lincoln struggled for words, so he settled on simply saying, "Renee." His voice was hoarse and barely audible.

"Lincoln, what are you doing? How did you get wrapped up in this?" Instantly, Renee was back in high school. The man beside her was no longer a man, but a teenage boy dying to fit in. She was no longer a queenpin, but a teenage girl willing to give her friendship.

"Your eyes . . . your eyes are so beautiful," he forced out clearly. The rest of his face swelled and was not far from matching the swelling of his eyes.

Since Lincoln had started seeing Carmen, he had constantly wondered what it was that attracted him to her. Of course, it was her looks, but there was something more. Something he couldn't put his finger on, and now that he was reunited with Renee, he realized it was her eyes. Carmen's eyes were the exact replica of Renee's.

"What have you done?"

"I proved myself." Lincoln breathed hard and erratically. His words ate away at his energy. "I was tired of being alone." He paused. "She told me to kill her, so I did."

Renee needed to hear her name, needed to hear for herself that Carmen had put out the hit. "Who? Who told you to kill Reagan?"

Lincoln coughed, and his face contorted before he answered, "Carmen."

Without warning, Dane stormed over and kicked Lincoln in his face with such aggression, pain, and force his body flew backward. "And you were dumb enough to listen to that bitch," Dane hissed.

Renee pushed her away. "Just give me a minute."

Dane walked away. Fury traveled through her veins and grief through her heart.

Renee grabbed Lincoln and helped him slightly sit back up. Her left hand secured his back. "Did you know Reagan? Why did Carmen want her dead?"

Lincoln's eyes were completely shut and his body still. Renee shook him, not intensely, but enough to try to bring him back. "Lincoln!" she shouted.

He opened his eyes. Although low, they opened.

"Did you know Reagan? Why did Carmen want her dead?"

"Her name was Reagan?" Lincoln tried to lick away the blood that escaped from the cuts on his lips. "Carmen wanted revenge."

"On who?" Renee feared Lincoln would either die or pass out before she got her answers. She used the bottom of her shirt to wipe away the blood on his lips. It hurt, but he reinforced a smile. "Who did Carmen want to get back at, Lincoln?"

"Her ex." He took a break from speaking, rested, and continued. "He left her, and she wanted to hurt him."

Renee believed every word that left Lincoln's mouth. She knew the story of the man who abandoned Carmen for another woman without leaving her a penny to her name. Nevertheless, all she could wonder was if Lyfe truly knew Benz's identity. *I guess we'll never know.*

"Carmen is my sister, Lincoln. The woman you killed was named Reagan, and she was her sister." Renee pointed to Dane tucked away in the corner stationed between Julian and Calloway. Her eyes burned holes into him.

Lincoln looked at Dane then back at Renee. "I didn't know." His hands still shook, and tears dropped.

"Carmen's no good, Lincoln, and I'm sorry you got caught up in this." Renee wished with every fiber of her being that this were still high school, because if it were, she would have been able to save him. But it wasn't, and there was nothing she could do. "Stop falling for a pretty face. They're not always who they seem to be."

Renee let him go and stood to walk away, but before she did, she had to ask him one more question. "I know your loyalty lies with Carmen, but, Lincoln, I need to know what else she has planned."

Lincoln found it funny that Renee truly believed that he would ever pick Carmen over her, but he had to remind himself that she never knew the love he had for her flowed so deep. So he told her the truth and hoped that one day she would discover his unspoken truth.

"She'll kill him." Lincoln put his hand on one of his stab wounds and grimaced. "She got his crew, offered him a cheaper price on drugs," he pushed out then coughed. "In a few months, she will kill him once she knows his operation." Lincoln lay on his back and gathered all he had to spit out his sentence. "Said she'll soon be in control of New York's drug supply. This will not end with Reagan. It's only the beginning."

Renee nodded her head and walked away. She couldn't bear to see what Dane had in store for him. She knew of Lincoln's loyalty, knew he was the one who informed Julian what Page had up her sleeve, but he made a bad move and started playing for the other team. Renee walked straight past Dane and out of the basement.

Julian took one last look at Lincoln and sent prayers up to heaven for him.

Dane walked over to Lincoln and bent down beside him. "Okay, Calloway!"

"Wait!" Lincoln forced out of his mouth. He surprised himself with how loudly he spoke. He had no energy left, so to be able to yell amazed him, even though it was accompanied by severe pain. "How did you know it was me?" he asked Dane.

Dane looked at the defeated man and, before she answered, decided to ask a question of her own. "Do you regret what you've done?"

Lincoln's body tensed up, and he swallowed. Of course he did. He took a life, all for the love of a woman he hardly knew, and he'd never see the next chapter of his life because he had cut it short. He wished he could go back in time and remove the day he ever laid eyes on Carmen. "With every fiber of my being."

Dane pushed her lips out and nodded. "I knew her husband was the enemy, so I planted cameras around her home. You're very photogenic."

Dane knew by the looks of Lincoln that he was no fit for the life he was pulled into. The reality of it was sad, but she buried those feelings and did what she had to do for her sister.

She stood, walked toward the stairs, and yelled out, "Calloway! Release the hounds!"

Chapter 34

At first, it was uncomfortable staying in Dane's aunt and uncle's home, but eventually, things worked themselves out. Renee and Julian spent a week in the Miami home her family moved to months after Reagan came to Florida. They wanted to lend their support to Dane and her family during their time of need, and Metro thought it would be best if they all went to stay with Dane's aunt and uncle and mourn the loss of Reagan together. When they gathered for the funeral, they had never spoken or been around each other outside of planning the service. They were distant and reluctant to come to terms with what happened. In their minds, if they sat in each other's presence when it wasn't needed, it meant accepting that Reagan was never coming back. Dane fought tooth and nail to stay in New York. Nothing was more important than planning the demise of Carmen and Benz. However, when Metro flew in from Jamaica and literary dragged her out of Renee's home, she had no choice.

Slowly, Dane was breaking down. Sleep was nonexistent, and her conversation related to nothing other than killing Carmen. When her sister was buried, she acted off emotion and set out to kill Carmen on sight, but after many tearful nights, her brain made the logical decision to take some time and handle the hit right. She made a living off being the grim reaper, and she was declared the best due to her well-thought-out, strategic hits. To act on emotion would do nothing but create a sloppy, painless job, and if anyone deserved to die in a way that would shake the nation, it was Carmen. Nothing would stop Dane from carrying out this murder.

The day Reagan died, so did Dane, and it pained Renee to watch her mentor drown in her own misery. The entire flight to Miami, Dane was mute and antisocial. She had no words for Metro for tearing her out of New York against her will, and she wanted to strangle Renee and Julian for allowing him to do so. However, when the four of them crossed the threshold of her aunt and uncle's house, her anger trickled away, evaporating into thin air.

When her aunt opened the door, she just stood there, her eyes falling only on Dane. Then without any warning, she fell into her arms and released weeks of regret, pain, and what-ifs. Dane was not a hugger. She hugged no one except Metro and her siblings. When her aunt forced her way into her arms, it opened a world of untapped emotions. Laura was the strongest woman Dane had ever stumbled upon, and seeing her cry broke Dane down. They cried and hugged for what felt like hours, and everyone remained where they stood, taking in the love this family had always denied.

A week in Miami surrounded by family was just what the doctor ordered. However, the only downfall to this trip was sleeping in a world of temptation. Dane could not allow her mind to forget that Benz's home was only twenty minutes from where she stayed. She craved to drain the blood from his corpse and punish him for not protecting her sister.

It was four in the morning when Dane slid out of bed with Metro and crept out of Laura and Ray's home. She drove to the boring and quiet neighborhood Reagan once resided in, and for two hours sat and watched as Benz snorted coke and drank Hennessy Black, glass after glass. He was in a downward spiral, guilt eating away at him because his wife was touchable and his mistress protected while in his presence on the day Reagan was gunned down. His wife's voice haunted him. She had always made her opinion known that the drug game would lead to one of two places: death or prison.

He missed the sound of her voice and her determination to make it in life the legal way. Her death made him reflect on why she wasn't enough and why he needed Carmen back in his life. That she died while he was laid up with another woman pushed him to the edge and made him contemplate suicide. His gun sat beside him at all times, waiting to be picked up when he gathered the strength to pull the trigger. But until that time came, he filled his body with poison and allowed his high to take him away.

Dane sat in darkness and took in Benz's surroundings. Her eyes zeroed in on the drugs, liquor, and gun. Her mind cheered for him to either overdose or blow his brains out. His soul lived in turmoil, and every indication that Benz was losing his battle with pain strengthened Dane. When she finally took off with a plan concocted in her distorted mind, it was 6:00 a.m. She made it back to her aunt's safely and slid back under the cotton sheets. Her heart felt a little less heavy.

The next morning, as Dane helped Laura prepare breakfast, Laura made an announcement. "I'm thinking of retiring, Dane." Laura's hands were submerged underwater while washing the dishes she planned to serve their meal on.

Dane's egg was inches from being cracked against the kitchen counter when her aunt's words stopped her in her tracks. "Why now? Since college, all I remember you doing was pushing drugs."

"Exactly, and I'm still doing the same shit. I'm getting too old for this, Dane. This game loves no one. And after losing Reagan, why stay? I only continued with it to help pay for tuition before she got married, and your brother is well on his way. He doesn't need any financial help. I think it's time I live and leave this business to the youngsters." Laura dried off the squeaky-clean plates and recovered from a case the silverware that she only brought out on special occasions.

"I have money, Laura. I don't know why you thought you needed to stay in the game in order to help my siblings. They always had me, but for some reason, no one wanted to open their mouths and let me know when they needed money. And you and Ray act like if you stop pushing this shit, you'll go into the poor house. You know I got y'all." Dane slammed her egg against the counter, the sound of the shells cracking added additional tension to the air.

"We're grown, Dane, we don't need any handouts. And since you always been hell-bent on us retiring, let me ask you something, when are you?"

Dane dropped the egg into the pan, and the sizzling sound erupted in their ears. "What does me retiring have to do with you?" Dane thought back to when Renee asked her the same question. It seemed like the world was waiting for her to put down her weapons.

"It has everything to do with me. It was because of my and your uncle's occupation that you even got in the game. And now that you've got revenge on your parents' murderers and made sure your siblings were protected, it's time to leave it alone." The kitchen table was neatly set, the sun shining through the Windex-cleaned windows.

"Is that so?" Dane chuckled.

"Yes, it is." Laura pulled her gray-streaked hair back into a ponytail, and it was then that Dane noticed how old she truly was. Her face and hands were slightly wrinkled, and makeup was caked on her face.

"Then why is Reagan dead?"

Silence stormed the room. They both knew why they were there, to mourn an angel, but every time her name was brought up in the same sentence with the words "die," "dead," or "death," time seemed to stand still.

Because she suffered from obsessive-compulsive disorder, Laura raced over to the table and fixed every fork and spoon she found to be uneven. With her back to Dane, she responded to her comment. "That wasn't your fault, Dane. You set out to protect your siblings from my enemies. How were you to know she'd be a victim outside of my foolishness?" Finally, the silverware was lined up straight, and Laura was able to breathe.

"I knew."

Laura turned to face Dane. "You knew what?"

"I knew her husband was the enemy. Reagan confided in me that she believed her husband was back to selling drugs and cheating."

"Wait a minute. Reagan was married to a drug dealer, and you didn't tell me?"

The eggs were on their way to burning until Dane turned off the fire. Hearing her aunt scream at her and racing to save the food caused her to become anxious, and her hands started to shake.

"I didn't know!" She broke. "She told me right before she died. I told her I would handle it and find out whether he was. When it came out to be true, I didn't tell her. When they met, she talked him out of being in the game, but he gravitated right back. I didn't want to break her heart and let her know her Prince Charming was nothing but a frog." Tears raced down her cheeks. "But he was, and to make matters worse, he was cheating with his ex, who is Renee's sister."

Laura marched over to Dane and grabbed her by the arm. "And you let that bitch come into my home and break bread with us?" Laura was enraged and disgusted all wrapped up in one emotion.

Dane snatched her arm away. "Renee had no idea what her trifling sister was doing. She just found out her damn self that she was even her sister!" Dane tried to keep her voice down, but her emotions were taking over. "I fucked up, okay? I should have eliminated him and his mistress before Reagan was even killed, but I moved too slow! I know this, okay? But I'm going to make this right. I have to!"

"Wait a minute. Are they the ones responsible for Reagan's death?"

"His mistress Carmen is. I killed the man she got to kill Reagan. Her husband knew nothing about it, but on the strength of him disrespecting my sister and bringing harm to her doorstep, he's dead. And when I get my hands on that bitch, every murder I committed will look like child's play." The intensity in Dane's voice confirmed that every word she spoke, she meant.

"How does Renee feel about this? Is she really going to stand by and allow you to kill her sister?"

"Renee's on board. Besides, even if she weren't, nothing will stop me."

Laura took a deep breath. She felt out of the loop and lost. But most importantly, her soul hurt for both her nieces. "What now?" she asked.

With her palms planted firmly on the kitchen counter, Dane told her, "What else? I'm going to kill her husband."

Laura's eyebrows caved in. "Is that why you came here?"

"No, but while you all slept last night, I found myself camped out in front of his house. For hours, I observed him, and I came up with the perfect way to wipe him off this earth. But nothing can be done until Thursday."

"Why Thursday? Today's Tuesday," Laura pointed out.

Before Dane got the chance to answer, she heard movement above her head, an indication that Renee and Julian would soon make their way downstairs from their room.

"I want him to suffer, but the poison I need is at home. I had to send Calloway to fly out and get it. He won't be arriving here until Thursday."

Dane opened the oven and removed the biscuits. She placed them into a bowl, and footsteps descending from the second floor of the house pounded against the steps.

"This is between me and you, Laura. Don't tell anyone, not even Uncle Ray."

"I won't, but there is one thing."

"What?"

"I want to go with you when it's done."

Renee and Julian walked into the kitchen, and seconds later, Metro followed them.

Chapter 35

Thursday came faster than Dane and Laura could have ever expected. Their constant thoughts must have willed time to move forward, because at the snap of a finger, Calloway was handing her over the fluoroacetate a half hour after stepping off her private jet. It was midnight, and the house full of killers had fallen into a deep slumber, everyone excluding Dane and Laura. When the women were positive their men would not feel them leaving their beds, they slithered away and fell into Dane's rental.

"I never got a chance to ask you, what type of poison were you waiting on?"

"Fluoroacetate."

"Rodenticide?"

"Yes."

"How exactly is this going to work?"

"Benz is a cokehead, and if he hasn't already, I'm sure he's preparing to snort that shit up now as we speak. We wait until he conks out, and then we replace his shit with that."

Laura's eyes looked in the back seat at the poison Dane pointed to.

"It's an odorless, tasteless white powder. Being as fucked up as he gets, he'll never know the difference. After he inhales it, he'll go through the motions and will eventually die due to respiratory failure."

"Good," Laura snarled, nostrils flared and eyes blinking uncomfortably.

Five minutes later, the women pulled up across the street from Benz's house. Just like two nights ago, the curtains were wide open, and he was seen sitting in his living room with liquor bottles beside five lines of cocaine spread out on the coffee table. Dane watched him partake in multiple drinks and snort up his drug. They waited in the car for three hours until he was nice and drugged up. Benz took one last drink and, on the plate, emptied more coke, which he struggled to cut up. The room was spinning, and in order to stop it, he threw his box cutter on the table and laid his head back against the couch. He dozed off, and ten minutes later, Dane and Laura made their move.

Dane went into her sister's kitchen and, with gloves on her hands, poured the fluoroacetate on a plate. She put the poison in the place of the cocaine and flushed the drug down the toilet. Dane pulled up a chair in front of Benz. Only a few feet separated the two while Laura sat in a corner, covered in darkness. Dane inserted a magazine into her 9 mm and released the slide, her firearm ready for battle. The slight sound the gun gave off in the noiseless home caused Benz to jump out of his slumber. When his eyes took in Dane's presence, his instincts kicked in, and he went for his gun on the table. He aimed it at her. When he pulled the trigger and nothing happened, he tried again. Repeatedly, he reenacted this action, and nothing changed.

Laura let out a monstrous laugh. "Damn, Reagan can sure pick them."

Benz jumped and turned his body in Laura's direction. His gun was aimed directly at her chest. "Who are you, and what the fuck are you doing here?"

Laura's smile never left her face.

"It's going to be pretty hard killing her with no bullets," Dane informed him.

He looked at his gun and slowly placed it down on the floor. "Who are you?" he repeated.

"Come on, Benz, don't offend me. You don't remember me? Dane, the woman whose protégé you thought you could get one over on?"

Benz's jaw tightened. He thought it would be a cold day in hell before he ever saw Dane again. "What do you want?"

"To kill you," Dane replied flatly.

Benz took in her appearance. She sat in the chair with her legs crossed, arms planted firmly on the arms of the chair, and with a gun comfortably situated in her lap.

"All because of what I did years ago? Aren't you a little late?" he antagonized. Benz wished he weren't so high. It took everything he had in him just to formulate a correct sentence. But in order to survive, he had no choice but to try to be alert.

"The past is the past. I'm more interested in the present. You're a sloppy motherfucker, Benz. Do you know that? It's not good to tell lies, and it damn sure isn't good to have your mistress put a hit out on your wife and succeed."

"What are you talking about?" Benz closed his eyes and shook his head. The room began to spin again.

"You told Reagan you were no longer in the drug scene when you really returned and with a mistress on your arm. You're a fool, Benz. You took back a scorned woman, and we all know what happens when you do that."

"What the fuck are you talking about?" Too many thoughts were racing through Benz's mind, and he couldn't put the pieces of the puzzle together.

"She killed her. Carmen put a hit out on Reagan and succeeded, and it's all your fault."

Benz's eyes blew up, and he fought to hold back tears. "You don't know what you're talking about, and how is any of this any of your concern?"

"Because Reagan was my sister, and I am my sister's keeper. Bitch ass should have learned the full family history of who he was marrying."

A tear dropped from his eye and landed on the carpet that hadn't been vacuumed in weeks.

"She got you. The second you gave Carmen just a piece of power, she already had it in her mind that she would take you for all you were worth and then kill you in the end. You slipped up, but I can't give a damn about you. What I care about is you putting my sister in harm's way."

Benz's heart was beating a mile a minute, and he tried to contain himself, but nothing worked. He had searched high and low for his wife's murderer and the reason she was killed, but he had come up empty. Now Dane sat in front of him, telling him it was all because he was sleeping with the enemy.

"But I will tell you this, Benz. Even if Reagan had never died, your days were still numbered. You were unfaithful, and you got into bed with a snake and upped her status without you even knowing."

"She told me she would be running New York. I just wanted to expand," he cried. It was no longer needed for him to save face. He murdered his wife. Therefore, his life was over.

"How naive can you be? You know that Jordan holds the Big Apple down. But then again, how were you supposed to know that Carmen is her sister, right?"

The punches just kept on coming. Everything now made sense. He now knew who was responsible for killing off his men. He lowered his head, then looked over at Laura. "And who are you? One of her goons?"

"Oh, no, you little prick. I'm Reagan's aunt. Don't you remember me? I'm that new connect you just linked up with. So you see, my dear, like my niece just said, either way, you were dead."

In the back of his mind, Benz doubted that Carmen would come through on her end of the bargain, so he reached out to his Miami competition and called a truce. She gave him a damn good price, so in his mind, if Carmen fell through, he still got more for his money.

"You're a cokehead, I see, so do yourself a favor and snort up the rest of your shit before you start pushing up daisies. You don't want to waste my aunt's stuff, now do you?"

Dane pointed her gun at him, and so did Laura. Benz looked at the drugs and vaguely remembered there being a lot less on the plate before he dozed off. But he pushed the warning to the back of his mind. He was an alcoholic gone druggie who couldn't tell his left from his right. He grabbed his box cutter and created four thick lines. Closing his eyes, he visualized Reagan, and when he opened them, he looked Dane in her eyes.

"I'm sorry," he told her. Then he lowered his head, and like a Hoover vacuum, he sucked the poison up back-to-back without the thought of having a break.

Benz inhaled so much of the poison that Dane knew the reaction would kick in any second. Just as she predicted, Benz grabbed his chest due to his irregular breathing.

"What's happening?" he forced out of his mouth.

Moments later, he turned away, his face twitched uncontrollably as he threw up everything in his system. His face became numb, and anxiety kicked in. Dane sat back and enjoyed the show.

This has always been my favorite part, watching death come for those who deserve it, Dane told herself.

Although Dane had killed for years, it still intrigued her how chemicals could break down the human body. She wanted to continue to watch for as long as it took him to die, but Laura had no patience or desire to see this man take one more breath.

"This is taking too long," Laura said. Without giving it a second thought, she emptied her entire clip into Benz's skull. She yearned to come to terms with her niece's death, yet the only way she saw herself being able to do so was if she took his life herself.

Dane rolled her eyes and put her gun away. "Not exactly what I imagined, but I got what I wanted."

She stood up and emptied the house of all the cameras she set up when visiting Reagan, and she searched for anything else Benz might have had installed. After exiting the home that was made into a bloodbath for the second time, Dane and Laura rode home in silence. When they made it back, they slid into bed with their husbands, nestled their faces into their chests, and cried as loud as the thunder spoke. Because after all they'd done, Reagan was still gone.

Chapter 36

If Carmen hadn't been in her right mind, she would have believed the world ended and she didn't get the memo. She couldn't get in contact with Renee or Lincoln and was beginning to have an unsettling feeling in the pit of her stomach. The last time she had seen Renee, they were at Lyfe's funeral and didn't say a word to each other. It was chilling how their relationship suddenly changed without her being aware of what was happening. She called Renee multiple times, only to hear the operator inform her that her line had been disconnected.

After flying back from Miami, she went over to her house and rang the bell, but no one answered. She repeated these actions for a week straight and never got a response. Carmen's instincts started to kick in, and she knew something was wrong. It wasn't normal for a woman who promised to give up her business to suddenly disappear into thin air without so much as a warning.

Taking heed to what the universe was telling her, Carmen barricaded herself in her home until she decided what her next move would be. The image of Benz broken and withdrawn was embedded in her mind, and it reminded her to reach out to Lincoln. She had to admit, she didn't think he had it in him to take a life. However, the horrified look on Benz's face when he came back from identifying his wife at the morgue proved Lincoln was anything but talk.

Benz's life had crumbled all around him, and as a man, he'd felt defeated. Within the privacy of his car, he'd broken down, mourning the life of the only woman he truly loved. However, once in the company of Carmen, he'd played the role of a man with power and prestige. He'd set out to find the person responsible for killing his wife, but he'd come up empty with every rock he turned over. Benz had been sure that whoever killed Reagan was responsible for killing his men. The only problem was that he hadn't any leads, and his heart had been torn between the wife he lost and the mistress he couldn't let go of. While he had been on the hunt for blood, Carmen gave Benz his space and flew back to the ghost town she once knew as New York.

Grateful for what Lincoln had done, she called him to show her appreciation and found it out of his character when he didn't take or return any of her calls. As she had done for Renee, she took a trip to his house, and she was disturbed when his neighbor told her she hadn't seen him in days.

Nothing was how she had left it, and all she could think of was whether Jared had reneged on their agreement and was out for blood. Maybe she came on too strong and he saw right through her. She was a fool for believing that she could tame him, and just like every other animal when they are cornered, Jared attacked, taking out her alliances and claiming his place as king. Carmen even went so far as to wonder if Jared had reconnected with Renee and told her their plans.

Alone in her brownstone, Carmen became paranoid and on guard. Every noise and voice she heard from outside she was sure was Renee and Jared coming for her. After three days of living in fear, she did the only thing she could do. She waited until Friday night, threw on her dancing shoes, and filled her purse with money. She was done with assuming and needed answers. Everyone knew that when one was in need of information, there was only one person to turn to.

Tina sat at the bar with large sunglasses covering her face and a dress that was two sizes too small. Her face was still swollen from the beating Jared had given her, and because no one could look at her without staring at her like she was the monster from the black lagoon, she decided to put her body on display. It was a trick she was trying out to take people's attention from her face. She then set out to drown her sorrows in a bottle of tequila.

Tina was afraid of Jared and had no idea how she could get rid of him. Her first answer was the easiest, and that was to do what he asked and get everything there possibly was on Carmen, but that was four days ago, and still she came up with nothing. Carmen was like another Renee, hard to get information on, and Tina found herself banging her head against a wall out of frustration from coming up empty. Carmen was a ghost whose identity never existed, and it sent Tina to a dead end. Out of fear, Tina wanted to get all the information she could on Carmen, but deep down inside, she knew it was impossible and dreaded the day she would meet with Jared again.

Back-to-back, Russell refilled every drink Tina ordered, and she turned down each man who asked her to dance. She knew every man's story and was aware that they were all lowdown men who didn't pay their child support and spent their days sleeping with random women. Weeks ago, Tina would have given them the

time of day, but today, all she wanted was out of an agreement she had been forced into.

Tina sat at the bar, drinking like her man left her, when
Carmen pulled up a stool beside her. The sight of the
beauty queen inching closer to her without a care in
the world forced Tina to detest her more than she already
did. She blamed Carmen for the ass whipping Jared laid
on her, and she wanted her to feel that pain that she had.
She knew she had no one to blame for her opening her
mouth except herself, but for some reason, she couldn't
help but blame Carmen for exposing her deep throat. For
nights, she tried to think of ways to get back at her and
get herself out of her situation with Jared, but no light
bulbs were going off, and she feared for her life.

"Tina, long time, no talk. I need to speak with you,
sista girl."

Tina slammed back the rest of her drink. She would
need it all if she was going to speak with Carmen. "What
else is new?" Behind her glasses, her eyes were bloodshot and swollen. She was glad she could at least hide
that, because her busted lip and bruised cheeks took front
and center.

Ignoring Tina's appearance and the stress wrapped
around her words, Carmen continued to speak. "What do
you know about Jordan and Jared setting out on a murder
spree lately?"

Tina shook her head. "I haven't heard anything new
about Jared, and as for Jordan, she's been so quiet, I was
starting to wonder if she was still in the game." Tina
wanted to inform her that the bruises and cuts that graced
her body came from Jared, but she kept that little information to herself.

"How do you know she's a she?"

Tina waved Russell down for another drink and laughed. "I know my shit. Why else would you and everyone else constantly knock on my door? Now is that all you want to know?" Tina's word's burned, and she hoped Carmen felt the heat. She then brushed Carmen off with a wave of her hand and planted her attention back on the liquor bottles that hung behind the bar.

Carmen didn't appreciate her attitude and snapped, "No, it's not!" Carmen grabbed Tina's wrist, forcing her to look her way. "My men were murdered, and I find it funny that it's occurring right before I take Jordan for all she's worth. So I need you to tell me everything you know."

"Take Jordan for all she's worth?" Tina swung her body in Carmen's direction. "Do you understand who she is? I don't know where you're from, but over here in this neck of the woods, talking like that will get you killed." Tina had been doing a lot of thinking, and she couldn't help but wonder if Renee was the one who had put a hit out on her brother. He warned her that if she opened her mouth, he'd die, and that's exactly what happened.

Russell handed Tina a shot of tequila, and she downed the burning poison like lemonade.

"I'm from Miami, where we don't give two shits about you little New Yorkers. And unlike you, I'm not afraid of her. My goal was to always claw my way to the top and be queen, and I'm getting just that." Carmen smiled. The thought of how she slithered into Renee's world was remarkable.

"What the hell are you talking about?" Tina was lost and had no idea where this conversation would lead.

Carmen looked around her, ensuring no one was listening. "She's living a life that should be mine, and I will die before I allow her to keep it. It was always my goal to take it all away, but after I saved her life, she offered me her empire when she retires."

"And why in the hell would she just hand everything over to a stranger, even if you did save her life?"

"Because I'm her sister, and my acting skills are impeccable." Carmen spoke with her hands.

"You don't know what you're talking about. Her sister is Page." Tina turned away. It was official. Carmen was a nut ball, and she was no longer entertained by her story.

"Her sister was Page. She tried to kill Jordan."

The words erupted in Tina's eardrums. Everything now made sense. Page had vanished after she supplied her with Renee's information, and magically, Carmen appeared. Slowly, she looked back in Carmen's direction. She was tempted to pay her for this groundbreaking information, but instead, a better thought came to mind.

The two women looked at each other. No words needed to be exchanged because they were now on the same page and understood that everything Carmen said was true.

"A pretty lady like you should not be over here without a drink."

A brown-skinned man who stood at six feet two inches, with the confidence and wardrobe of an NBA player, sat himself next to Carmen and immediately tried to woo her. The alluring sound of his voice forced Carmen to break eye contact with Tina and swing her body in the direction of this stranger. Grateful for the distraction, Tina locked her eyes on the two while rummaging through her purse. When Carmen let out a fake laugh three minutes into the conversation, Tina turned on her cell phone's recording device. Seconds later, she looked around for Russell, who was already bringing her drink.

"Thank you," she flirted.

Five minutes later, Carmen was back in business mode with a new number to add to her collection and a free drink to wet her throat.

"Like I was saying—"

"Wait a minute. You're blowing my mind with all of this, so let's take this to my car. The walls have ears," Tina pointed out.

Carmen agreed and followed Tina out of the club. However, without her noticing, Tina's and Russell's eyes locked, an indication that when he was on break, he would be the next one to get in her car. Undetected, he nodded his head, his STD-riddled body in need of a release.

Chapter 37

"I never knew Jordan had another sister." Ever since Tina found out Jordan's identity, she felt weird calling her by her alias. However, if she didn't want to come up missing, the name Renee could never leave her mouth.

"Neither did I. We didn't find out about each other until my uncle told us a few months back. In Miami, I was a kept woman while she was running all of New York. Ain't that about a bitch?"

Carmen shook her head, looked out the window, and watched women accompany men into their cars for a night of sex. That used to be her, using what she had to get what she wanted.

"What's wrong with that?"

"Everything," Carmen replied. "Like a princess, I had everything given to me and thought I had my shit together. I was given a reality check when I saw how she was living. Have you ever seen her home?"

Tina shook her head no.

"It's gorgeous, fit for a queen. If it weren't for my uncle laying it all out for me, I would have never believed she acquired all of those things alone. The only time I even achieved half of that wealth was through my ex. I got nothing on my own, so seeing how she lived made me want to be a boss. Her success made me want to stop being a princess and start being a queen, but I refuse to start from the bottom, so I set out to gain her trust and take what I deserve. But things didn't turn out that way. Before I had a chance to fully slither into her life, she crowned me her protégé after I saved her from being killed at the hands of her sister." Carmen was in a trance, her eyes moving with every partygoer who entered and exited the club.

"That's a good thing. Now you don't have to go through all that trouble."

"Yeah, it's a good thing, but still, work must be done. Because even though she's handing everything to me, I still have to get rid of her once she retires. I can't risk her taking it all back and coming back for Julian."

"Julian?"

"Her best friend, her partner, her lover. Before I found out about Jordan, I met Julian while vacationing in Jamaica. Instantly, we were attracted to one another and had wild sex like animals. I never thought I'd see him again, but life has a funny way of making things happen, because there he was sharing a bed with my sister. An additional thing I added on my 'Must Have' list."

Carmen never took her attention away from the window, so Tina's eyes peeked in the crack of her bag, confirming that her phone was still recording. "It's suicide what you're trying to do, Carmen, pure suicide."

"Only if I get caught." Slowly, Carmen's head turned in Tina's direction. "So are you sure you know nothing about any murders?"

Tina inched her hand closer to the door handle. The way Carmen looked at her set off alarms. "I'm positive."

"Okay, but I have one more question for you. Then you can get out this car." Carmen's eyes nodded toward Tina's hand, and she quickly removed it. "Have you heard anything about a dude named Lincoln? He seemed to disappear into thin air."

Tina took a deep breath. It always disturbed her to think of Lincoln. Her eyes dropped to the floor mat. "He's dead. Almost a week ago, pieces of him were found on his mother's doorstep."

Carmen stopped breathing, and her stomach began to turn. As quickly as she could, she flung the car door open and threw up on the concrete. The image of Lincoln's body parts littering his mother's doorstep ripped apart her psyche. Something wasn't right. It was no coincidence that Lincoln and her entire team were wiped out. Chills radiated through her body, and after wiping her mouth off on the sleeve of her coat, she sat back in the car and slammed the door.

"Who's responsible?"

Tina's shoulders rose, then fell.

Carmen jammed her hand into her bag, pulled out a stack of money, and didn't bother to count it before slapping it into Tina's lap. "Here."

Before jumping out of the car, she looked around the parking lot. When the coast was clear, she made a dash for her Mercedes.

Tina watched as Carmen raced out the lot, leaving nothing except her tire marks behind. Calmly, she counted the money Carmen gave her and tied a rubber band from her cup holder around the crisp bills. When her wad of cash was neat and to her liking, she opened her purse and placed it right beside her cell phone. Her fingers tapped the screen and ended the recording.

Chapter 38

Watching Dane with her family made Renee want one of her own. It was things such as visiting relatives' homes where you gossiped, laughed, ate dinners, and connected that made Renee wish she had kept Lyfe around. While sleeping in Laura's guest room, Renee would stay up during all hours of the night imagining how life would have been had her mother loved her, her father never died, and Page been halfway sane. She thought long and hard about the what-ifs and listened to the nights Dane made her escape. The cries the women poured out the night they killed Benz shook Renee to the core simply because it was proven that every woman she knew was cursed, just like her.

Back home in the comfort of her own bed, she listened to the sound of Julian's heartbeat. There was nothing more soothing than resting her head on his chest and listening to his very existence. Thoughts of marriage and motherhood walked their way into Renee's mind and took a seat. It surprised her how at ease she became once she painted a picture of her very own family, and she was surprised twice as much when she heard herself expressing these emotions to Julian.

"What if we gave it a try?"

"Gave what a try?"

"Getting married and having kids."

Julian sat Renee up so that he could look at her. "Where is this coming from?"

"From here." She pointed to her heart, the strongest muscle in her body that leaked out love.

Gazing into Renee's eyes, he saw the woman he'd fallen in love with who fought to come out of her dark corner. He saw his lover and friend, the reason for his existence. When she smiled at him, he saw the woman he betrayed.

"So what do you think?" she asked, pulling him out of his guilt-ridden thoughts.

"I think it's gonna happen, as long as you forgive me."

"Forgive you for what?"

Julian failed the first time he tried to come clean, so he refused to fail again. "Renee, when I went to Jamaica to speak with Dane, I—"

"Renee! Get down here!"

The urgency in Dane's voice caused Renee and Julian to look at each other in confusion and exit the room. As frustrating as it was to be interrupted for the second time as he'd tried to tell his secret, Julian was relieved that Dane announced herself. The last thing he wanted was to spill his guts when they weren't alone. The conversation was personal between him and Renee. No other person's input or opinion was welcomed.

The couple walked down the stairs, and their vision took in Dane standing directly in front of Tina. Julian felt his mind fading in and out. The last he had seen of Tina was in photos taken by people he had following her. After putting a hit out on Waves, he dropped the ball and never got around to shutting Tina's trap for good.

"What are you doing here?" Julian growled. In protective mode, he stood in front of Renee.

Renee's eyes never left Tina as she tried to figure out who she was.

"I'd like to know the same thing. I found her standing in front of the door on my way here," Dane chimed in, Renee's house keys clutched in her hand.

The color was drained from Tina's face, and her heart was racing. The look in Dane's eyes made Tina uneasy, and she slightly regretted coming to Renee's home. All eyes were on her. Her brain told her to speak, but her mouth wouldn't comply.

"I suggest you answer him," Dane warned.

Terrified, Tina opened her mouth, and words finally fell out. They tripped over one another, and Tina stuttered with every word she formed. Midsentence, she stopped, closed her eyes, and took a deep breath while telling herself, *relax and tell them what you know.*

"There's something I think you should know." Tina looked around Julian, her sight landing on Renee.

Julian never moved from in front of Renee, his stance giving off the impression that he thought if he did, she would be in danger. She stepped from behind him, her touch letting him know that it was okay.

"I don't recollect ever meeting you, so what could you possibly have to tell me?" Renee asked.

"I know you don't know me, but I think you should know that your sister, Carmen, can't be trusted."

Tina was holding her breath while waiting for a response from Renee. However, the only thing Renee did was play a game of "don't blink." She gave off no indication whether she was angry.

Seconds passed before she finally replied, "What do you know?"

Dane walked over to the door and guarded it as reassurance that Tina would tell them everything she knew before leaving.

"I know that the second you retire, she is going to place a hit out on you. From the moment she met you, her plans were to suck you dry then dispose of you. Carmen envies you. She'll do anything to take your place."

"You're the one who told Page about me."

Surprised by her comment, all of the strength Tina mustered up to speak rapidly deteriorated. "Yes, I am. And I'm sorry about that. I had no idea what her intentions were."

"So you understand why I am wary of you. How do I know you didn't tell anyone else?"

"I promise I didn't!" Tina walked closer to Renee. She needed her to believe that she told no one else about her identity. "I know I don't have the best reputation, but I'm trying to right my wrongs. Instead of my mouth hurting people, I'm trying to actually help for a change," she lied.

There was nothing positive about what Tina wanted to do. She had two goals in mind and two goals only. The first was to expose Carmen, payback for giving her up to Jared, and the second was to get both of them off her back. To see the damage Jared did to her body whenever she looked in the mirror was heartbreaking. Before those two came into her life, things were decent, and now all she wanted was for things to go back to the way they were. If she wanted any type of normalcy, she had to fight fire with fire and get Carmen and Jared out of her life for good.

Renee didn't respond. The silence only heard in libraries filled the room and caused Tina's teeth to chatter. She had no idea what ran through Renee's head, and the suspense was killing her until Dane opened her mouth and spoke up.

"I want proof. I trust no one who runs in the same circle as Carmen."

Tina jammed her hand into her back pocket and pulled out her phone. She pushed the touch screen, and the device played the conversation between her and Carmen:

"I never knew Jordan had another sister."

"Neither did I. We didn't find out about each other until my uncle told us a few months back. In Miami, I was a kept woman while she was running all of New York. Ain't that about a bitch?"

"What's wrong with that?"

"Everything. Like a princess, I had everything given to me and thought I had my shit together. I was given a reality check when I saw how she was living. Have you ever seen her home? It's gorgeous, fit for a queen. If it weren't for my uncle laying it all out for me, I would have never believed she acquired all of those things alone. The only time I even achieved half of that wealth was through my ex. I got nothing on my own, so seeing how she lived made me want to be a boss. Her success made me want to stop being a princess and start being a queen, but I refuse to start from the bottom, so I set out to gain her trust and take what I deserve. But things didn't turn out that way. Before I had a chance to fully slither into her life, she crowned me her protégé after I saved her from being killed at the hands of her sister."

"That's a good thing. Now you don't have to go through all that trouble."

"Yeah, it's a good thing, but still, work must be done. Because even though she's handing everything to me, I still have to get rid of her once she retires. I can't risk her taking it all back and coming back for—"

"Cut it off," Renee instructed. Although Renee had made up her mind and considered Carmen dead seconds into the recording, she still had an apology to give Julian and Dane. From the very beginning, they had seen Carmen for who she was and had warned her, but still, she chose to ignore them and believe what she wanted. Now that everything was out in the open, she felt she must apologize.

"I'm sorry," she said, her eyes stationed on the front door.

"Who are you apologizing to?" Julian asked.

"To you and Dane. You both tried to warn me, so what better time to apologize?"

No one spoke, but the silence alerted Renee that her soul mate and best friend accepted her apology.

"How did you meet Carmen? She's fairly new to New York. Was that your first interaction with her?" Dane asked.

Things were running smoothly, but Tina's nerves were still in disarray. Her legs were shaking, and she feared she'd collapse at any minute. "May I?" she asked, pointing to the couch.

Renee nodded her head, and Tina's spaghetti legs wobbled their way across the room and took a seat. Her hands were full of sweat, so she placed her phone down and thoroughly wiped her hands on her jeans.

"That wasn't the first time we met. The first time we met, we were at a club, and she wanted to know if I knew any men who were willing to put in work. I let her know that all the guys I knew about were killed a few months back. However, there was one I told her about."

Tina's head dropped, and her hands began to shake. Everyone noticed how uneasy she was, and they waited for her to finish. When moments passed without another word leaving her mouth, Renee stepped in. Her tone was soothing and caring.

"Who did you tell her about, Tina?"

She sat down beside her and rubbed her back in order to calm her down. Because of her kind gesture, Tina felt a little more willing to tell her about Jared and not fear so much for her life. "I told her about Jared."

They all tried to fight it, but their laughter slipped through their lips.

"Obviously, you're not up on your current events like we all thought," Dane chuckled.

"No, I'm ahead of them," Tina whispered. "He's not dead. I know a nurse in the hospital he was treated at who can verify that."

The way Tina spoke caused the laughter to die down and everyone to look at one another. Tina removed her shades, her face a long way from being back to normal.

"He found out I told Carmen he was alive, and he did this to me." She pointed to her bruises. "Today, Carmen asked me if I knew anything about you and Jared killing her crew, and I recorded it. I have a feeling she thinks you're on to her."

Dane rushed toward Tina, her knee-high boots stomping against the floor. "This shit coming out of your mouth will get you killed. My men got rid of Jared's body. There's no way he's alive."

Once again, Tina's heart rate sped up, but she needed Jared taken care of just like she needed Carmen gone, so she pushed herself to tell everything that needed to be told. "It's true. He's walking and breathing just like everyone in this room."

Dane was a true believer that if someone lied, they did not look you in the eye. Never once during this debate did Tina turn away. She tried to fight what her mind was telling her, but she knew there was no running away from this one. Fergus and Calloway had lied.

"What do you want?" Renee intervened.

Julian stood against the wall, his eyes staring a hole into the ceiling. The saying "The more things change, the more they stay the same" sprinted through his mind.

"I don't understand," Tina said.

"Nothing is for free, especially this information. So what do you want?"

It's now or never, Tina thought. "I want them out of my life. I want you to do what you do best. After what Jared's done to me, I'm living in fear, and it's all because of Carmen, so I need them to go away."

For the first time since she'd been there, Tina looked at peace as she told Renee her wish. Even though all of her information was accurate, Renee didn't believe for a minute she was telling her all of this out of the goodness of her heart, and she was just happy that Tina finally admitted it.

"Consider it done."

Tina observed Renee. She needed to see for herself whether she was serious. When she never blinked an eye, she knew Renee was the real deal. "Thank you!"

Tina jumped into Renee's arms, showing her appreciation for giving her her life back, squeezing her like a child squeezes a teddy bear. Renee stared at Julian until he looked down from the ceiling. The cold, withdrawn look told him everything he needed to know. Instead of looking at Dane, he walked past her, his shoulder grazing hers, an indication that they had business to take care of.

He opened the door, and Dane walked out of it. She stood in the hall, waiting for Tina to exit.

Renee backed out of Tina's hold and continued to speak. "Thank you for coming here to warn me. That took a lot of guts. But you no longer have to worry. Everyone will be taken care of."

Tina smiled, and a weight lifted off her shoulders. "Thank you."

Renee returned her smile and walked Tina to the door. "They will take you home. Take care, Tina."

Tina smiled at Renee one more time before leaving her sight. Dane followed close behind her when she left the house. Julian grabbed Renee into his arms, the two wrapped up in each other's grasp.

"Make sure they make it as painful as possible, Tina included," she whispered in his ear.

"I will. I'm going to do what I should have done a long time ago."

The two kissed with the thought of starting a family lingering in both their minds. Renee watched Julian walk farther into the hall, and when he was out of sight, she went back into her home. She walked through the living room, and her eye caught a glimpse of Tina's phone. Picking it up, she flicked through it until she found the conversation between her and Carmen. She listened to the conversation Tina played for her and became angry with herself for not seeing the signs. Each word she listened to made her laugh for how stupid she had been, but when the recording kept going where it should have ended, her eyebrows caved in, and her heart fell to her feet as she listened to the remainder of the recording.

"I can't risk her taking it all back and coming back for Julian."

"Julian?"

"Her best friend, her partner, her lover. Before I found out about Jordan, I met Julian while vacationing in Jamaica. Instantly, we were attracted to one another and had wild sex like animals. I never thought I'd see him again, but life has a funny way of making things happen, because there he was sharing a bed with my sister. An additional thing I added on my 'Must Have' list."

"It's suicide what you're trying to do, Carmen, pure suicide."

"Only if I get caught."

Chapter 39

With tears in her eyes, Carmen drove as fast as she could to Lincoln's home. In her heart, she knew that what Tina had told her was the truth, but she refused to believe it. The sky began to roar, and in the snap of a finger, raindrops the size of basketballs saturated the streets. God's tears drenched the windshield, making it hard for her to see what lay ahead. With the back of her hand, she wiped her tear-streaked face, but it was no use. Every time she rid her cheeks of her pain and guilt, they were automatically replaced with brand new drops of misery.

It's all my fault. It's all my fault, were the only words racing through Carmen's head. She knew she would be Lincoln's downfall, knew that with her in his life, she would inject her poison and watch him die a slow, undeserved death. But for it actually to happen demolished her soul and sent her into a whirlwind of emotions she could not escape. The thought of Lincoln being dead sent Carmen's heart rate into overdrive. Her body went numb.

She raced down the empty neighborhood streets. On the first corner, she pulled her vehicle over, and when she tried to dive out, she was pulled back into her seat by her seat belt. With the speed of Sonic the Hedgehog, she released herself from its grasp while her mouth blew up like a blowfish. She rushed out of the car and tripped on the curb, her tuxedo jumpsuit pant legs tear-

ing at the knees. Unable to hide in the bushes, she threw
up right there on the sidewalk. On all fours, she cried like
she never cried before. Maybe it was because of Lincoln,
maybe it was because of Lyfe, or maybe it was because
of the stress of taking Renee's place and being so close
she could smell the money, only to have it torn from her
hands.

Something wasn't right. Carmen could feel it in her
soul. When she looked up from where she sat, she noticed she was on the side of the park where she and Renee
had watched that young man play ball. Life had come
full circle, and she was right back where she started. Her
short hair stuck to her face, and her makeup became a
pile of mud smeared on her cheeks.

Carmen didn't move. She had become one with the
concrete and allowed the rain to wash over her. She was
cursed, and she had spread her bad luck to an innocent
soul. Unable to accept what her spirit told her, she finally
turned over, her behind bashing against the concrete, and
the rain washing the vomit from under her body and into
the city's storm drains. With Lincoln gone, there was no
turning back. No way would Carmen ever experience
true love.

Being with Lincoln at the present time had been out
of the picture because her greed was too strong to allow
love to take front and center, but deep inside, where no
one except her knew the truth, she'd planned to turn to
him after she had sown her wild oats and settled down.
Then and only then would she accept love and let go of
her materialistic ways, but now that would never happen.
Perhaps that was the true reason she sat on the wet streets
of New York, cold, shivering, and mourning the loss of
her future love.

***

Carmen turned the ignition off, and her eyes gazed into space. So that she wouldn't stay in denial, she replayed her conversation with Lincoln's neighbor over and over in her mind.

"Young lady, I'm sorry to break the news to you, but his mama informed me just yesterday he passed not too long ago. Poor thing was found on her doorstep in pieces. His mama just left. She's been here twice this week cleaning out his place. I pray they find the monster responsible for this."

Carmen's heart sank, followed by a sharp pain that gripped her chest. "He's dead?" *she asked.*

"Yes, baby, I'm so sorry." The old lady allowed Carmen a second to process the tragic news before she continued to speak. "He really cared for you, suga, always talked about you whenever I bumped into him. I hope you can find comfort in knowing that."

Just to feel his presence, she lied to the elderly woman who she knew had a spare key, telling her she needed to retrieve a few of her belongings she'd left behind.

"Take your time, sweetheart. I'll be right next door if you need me." She looked Carmen up and down, and her facial expression could not hide that she wondered what happened to her that night.

For hours, Carmen lay in Lincoln's bed. Her body was wrapped around his pillow, and her nails dug into the sheets. She wished his body were there to fill its flat surface. It was amazing how much her love for him showed now that he was gone. When she was in Miami, she didn't take his calls, and now that he couldn't speak, she would give anything to hear his voice. Tearing herself away from the one person in her life who gave off positivity, she walked out of the apartment and told him goodbye.

The moonlight had kept Carmen company for hours. Daylight had long fallen behind along with the news of Lincoln's death. In her car around the corner from her home, she sat for hours. She was emotionally exhausted and suffered from a migraine that throbbed with every minute and prevented her from moving. Finally, strong enough and capable of leaving her vehicle, she prepared to go into her brownstone, when from the passenger-side window, she saw her front door was wide open. Carmen's head looked up and down the block, searching for anything or anyone who looked out of place. However, nothing looked suspicious, and instead, everything reeked of normalcy. Snatching her purse, she walked into her home, her mind preparing her for the worst.

Chapter 40

It was nights like this when the ghost of Jared's past came back to haunt him. He could hear the voices of all his kills whispering in his ear, but lately, the loudest were Waves and Janae. The most peaceful nights were spent with Jared stuck in his home, listening to Waves's howling. *You're choosing her over me? Your loyalty lies with her? You're choosing a bitch who isn't yours and doesn't even want you!* Not too far behind was Janae's insecure, irate voice slithering into his eardrums and questioning where he'd been the night before and who was the cause for his deceit. He'd see silhouettes appear then disappear, and when he'd least expect it, the visuals would walk his way, threatening to invade his privacy and what small peace of mind he still inhabited. Years ago, sights of spirits from those he prematurely sent to the afterlife would awaken his anxiety and trouble his mental. However, the more he encountered the visits, the more used to the hauntings he became. From time to time, he smiled if not laughed at the talkative voices. Jared's past could never be forgotten or his actions forgiven. He was placed in a mental jail, and the only way to retreat was to take a midnight drive around the city when he craved silence in order to hear himself think.

On the Brooklyn Bridge, Jared felt a sense of freedom with the windows rolled down and the cold slapping him in his face. There was nothing at the precise moment he wanted to hear more than for the wind splashing past him and the car tires tumbling against the asphalt. Life was hard, but the longer he survived, the harder it was without Renee. He dreamed of her every night, and the vision of her face made him want to kick down her door and drag her out of her home, this dominance and demanding presence triggering Renee to do all of two things: kick and scream. Although the human imagination could conjure all and anything, Jared's still revealed bits and pieces of reality and what he knew must take place even when he didn't want it to.

Ever since Carmen approached him, he imagined himself killing her and getting Renee to love him, the murder of all murders, but after countless sleepless nights, he came to the conclusion that Carmen was a genius. Although he was dangerously in love with Renee, he promised to destroy her world for the pain she'd caused, and working with Carmen, her unknown enemy, was the best way to seek revenge, right next to killing Julian. Love conquered all, yet even Jared knew if actions went without punishment, history was bound to repeat itself. When it came to the love he craved, boundaries had to be set and respect established. Before Jared could shower Renee with love, he had to make her pay. To gain a healthy relationship, he'd train her and show that denying him her love had consequences. Once he put in work with Carmen, he planned to kill Julian right in front of Renee's alluring eyes, then snatch her off her throne and create a life all their own. *The past must live and die there.*

The clock read three o'clock in the morning, and Jared felt confident that if he returned home now, all the ghosts of his past would be retired for the night. Even souls living in limbo had limitations. Twenty minutes later, he was one block from his home when he saw a checkpoint set up straight ahead. He made a right to avoid the police, and his cell phone went off. Stopping at a red light, he opened the text, and his blood chilled.

Fergus: Get out the house. Tina told them you're alive, which now has my ass in a sling. If you don't hear from me or Calloway within forty-eight hours, kill them all. And don't forget, you owe me.

Chapter 41

Carmen's ankle boots crushed the broken glass beneath her feet. Huge holes punctured the walls rats swarmed in and out of. Petrified the rodents would move her way, Carmen froze. The sound of rat nails scratching and racing inside the walls and across her damaged goods scattered on the floor tormented her ears.

My fuckin' walls. My walls were made into a rat hotel.

Carmen grabbed her chest and with caution slowly walked around her demolished home. Her eyes zeroed in on every corner, and her ears tried to delete the sounds of rats scurrying and focused intently on any clue her intruders still lingered. Her heart raced and fingers fidgeted. She fought to keep the vomit her nerves produced at bay.

Fuck, my pepper spray is in the car.

In order to walk, she had to make a path that led from the front door to her bedroom. She kicked aside slashed couch cushions, books, shattered crystal vases, old DVDs, and cracked picture frames. She was even forced to flip over her coffee table and stand her bookshelf upright. As much as she wanted to run full speed around her home and check out the damage, she couldn't. Her legs would only allow her to move at the speed of a snail, her eyes absorbing all the damage.

Slowly she walked up the stairs. The steps were rickety. Whoever had invaded her space damaged everything.

She prayed the steps wouldn't cave in. The handrail lay on the floor in pieces. Rats ran into the holes, forcing Carmen to skip a step or two. This was no longer a home but a war zone.

"My house." The words slipped out of Carmen's mouth in a low, fearful, childish voice. She no longer recognized her place of comfort.

Her body shook. Her life was literally crumbling all around her. She placed her hand on her bedroom door-knob and braced herself for what she would see next. All that Carmen cared for in her life were her material objects, and for those to be taken away from her would make her feel alone and broken. Scared and nervous, she pushed open the door.

The instant Carmen pushed open the door, it flew off its hinges and crashed against the polished hardwood floors. A cloud of dust exploded into the air and tempo-rarily blinded her. Instantly, her eyes shut, and violent coughs escaped her mouth. Her chest heaved in and out, and she held on to her neck, the dust proving to be too much.

Finally, the dust settled, and particles trickled down to the floor. Her eyes opened, and her once-seductive eye shape turned as wide as dollar coins.

"Oh, no," she whispered.

Snakes of multiple colors and sizes slithered out from every corner of her bedroom and joined those already sta-tioned at the center of the room. Just like the rest of the house, her bedroom had been vandalized, minus the rat-filled holes in the walls. Snakes slithered across the door and on Carmen's feet. The feel of cold, heavy flesh re-pulsed and frightened her in a multitude of ways. She kicked the reptiles off and stumbled farther back into the hall. Her back slammed against the hallway wall, and a rat fell on her shoulder. Carmen hollered, hopped around, and slapped at her body with her hands. Rattled and at a loss for breath, she looked back into her room.

Chills raced through her body. The serpents' slow movements and hissing sounds caused Carmen to tremble and a thin layer of sweat to coat her body. Her heart galloped in her chest, making it complicated for her to breathe. Her eyes roamed around the room and landed on an item that lay comfortably on her satin pillow. Lost in the visual of what was on the pillow, her mind told her to depart, but curiosity got the best of her and forced her to stay.

Carmen collected all the courage she had and made herself stand in front of one of the large holes in her wall. She waited for the next few rodents to appear, and when two obese, gray rats appeared, she grabbed them both by their tails and, in one swift motion, flung them inside the snake-infested room. Like bees to honey, the snakes flocked to the corner of the room where the rats landed, far from where her bed sat.

Carmen knew she didn't have long, so she ran to her bed and grabbed what she discovered were three photos turned facedown on her pillow. She dashed out of her room, made a beeline for the kitchen, and tried her best to move swiftly without tripping over the multiple pieces of furniture. Relieved that she was away from the snakes, she placed the pictures on the granite countertops. One word written in black permanent marker stained the back of each photo. Carmen arranged the photos in the proper order, and together they read, "I Declare War." Her jaw locked, and her pulse sped up. Those words together were only a foreshadowing of what was on the other side of those pictures.

Slowly, she flipped the picture with the word "I" written on it, and a wave of shock bolted through her. There Benz was as clear as day, dead in what appeared to be the home he shared with Reagan. His eyes held a blank stare. However, when Carmen looked closely, there seemed to be a sense of peace visible on his face. She pushed the image to the side. As much as she wanted revenge, she couldn't stomach seeing him like that.

Her fingers inched over to "Declare," and she questioned whether she wanted to see its photograph, but the mystery pulled her in. She turned the image over. A lone tear dived from Carmen's eye, and her bottom lip quivered. Lincoln's body was slaughtered into pieces, and the only reason she knew it was him was because his head was front and center. Her body turned cold, and her emotions jumped off a cliff. The pain of having someone ripping her heart out of her chest would have felt better than what she was currently experiencing. This was a dream she wished she could wake up from right now, so she glanced around the room. When the photographs didn't disappear, she gave up on escaping her nightmare.

Her hands shook, and her thoughts ran to the ends of the earth as she thought of who could possibly appear on the next and last image. Before she turned it over, she made her right hand form a fist, forcing herself to maintain a sense of control and ease. When she felt she was prepared to open that last door, she flipped the picture over, and her entire world dissolved.

The wind was knocked out of her, and all of her innocence vanished. The past came to the present, and she saw herself with the only father figure she had ever known. She looked down at Lyfe's coffin, but the photo was divided into two. On the right side, it showed him

burned to death inside his home. Carmen had no idea
how that half of the photo was taken, and at that point,
she did not care.

The floodgates opened, and she let out a loud howl.
Looking at Lyfe in that state demolished her whole existence, and she was left scrambling for life. She threw
the photo off the counter and broke whatever was left to
break in her kitchen. She added to the turmoil Renee left
behind and felt not an ounce of regret afterward. After
trashing what little was left of the kitchen, she took all
three photos and burned them. She didn't need to remember them that way. She deleted the memory Renee tried
to leave behind, and maintained how she remembered
them.

She stood in front of the counter where the pictures
once sat, and her nails tried to dig into the granite, but
nothing happened. Instead, they chipped off and fell to
their death. She wanted to cry and lash out, but she refused to give Renee the pleasure and instead held it all
in. The vibe she gave off screamed rage, and after each
picture was nothing more than ashes, she turned off the
stove's flames and stomped her way to her coat closet.
Inside sat the luggage she had taken with her to Miami,
and right in front of the closet, she stripped out of her outfit and ankle boots and threw on a gold blouse with fitted
jeans and high heels. She snatched a brush from her purse
and put her hair back in place. Afterward, she fixed her
face and applied some makeup.

She then ran up to her room and, with leather gloves
stuffed on her hands, dug her hand into the wall and
pulled out more rats. Held by their tails, they twisted
and turned until she released them into the room for the
snakes to devour. Once their attention was placed on

their next meal, she opened her closet, took handfuls of clothes off the hangers and out of the drawers, and threw them into her suitcase. The snakes were making their way toward Carmen, but she kicked and stepped on them as she left the room.

Downstairs, she opened her Miami luggage again and retrieved all of the important paperwork needed to survive, such as her passport, birth certificate, and social security card. She never traveled without them and was happy she didn't put them away, because now that she was in a rush and had to evacuate, she had no time to search for them. With her purse flung over her shoulder, she grabbed her luggage and made her way out the door. Two feet away from her house, she stopped, looked back, and pulled a pen and paper from her purse. She rushed in her dismantled kitchen and was relieved to find Scotch Tape in the only drawer that hadn't been emptied. Back outside on her doorstep, on top of the blue lines, she wrote:

> *You got this one, but I get the last laugh. I'm not the only one born outside of your parents' marriage. There's one more, one more girl, who shares our father and received just as much attention as me. And the best part of it all is that she's older than us. Yes, Renee, there is someone walking this earth who outranks you. And if I haven't already turned the knife in your back, maybe this will: I don't need Julian to be a part of my crew, because I've already had him and I will have him again.*
>
> *Love you sis, xoxo,*
> *Carmen*

She sealed the letter with a kiss and taped it on the front door. She hoped Renee would return, hoped she tried one more time to catch her off guard, and when she did, she would find the last of their family secrets. Carmen knew nothing about Renee growing up, but she knew everything about her sister. After sticking the paper to the door, she slammed it behind her and went on her merry way.

"Next stop, Miami," Carmen said to herself. Then she planted her sunglasses on her face.

Chapter 42

Carmen held her cell phone in her hand and waited for the cab to stop in front of LaGuardia Airport. She wanted badly to drive her car, but what was the use? She already knew that the moment Renee discovered that letter, she'd make her way straight to Miami. Why make it easier and confirm that she had retreated by having her car parked in the airport's parking lot? She didn't plan to stay in Miami forever, but she needed to be in her element and surround herself with what she knew in order to get back on her feet. The fight between her and Renee was far from over. She might have won the battle, but Carmen would definitely win the war. There was always more than one way to skin a cat, and she didn't care if it took her nine tries, Carmen would dethrone Renee and take her for all she was worth.

This time, she would be smarter and more patient. Her biggest mistake was underestimating Renee and not having a bulletproof plan for every time a monkey wrench was thrown into the equation, but never again. Never would she make the same mistake twice. Those pictures were all the motivation she needed to claw her way to the top, and she wouldn't stop until Renee's blood was shed and she sat in her seat.

Carmen paid her fare and waited for the cab driver to empty his car of her belongings. Once out of sight, she

pressed a few buttons on her phone and placed it to her
ear. She waited for the other end to pick up. She looked
down at her watch. It was 5:45 a.m. Being the early bird
her mother was, Carmen hoped she was in her office.

"Priceless Realty, this is Raquel Hunt speaking. How
may I help you?"

Good, she's in the office. "Hey, Ma, how are you?"

"I'm good, baby, how are you? I haven't heard from
you in a while, and I was starting to get worried."

"Actually, I tried calling but never could reach you. I
left messages."

"Oh, that's right! I'm sorry, the first time you tried, I
was with a client. A lovely girl just about to finish school.
I was showing her that gorgeous property in South Beach.
You remember the all-glass building I keep talking
about?"

Frantically, Carmen shook her head. Her mother's job
and clientele weren't what she wanted to talk about. She
needed to cut to the chase and talk about the real reason
she called.

"Yes, yes, the glass one. I remember. Listen, Ma, I need
a favor." Carmen could hear her mother taking a deep
breath on the other end.

"What is it, Carmen?"

"I'm coming back to Miami for a while, and I need you
to get me a place, like yesterday."

"What's wrong with New York? Is it because your uncle is no longer with us?" Raquel waited for the day
Carmen would return home after she found out Lyfe
died. Carmen was not meant to be alone. She depended
on anyone except for herself to take care of her.

"That's one of the reasons, but I just want to come
home. I need to get some things in order that I can't do
here."

Raquel wanted to interrogate her daughter, but she was having a good morning and wasn't up for an argument. To shut her daughter up, she'd do as she asked in order to carry on with a positive day.

"Fine. I have a few places I think you will like." Raquel scribbled down locations of the places she had in mind, then forced herself to say what she thought her daughter needed to hear, even if it did ruin her day. "And, Carmen, get yourself together. I don't need to see you like your sister, swinging on some pole somewhere."

Carmen didn't reply right away. Although she wanted to give her mom a good tongue-lashing, she knew it wouldn't be right. The biggest pain Raquel had encountered, next to losing her lover, was having her daughter wind up so lost in life that she turned to stripping. She never spoke about her sister, so for her to bring her up now led Carmen to believe that she sensed she was in a downward spiral known as her life. She grabbed the handle of her luggage and absorbed everything her mother was saying.

"I won't, Ma. In order to live how I want to, I need to come home and get myself right. I will never turn out like Madison. I promise you that."

Carmen missed her sister, but she was a lost soul. A few years ago, misery plagued her and swallowed her whole. Her bad decisions ripped apart the remainder of their family and devastated their mother. Carmen never told Raquel, but after turning over a few stones, Carmen learned right before Benz left her that Madison was stripping somewhere in New York and going by the name Misery. Not a day went by while living in the city did Carmen not think of seeing her sister, but her feet would never move, and her eyes would never allow her

to see her sister that way. With Raquel unwilling to talk
about her firstborn, whom she'd handed over to her sister once she gave birth, Carmen was left with no one to
open up to. Lyfe knew nothing about his brother's firstborn. It was Carmen and her parents' little secret, meant
to be taken to the grave. The three of them had visited
Madison frequently, but Carmen knew deep down inside that Madison became who she was because she had
a father who was a cheater and a part-time mother who
was too frightened to take responsibility and care for her
when she was born.

"Thank you, baby, and I'm going to hold you to it."

Carmen could hear her mother's smile beaming
through the phone, and it made her smile herself. Her
mother was her best friend, the woman she set out to be.
"I'll see you soon, Ma. I'm about to jump on this flight. If
I want to get myself right, I need to act now."

"Wow, you're serious, aren't you? Okay, baby, let me
go so I can get you into one of these places as soon as
possible. I thought I had a little time, but I see my baby
girl ain't playing." Carmen and Raquel shared a heartfelt
laugh, one needed to ease the pain over Madison.

"Okay, Ma, I'll see you soon. I love you."

"I love you too, Carmen."

After everything that took place within the last couple
of months, Carmen wanted to break down and cry, but
her pride wouldn't allow her to. So she walked into the
airport with a smile so confident that it made everyone
passing her envious, wishing they walked in her shoes.

Never let them see you sweat, were her thoughts.

It was a new beginning when Carmen made her way
through airport security. She removed all metal and anything else she suspected would trigger the metal detector,

and she put each item into the plastic pan they supplied. She put her carry-on luggage and purse onto the conveyor belt and briefly watched it travel through the X-ray machine. Quickly, she stepped through the metal detector and met up with her belongings. The last thing to go through the X-ray machine was her purse, and it was then that she smiled long and hard. She laid eyes on the frivolous objects her purse contained, such as her keys and cell phone, but her happiness didn't stem from that. It came from the thought that, one day, right next to those items would be Renee's crown, and her dreams would be accomplished.

She got herself together, grabbed everything from the conveyor belt, and walked to gate 44 with no regrets. As much as New York had dragged her through the mud, she refused to say goodbye. Oh, no, goodbye was forever. Instead, she looked out the airport's window and told the Big Apple, "See you later," because when she returned, there would be no more running.

Discussion Questions

1. Was Renee naive for wanting to give Carmen her empire?
2. Now that you know Jared's past, do you believe his actions are justified?
3. Dane has shown a lot of emotions in book two, what are your thoughts of her now?
4. If you were Lyfe, would you have retired for Renee?
5. Do you think Renee made a mistake by killing Lyfe?
6. Do you think Lincoln deserved to die?
7. If Lincoln would have never died, do you believe that he and Carmen would have become the next Renee and Julian?
8. Which sister do you prefer, Page or Carmen?
9. Which character who was killed off do you wish had made it to the end?
10. What were your thoughts when you discovered Renee had a third sister? Do you see Madison being a problem in the future?

About the Author

Born and raised in New York City, where she lives with her husband, Brandie Davis-White graduated with a bachelor's degree in English from York College and is the founder of My Urban Books blog and Facebook book club. From home, she continues to pen drama-filled novels.

Follow Brandie on Facebook at:
www.facebook.com/brandie.davis.948

Join her Facebook book club My Urban Books Club at:
www.facebook.com/groups/232356380133003/

Twitter:
@AuthorBrandieD

Instagram:
@authorbrandiedavis